The WILD CARD

JUDY
MURRAY

The WILD CARD

ORION

An Orion paperback

This edition published in Great Britain in 2024 by Orion Fiction
an imprint of The Orion Publishing Group Ltd
Carmelite House, 50 Victoria Embankment
London EC4Y 0DZ

An Hachette UK Company

1 3 5 7 9 10 8 6 4 2

A CIP catalogue record for this book is
available from the British Library.

ISBN (MMP) 978 1 3987 1135 8
ISBN (eBook) 978 1 3987 1136 5
ISBN (Audio) 978 1 3987 1137 2

Typeset at The Spartan Press Ltd,
Lymington, Hants

Printed and bound in Great Britain by Clays Ltd,
Elcograf S.p.A.

www.orionbooks.co.uk

Chapter 1

NOW

The discreet black car eased its way down the sloped driveway, leaving the neat hedges of Belvedere Villas behind as it headed onto the main road.

'Ladies' quarter-finals day here at the All England Club, and the first match of the day sees one of the biggest surprises of not just the year but the entire tournament's history...'

The voices coming from the radio were familiar to Abi Patterson, as was the story they told. The car drove away from the basement flat she had hastily rented in time for the first week of the Championships and the voices continued. Radio Wimbledon. Of course that was what would be playing in her slick courtesy car – standard for all competitors in the event. But this time, those voices, the ones that Abi had spent the last twenty years listening to on the school run, on her way to work or while waiting for the kettle to boil, were discussing *her*.

'Absolutely, Barry, it's just a couple of hours until we see a British wild card hit the second week – an unprecedented situation! Abigail Patterson will be facing world number 12 and the fans' favourite, Carly Cunningham in this year's ladies' quarter-finals. And it's not only Abigail's unexpected progress through the first week of the event that has shocked the tennis world, it's the fact that at thirty-six she is the oldest player here – and by some margin ...'

Abi shifted in her seat, smoothing the seat belt across her chest and picking a speck of dust off her immaculate white tracksuit bottoms. Trying to block out the noise of the radio, she stared out of the tinted windows at a local Wimbledon resident pretending to prune the roses creeping up the outside of her adorable, but no doubt eye-wateringly expensive, house. Secateurs in hand, the woman was making the occasional snip-snip while making very little contact with her roses – she could not fool Abi that she wasn't actually using her enormous sunglasses to hide, while scanning the road for passing celebrities, or perhaps even a royal or two on their way to the tournament grounds.

'Let's get this into perspective, shall we – these days, it is not uncommon to see players nudging towards the higher end of their thirties while still riding high in the rankings, is it?'

'No, absolutely not. We've had Serena Williams and Roger Federer playing in their forties after all. But the difference here is that Abigail Patterson retired from the game entirely for the best part of twenty years.'

'So, she really has come out of nowhere?'

'Oh, totally. She was apparently just a local coach for all that time. She has no form whatsoever, and no sponsors when the tournament began ...'

Just a coach. Abi swallowed, determined to stay calm.

'And what about her team? Who is coaching the coach?'

'Well, this is the question on everyone's lips ... and no one's quite sure. She seems to be working with Max Chamberlain, a

Brit who's an agent for a sports-management company based over in Miami. Good reputation. Well-liked on the circuit...'

Abi looked over at her best friend, Georgie, in the seat next to her. The women grinned at each other and Georgie rolled her eyes at the mention of Max. Of course everyone liked him.

'But we don't know who her coach is. Or even who she's worked with in the past. We last saw her in SW19 two decades ago. Back then, she was one of our most promising juniors, but she left the tour while still in her teens.'

'What do you make of her, Mel?'

'Well, she's a real dark horse. I remember all the hype about her when she was a junior. Great hands, good feel. Lots of variety. Pretty good little athlete, but needed work on her serve. That just wasn't a weapon – but she was tipped for the very top. She had the X factor, no doubt about it... but then she just disappeared from the circuit. Boom. Gone.'

'I wonder how she filled those twenty years?'

The women were no longer sharing a smile, but listening intently now. Abi held her breath, keen to know if there was going to be any mention of her son, Robbie, now eighteen, and only a few hundred metres away in the flat they had just left. Robbie. The reason she was here at all today.

'You're not the only one. But now she's back. How did she get here? Well, she somehow got herself a wild-card spot in the all-British pre-qualifying event, worked her way through that and then won three rounds of qualifying to reach the main draw. Now, to everyone's astonishment and delight, she has ripped up the form book and made her way through four rounds with relative ease to book a place in the last eight. It's fairy-tale stuff.'

'It's an unusual streak, that's for sure, but perhaps doubly so in one who has taken such a long career break and is now one of the tournament's older competitors?'

'That's it, Mel. This sort of a journey through the tournament would be notable under any circumstances, and it's doubly so from a player with this history.'

'And you can bet that if she does well today, every newshound in the country will be trying to find out where she's been all this time.'

'Absolutely.'

'So this is the comeback of all comebacks, then, isn't it?'

'It certainly is…'

The car stopped at a set of traffic lights, and Abi shifted her gaze from the window to avoid making eye contact with any passers-by. She found herself wishing she had on an enormous pair of shades too.

Thank God for Georgie, her oldest friend and the one who had been there in the early days on the circuit. Back then, they'd been competitors and best friends, travelling the length and breadth of the country on the junior tour, and dreaming of travelling much further. These days, Georgie was a powerhouse sports PR, the sort of woman who sports stars dreamed of having to clear up their reputation and young athletes depended on to bag the big sponsorships deals. But to Abi, she would always be the nerdy thirteen-year-old tennis geek with feet the size of her dad's and an uncanny ability to remember tournament stats.

Today, Georgie was keeping herself discreetly behind an enormous pair of tortoiseshell cat's-eye sunglasses, dressed in immaculately cut trousers and a silk blouse. Her ever-present jewellery caught the light, huge chunks of onyx, moonstone, topaz, glistening in the sun as she reached across the back seats to Abi and gave her hand, resting on the butter-soft leather of the central seat, a squeeze. The women smiled at each other.

'You're going to smash it,' Georgie said, raising her shades to reveal her twinkling grey eyes. Abi looked down at her lap, and took a huge breath, sick with nerves, yet also tingling with excitement. 'Even if they're not bloody mentioning *me* on the radio . . .'

Abi giggled, despite her nerves. She felt her phone buzz in her lap and turned to see her son's name.

You got this mum. And if you don't I am really sorry I got you that wild card lol

She smiled at her phone. Robbie's birth might have been the reason that she'd had to pause her career almost two decades ago, but, today, she was only in this tournament because of him. Well, because of a plan hatched between himself and Max, who, the radio had failed to mention, she had known as long as Georgie – but who was, indeed, a 'well-liked' agent based in Miami. So far, it was the only fact the press had managed to find out about her this week. Small mercies.

Oh, piss off! And make sure the washing-up's done by the time I get back. 😉

Important to keep his feet on the ground, she thought to herself as she pressed send with a smile. Because none of them could quite believe that things had gone the way they had over the last few months. Abi suspected that Robbie's original wild-card plan had been meant as a gesture, more than anything else. But now . . . well, now, her whole world had been turned on its head.

It turned out that Robbie – after lots of furtive chats with Max over Christmas – had written to the Lawn Tennis Association's board in January, asking them to consider Abi for a place in their all-British wild-card play-off at Raynes Park. After much prodding and pushing, he'd finally admitted to Abi that in his letter he'd explained that at seventeen years old, she'd been one of the nation's top juniors, before quitting in order to have him. But Abi knew that a sob story would only get you so far – it turned out that Robbie had gone on to list *all* her achievements since, explaining that at seventeen she had been number three in the British junior rankings, with a string of regional and national titles to her name. He'd detailed how she had just started to attract the attention of top coaches, pundits and agents when she'd quit to have him, later taking on a role as a coach, mentor and hitting partner to many of today's top juniors in Hampshire, before making a return to the county championships last year and winning the title without dropping a set.

As luck would have it, one of the board members, Iain Donoghue, had also witnessed her impressive victory in the county championships. It wasn't every day that a late-thirties 'nobody' lifted the trophy – and Iain had been doing some digging into Abi's tennis career himself. And so, very soon, Abi had found herself playing at Raynes Park for one of the wild-card spots. And then, more to her own amazement... winning.

The car lurched forwards as the traffic lights changed to green and Abi's thoughts jolted back to the present, the voices on the radio still happily discussing the biggest day of her career to date.

'What can we expect to see in the match today, then? Why is this one such a special one?'

Abi noticed the driver's eyes flicker towards the rear-view mirror to take a brief look at her. Her own eyes darted away instantly.

As the car rounded the corner towards the All England Club, lines of eager fans started to appear, some of them spilling into the road, causing taxis to jam up the route ahead. Abi chewed the inside of her lip, nerves floating like jellyfish inside her. She was numb with stress and alive with excitement, each only a heartbeat apart, flicking back and forth, back and forth.

'Do you think we could have the radio off, please, mate?' said Georgie, leaning forward towards the driver, who immediately nodded and pressed a button.

'Thank you,' mouthed Abi to Georgie, who gave a dismissive wave.

'What? Are you edgy or something?' she said with an impish grin. For a moment, it felt as if they were teenagers again. Stuck on a train on their way to compete in some junior event, with little more than a bag full of clammy cheese sandwiches and a shared copy of *Just Seventeen* to their name.

The car approached Gate 16, the players' entrance, taking the corner especially slowly as a swarm of cameras – both media flashlights and fans with camera phones – thronged towards it in the hope that Abi was inside. The thick tinted glass kept the noise of the crowd out, but she could still see the phone screens being thrust forward, blocking the faces of the fans, the flashes blasting into her eyes causing her to dip her head, staring down at her pristine new grass-court tennis shoes.

The car swung into the gates and the driver got out to open the door for Abi.

She had arrived. At last.

Chapter 2

THEN

The sun beat mercilessly on the back of Abi's neck as she bent forwards to tie her laces. It was only June. Her seventeenth birthday was two months away, but her tennis shoes were already looking pretty battered, covered in scuffs, grass stains and the mud from a puddle that one of the laces had trailed across as they'd run from the rain a couple of weeks earlier. The shoes would have to last; she knew she couldn't ask her gran for anything else right now.

On the other side of the immaculate grass court, Georgie was pulling her visor down over her pale grey eyes, before swigging from a bottle of water that she then slung to the side, leaving it to roll towards the wire netting. The air smelled of freshly cut dried grass and sun cream. It was the sort of day when anything might be possible.

'OK, Hingis, ready for set two?' she asked with a grin.

Abi smiled back and rolled her eyes. 'Yep. Let's do this, Davenport…'

Georgie picked up a discarded tennis-ball tube from the

side of the court and put it over her mouth, speaking into it to recreate the tannoy of an All England Club official. 'Seats, please, ladies and gentlemen, seats, please. Play will be resuming shortly.'

Abi wiped the sweat from her eyes and flicked her long dark plait off her shoulder and back behind her as she stood up. She readied herself to receive Georgie's serve, as keen to beat her mate on court as she was to have a laugh with her off it. Relatively small for a tennis player, Abi was quick and smart, just like her role model, Martina Hingis. She needed to be when she was up against Georgie, who was not just her best mate but also her closest rival in the county.

At almost six feet, Georgie Blackwood was nearly as tall as her own idol, Lindsay Davenport. Her height made her a daunting opponent, especially to anyone who didn't know her, but she had to work hard on the agility that came effortlessly to Abi. While Abi loved Hingis's ability to change pace, height and depth, and spent hours watching her matches over and over, trying to emulate her repertoire of shots and footwork patterns, Georgie's size ten feet often seemed to get in the way – both on court and off. Then again, her height did enable her huge serve, and it was that which Abi was steeling herself for now.

And so began the next set of their usual back and forth, interspersed with Georgie's 'tannoy announcements' and the odd bit of ultra-posh 'BBC commentary' from Abi. This game of Wannabe Wimbledon was one they had been playing in every out-of-school moment since the actual tournament had begun a week ago, and it was bound to continue long after the real finals were played.

Just as summer had shifted from the grassy promise of late May to the hazy heat of June, playing tennis had blossomed for them too, making a slow but definite shift from their hobby to something that the young women were starting to take seriously. Was there really a chance that if they worked hard enough, they could do this all day every day? That they could turn it from something they spent every penny on to something that might actually pay them? Perhaps. But every time she let herself dream for a moment too long, Abi reminded herself that it wasn't that simple. Georgie Blackwood, however, had no such worries.

Abi was dealing well with the fierce serves coming her way, but as fast as she returned them, she was faced with a barrage of huge, clean groundstrokes in return. She was darting all over the court, while Georgie seemed to take – at most – half the number of strides and to achieve just as much with them. No wonder her shoes were more worn out, Abi thought as she skidded towards the net, leaving a plume of dust and grass in her wake.

But differing match styles weren't the only thing behind Abi's scruffier kit. After all, it was a tennis court in Georgie's back garden that they were playing on: the difference in the girls' upbringing was as undeniable as the difference in their games. While Abi was making the pair of trainers she'd received for Christmas last as long as possible, Georgie had on an almost box-fresh pair of grass-court shoes from the same brand as Davenport herself. While Abi had had to save up for her two rackets for the best part of a year, and now looked after them, knowing they would have to last for even longer, Georgie had a holdall full of rackets and treated them with the nonchalance of someone who knew they could easily be replaced. She was right. Because while Abi's parents had died in a car crash when she was only twelve, leaving her to be brought up by her well-meaning but somewhat out-of-touch grandparents, Georgie had her whole family – and their considerable wealth – behind her when it came to making things happen in the tennis world.

Abi's grandmother had only quite recently come to realise that Abi was serious about tennis – that this bouncy teenager who had once just seemed little more than 'sporty' was actually hell-bent on this being her future. As a small child, she had told her Grannie Annie that she 'dreamed about playing tennis' and her grandmother had thought it was just a sweet anecdote. Now, she was accepting that it was very much an ambition rather than a mere fantasy. Yes, Abi *literally* dreamed of tennis when she couldn't be playing it, leaping and reaching through the air as she slept, her body itching to get back on court the minute she was up. But, crucially, she *loved* winning.

Since her parents had died, nothing else had given her the same buzz as working out the tactics to beat her opponents, knowing that she had the skill, the power, the fitness to deliver the plan and get the win. And to do this again and again, to achieve this lambent sense of belonging time after time, she was ready to take it seriously, to put in the hours of training and travel required, and to strive for the very top. The trouble was, she had run out of ways to try to explain this to her grandparents, and was just hoping that the consistency of her message was getting through.

Meanwhile, Georgie had barely ever had a choice in it. Early family photos of her in tiny tennis whites were crammed onto every spare inch of wall space in the Blackwoods' house, the hopes and dreams of her family reflected back at her in a constant loop.

Abi sometimes felt a shard of envy about these advantages, but Georgie was such a genuinely good friend, she found it almost impossible to sustain any ill will for too long. Especially as Georgie seemed as sincerely enthusiastic about Abi's success as her own, as keen for a mate who enjoyed playing as much as she did, and as full of infectious giggles and silliness as anyone Abi had ever met. How could she begrudge such good fortune when it had been bestowed on someone as full of sunshine as Georgie was? Someone who wished as much success for her as she did for herself?

Abi was never quite sure about the specifics of Georgie's father, Derek Blackwood's job, but he seemed to have made a lot of money in property in their corner of Hampshire. And Mr Blackwood seemed equally relaxed about spending vast swathes of it on keeping both his wife and daughter happy.

Keeping Georgie happy was pretty simple: she wanted to play tennis, and lots of it. Georgie's mum, Barb Blackwood, however, wanted more. Not just for herself, but for her daughter too. Ever-present and always audible, Barb – *never* Mrs Blackwood, as it 'made her feel old' – saw herself as one of the game's greatest authorities, despite never having made it beyond the ladies' second team at Bracken Lane Tennis Club in Winchester. The fact that she was a committee member, and one who liked to have her voice heard, was enough. People deserved her insight! And she was relentlessly generous about sharing it – a generosity matched only by her commitment to looking the part.

Barb saw keeping up with tennis-wear trends, staying aware of the big brands and who they sponsored, as an intrinsic part of her role at the club – and in Georgie's life. With the enthusiastic use of her credit cards, she encouraged her daughter to stick to one or two of the same labels, dressing head to toe in outfits straight from the latest catalogue, so as to hint at the possibility that Georgie might already be being sponsored by some big names. And Barb did the same, making sure that even when she had no intention of playing, she was wearing branded loungewear that might conceivably have been gifted by a big-name sponsor.

She saw grass stains as an enemy on a par with simple carbohydrates and the entire family's kit was never less than immaculate. It was only Barb's hair – long, burnished red, diligently straightened to glass-like perfection – that seemed to betray the fact that the energy she spent on any actual match skills always came second to the energy she spent on living the life of a key committee member of Bracken Lane Tennis Club.

But Barb's ambition didn't stop at Bracken Lane: she was as determined to make it to the All England Club as Georgie was. Indeed, there were times when Abi wondered if Barb's determination that Georgie made it as far as playing Wimbledon was as much about her daughter becoming a successful professional as it was about Barb being accepted there herself. Yes, she longed to sit in the players' box on Centre Court, having her outfit discussed on the pages of the next day's papers. But what she *really* longed for was a life spent discreetly networking from the chintz-bedecked comfort of the sofas in the members' lounge. Just to sit in that ladies' steam room and listen to the members chat while the condensation dripped down on them, she had once confessed to Mr Blackwood, now *that* would really mean success. And if it took indulging Georgie's every training whim to get there, so be it!

It wasn't that Abi didn't envy Barb's boundless enthusiasm for the game now and then. Her grandparents did what they could to support her, but their funds were as limited as their knowledge and understanding. They had never played it in their youth and they only really saw it on television for a fortnight every summer. This had its frustrations, but Abi sometimes felt awash with relief not to be the focus of Barb's red-hot ambition. Georgie was wearying of Barb keeping such a watchful eye over her diet, talking over her when she didn't even seem to realise she was doing it, and making an increasing number of decisions about her future without any real consultation.

Georgie loved tennis, but it was the playing that she loved. She wasn't so keen on the drama that her mother surrounded it with, but she had figured out early on that the more you played, the more you won… so the more you got to play.

Having a grass court in your garden had seemed like an unimaginable luxury to Abi when she had first found out about it two years ago, but now she saw more clearly that it came at a price, and that that price was bearing the weight of Barb's ambition.

The results of this pressure became increasingly evident as the day's Wannabe Wimbledon match proceeded. Abi, happy to have such a gorgeous court to practise on, was delighted to be playing at the Blackwoods' again. Each time she leapt or leant towards the ball, sensing her body grow stronger and her technique become a little more polished, she felt lucky to be where she was, to be enjoying the Blackwoods' generosity. And she was sure that Georgie had started the match almost as carefree. But as she heard the enormous patio doors open behind her, Georgie's playfulness was quickly replaced by a renewed focus and a fresh sense of competitiveness.

The distant clink and scrape of Barb making her way out onto the terrace, arranging the white cast-iron furniture and laying the table for one of her ladies' lunches, seemed to remind Georgie that she was being watched. That there was a goal in sight. That in return for the vast amounts being invested in her game, she was expected to pay for it with results.

Abi glanced up at the patio, leg raised behind her, tapping the grass out of the dimpled sole of her shoe with her racket, and saw Barb, hand up to shield her eyes, watching the girls. Georgie, clearly listening despite having her back turned to the patio, experienced an obvious dip in concentration.

Break point approached and the ball caught the top of the net, Abi reaching it just in time. Georgie fluffed the next shot, and at exactly that moment, three of Barb's friends appeared on the patio, scraping their chairs on the concrete as they pulled them out to sit down, the tinkle of ice cubes hitting glasses as they fell from the giant jug of Pimm's No.1 almost as loud as the high pitch of their laughter.

'Woah, amazing serves today!' called Abi to her friend, whose disappointment at messing things up just as they had an audience was obvious. 'Your serve's going to be bigger than Davenport's before long!'

On the advice of the county coach, both girls were enjoying spending time watching any recordings of their 'sheroes' matches they could get their hands on, and trying to replicate what they saw. They loved having an excuse to watch endless tennis together whenever they couldn't actually be playing it, and to their delight they were now reaping the benefits too. But it was starting to look as if it was going to take more than some recorded matches to keep Georgie on an emotional even keel with Barb breathing down her neck. It had only taken a couple of games for Abi to win the match once she had broken her friend's serve, and before long they were walking up the lawn from the court, as the sound of stiff applause from the patio made its way down to meet them.

Inside, Abi was glowing with satisfaction that she had once again won the match, but she knew that now was not the time to celebrate.

'Well done, girls,' said Barb. 'Lots to work on ... lots to work on ...'

'Thanks, Barb,' replied Abi as she skipped up the steps towards where the women were sitting. She had been planning to get past the lunch party as quickly as possible to avoid too much chat from Barb – for Georgie's sake as much as hers. But just as they approached, Billie, their white bichon frise, came scurrying out of the house, almost tripping up Barb, who was carrying a huge platter of salad, topped with glistening slices of halloumi. She'd clearly been watching Nigella again, thought Abi, who had long been envious of the TV in the Blackwoods' kitchen.

'Would you like to join us for some salad, girls?' asked Barb, a smear of lipstick visible on her front tooth as she smiled towards them.

'I'm desperate for a shower, Mum ...'

'Yeah, I should probably have one too, if that's OK, Barb.'

Barb sighed, clearly a little put out not to be able to deliver a few pearls of tennis wisdom, or to have Georgie to show off to her pals. But Georgie just kept moving and the girls made it to the cool and calm of the kitchen, leaving the women to gossip. Moments like these left Abi with a small pebble of anxiety in the pit of her stomach, so she could only imagine what they did to Georgie, who already had her head in the fridge, hunting for a snack. She pulled open the bottom drawer and reached past a punnet of strawberries to find two chilled green apples. As she stood there, snippets of the women's conversation outside drifted in through the Crittall windows.

'Honestly, he has to be seen to be believed – he's in *such* great shape – but he's a charmer with it…'

'Snake charmer, if you ask me…'

A sprinkling of laughter, then the women lowered their voices. Abi suspected they were discussing the incoming club coach, who Georgie had already told her had more than piqued Barb's interest. Mr Blackwood was apparently less impressed with tales of the Californian hunk.

'The name, though – it's so *Sex and the City*!'

'What do you mean?'

'Cole Connolly Jr. It's American, but very American, no?'

Barb's voice rose above the shrieks of excited laughter.

'He *has* got the talent, though. And the international experience. He's fresh from the States and his CV is impressive…'

'Oh, come on, Barb, he's easy on the eye and that's going to be great for the club either way – you don't have to be shy about it.'

The laughter was only interrupted by Georgie turning from the fridge and shouting, 'Catch!' as she lobbed an apple across the mottled granite of the island. Abi snapped out of her earwigging and leant back, easily catching the apple with one hand. Grinning at her friend, Georgie poured them each a glass of water from the neat white filter jug in the fridge door.

'Strawberries and cream next year, babe,' she said, closing the fridge.

'Maybe one day,' replied Abi. As she sat on an elegant designer stool at the island, it seemed an act of wild imagination that raw ambition could get her to Wimbledon any time soon, especially in comparison to all of Georgie's advantages. But as she bit into her apple, Abi knew she had it in her to give it her very best shot.

Chapter 3

NOW

The security staff rummaged through Abi's kitbag as she stood at the front desk smiling nervously. What were they looking for?

After what felt like an unnecessarily long poke about in her belongings, the staff, apparently oblivious to the fact that they were dealing with one of the final eight, handed it back and waved Abi and Georgie in towards the player-services area. As they entered the building, the two women passed a spread of the day's papers laid out along part of the reception desk, several of which were emblazoned with either Abi's face or name – or both.

They shared a quick glance and swiftly turned left towards the main warm-up area, heading past the players' gym, with its bank of running machines and static bikes. Above them was a row of TV screens, two of which were playing footage of her arrival only minutes ago as part of the hourly headlines. It felt as if Big Brother were watching her wherever she went. Abi bit down on her lip, feeling her heart race, momentarily bamboozled by the bustle of the club, the hum of the crowds outside – making their way towards food and drink concessions, finding their seats, seeking out a good spot on the hill. She had anticipated feeling out of place because of her age; instead, she felt like a teenager again. An impostor in an adult world. Who *did* she think she was, turning up as if she belonged here? She spun on her heel to face Georgie.

'I need to get out of here – let's go to the practice site.'

'Up to the Aorangi Park courts?'

'Yes, please.'

Ten minutes later, they'd made the short golf-buggy ride along the secret tunnel running the length of the grounds. While the other competitors had a ready supply of 'hitters' – would-be or ex-professionals who could be hired to warm players up in the style of their next opponent – Abi and her team had thus far been making do with each other. She'd grown up playing Georgie and Max, and they knew her style, her weaknesses and the chinks in her psychological armour. So, while working with an amateur's budget, who better to rope in than her oldest friends and competitors? And today was no exception. Georgie had slipped out of her PR-maven uniform and into oh-so-chic whites, readying herself to give Abi a run-around before the match itself. Aware of the press's increased interest, they had snuck away to Court 22, out of the way and largely out of sight.

Anxiety loosened its grip and Abi's muscles began to relax. Her heart found a steady beat as she focused on keeping her breathing deep and slow. Georgie's forehands were no less fierce than they had ever been, and she was sending Abigail shots just like the ones she knew she'd be facing from her opponent before too long. But Abi was absorbing the shots comfortably, settling into a rhythm – her body feeling at home, injury-free, ready to throw the kitchen sink at the match.

As she waited for Georgie to fire down some of her rocket serves, Abi pulled at her shirt, loosening it from her skin, before flicking her long auburn French plait behind her. Her skin was as freckled as it had been as a teenager, if a little more weather-beaten from years spent coaching outside, often squinting into the sun.

There was an audible cheer from the distant crowd on Murray Mound as the sun came out from behind a bank of cloud, and as the rays reached Abi, she closed her eyes for just a minute. Was that Carly, today's opponent, arriving? At the same gate, with its crowds of fans, where she had so recently arrived?

Carly was, in many ways, a very similar player to Abi – or at least to the player that Abi had been at the same age. A right-handed eighteen-year-old with short, tousled blonde hair, she was effortlessly athletic, and as comfortable playing on grass as Abi had ever been. Robbie had noted this last night without apparently realising the weight of what he was saying, that Carly Cunningham was the closest Abi could come to playing her younger self.

But in contrast to Abi's outsider status as a literal wild card, Carly was very much an insider: the daughter of former player Bradley Cunningham, who had a handful of tour titles to his name and was a member of the Australian team that won the Davis Cup in 1986. He was a national hero and a bit of a heartthrob (or 'legendary dreamboat', according to Barb). It was this inherited ease with which Carly and her dad handled the big occasions that was preying most on Abi's mind today, but Georgie had clocked that long ago.

As the cheers from the crowd floated up the hill towards

Court 22, Georgie paused before her next serve and eyeballed Abi.

'At least you know she's going to be pretty easy to read,' she said with a hint of a shrug. 'You just need to think about what your fifteen-year-old self thought were your smartest tactics.'

'Hmm.' Abi was unconvinced, but reluctant to admit to it out loud.

'It's true! The experience gap is more of a canyon! You've taught kids on the Hampshire circuit more mature than her! You'll be surprised how easy she is to read...'

Abi chuckled, bouncing up and down on the baseline, waiting for Georgie's mini lecture to wind up. Was she just trying to distract her? Was this part of the warm-up?

'And then there's the fact that we all know she must spend half her life wondering what percentage of the crowd is just there to get a glimpse of her old man...'

Abi nodded, silently conceding this point was undeniable. A heartbeat later, the ball came hurtling towards her again, and her mind returned to the game itself. Back and forth, they went, until it was time to head to the ladies' dressing room to get ready for the 2 p.m. match.

They reached the door to the players' dressing rooms without attracting any attention from fans or press, and Georgie put her bag down, hugging Abi tightly.

'I'm off to get myself match-ready,' she said, nodding at the smart trouser suit and silk blouse in its chic suit holder. 'But listen, there won't be a moment on that court that you're there alone. We're all going to be there, not just in the box, but in spirit. I know you know that, but it can't hurt to tell you again. The pressure and the expectation is on her. Not you. You can own this match. Let yourself own it.'

'Thank you, babe,' said Abi into Georgie's hair, before letting their embrace loosen.

Georgie looked square at her now, face to face as they had been so many times, before so many matches. 'I know what you can do. You know what you can do. Do it.' Then Georgie blew her a kiss, turned on her heel, and walked away before either of them could let emotions slide into centre stage.

While Georgie headed off to meet the rest of her on-site PR team, Abi made her way into the changing room and started her little ritual of checking the contents of the kitbag she'd be taking on court.

Her phone buzzed on the bench beside her. Max.

You've got this. You've always had it. But now is your time. Bracken Lane Ballers Forever! 🤟

Abigail felt her face soften as she smiled at the screen. Max. She hadn't realised until the last few weeks, now that he was her agent and they spoke multiple times a day, how much she'd missed his warm, solid presence in her life. Of course, he'd always been a great friend – and a father figure to Robbie – but his work in Miami always pulled him away.

Don't let yourself get distracted now. It's his job. But she still found herself wondering if the flutters in her stomach were solely down to pre-match nerves.

Don't. Get. Distracted.

Abi blinked. Back to the bag. She had already applied her sunscreen but made sure that the rest of the SPF spray was in there. She had a couple of spare T-shirts, neatly folded, complete with the new sponsor patches from two of the brands who had been in touch with Max earlier in the week when she'd smashed into the final eight. Now that she was going to be making a Centre Court appearance to a global audience of millions, apparently every inch of her kit counted for something.

But, as she ran her hand across the embroidered logos, it was the fact that Max had swung into action for her with such speed and enthusiasm that had meant the most. She had her visor, extra socks, spare shoes, spare laces, several sweatbands, each of them nicely worn in so that the seam didn't rub. There were spare hair ties, some over-grips and the four rackets themselves, each one freshly strung and stencilled, just as if she were a real pro, and not someone who still felt like something of an impostor, an afterthought. Her competitors' pass told a different story, though, and was positioned on top of the pile of her belongings, not least because Max had repeatedly warned her not to lose it as she wouldn't be able to get back into the clubhouse without it – even if she *was* a quarter-finalist.

In one of the side pockets of her bag was her stash of jelly beans, the best source of instant energy she had ever come across, and something that always reminded her of the fun of her childhood matches. She couldn't bear the wholesomeness of the scientifically created energy bars that were so in vogue now – how were you even supposed to swallow something so dense and tasteless when you already felt as if your heart was in your mouth? If you were going to have to eat on court in front of millions, surely it should just be something that felt like a bit of a treat?

As Abi had packed and unpacked her bag last night, Robbie hadn't been so sure, questioning the professionalism of it, and how it might look on camera. The cheek of him! But Georgie had hushed him away from discussing it again. A whispered,

'She's *always* done this; she's not going to change now, when so much else is changing...' and a hard stare followed by a conspiratorial wink seemed to have kept him quiet. Abi hadn't let nutrition fall entirely by the wayside, though, because Georgie had carefully prepared several bottles of energy drinks, meticulously measured with all natural ingredients and real fruit.

Abi wondered if Georgie had had her own shower and made her way up to Gangway 211 yet. For years, it had been the stuff of legend, as it marked the entrance to the players' box. To gain access at this point, you were more than a tennis fan, a wealthy corporate donor or a well-connected celebrity – you were *invested.* Some fans called it the best seats in the house, but to many a parent or partner, Abi knew it often felt like more of a pressure than a privilege. Were Georgie, Max and Robbie together now, feeling that weight? She tried to imagine them sitting there, staring out at the immaculate grass, trying to chat discreetly, while no doubt aware of the army of cameras at all angles around them.

She had imagined looking up at that iconic box a million times as a teenager. Night after night, she had told herself that the aching muscles, the parties missed, the money spent, would all be worth it when she looked up for the first time and saw her own crew in the Centre Court players' box. She had pictured them whooping as she dived for shots, punching the air as she scored a winning point. Back then, it had been Grannie Annie and Grandad Bob sitting there that she had visualised, with perhaps the Blackwoods and a teenage Georgie and Max.

A momentary thud of grief passed through her at the thought that it had taken her too long to reach Centre Court for her grandparents to see her childhood dream come true.

The hours she had spent on the phone to Georgie, on their early, clunky mobile phones, discussing who they would allow in their box, how many could fit – and if another school friend crossed them, they'd wickedly announce, 'Out of the box!' She wondered if Georgie was thinking the same, now this childhood dream was coming true. Abi wasn't sure she'd even believe it when she saw them all sitting there, when she walked out onto court in just a few minutes' time now.

Her stomach lurched and, finally convinced there was little more she could do to prepare, she looked down at the contents of her bag. Lying at the very top was her notebook full of motivational quotes and key tactics for the match, and a Post-it note on which Robbie had scrawled *Good Luck, Mum*. It was these that she wanted to see first if she opened her bag courtside at any point, and she was pretty sure she had figured out how to position them so that she could glimpse the pages while prying eyes and long-range cameras couldn't.

A cleaner bustled into the dressing room and as the door opened, she heard the familiar sound of Bradley Cunningham's voice booming out from the hallway speakers. He loved the limelight almost as much as he loved himself and had become an expert in self-promotion. He took every opportunity to face the media and speak on behalf of his daughter. And, of course, in his typical maverick style, he wasn't averse to belittling his daughter's opponents at any opportunity.

'Abigail who?' she heard him say in his broad Aussie drawl. 'Till yesterday I'd never heard of her. Bit old for it all, isn't she? Now, I know she's going to have all the pressure of being home favourite. Wouldn't like to be in her shoes … I'd imagine she'd prefer to be tucked up at home with a cup of tea and some fluffy slippers.' He guffawed.

Abi looked down at her brand new grass-court trainers, the laces triple-checked and knotted. Broken sunlight fell through the frosted window like glittering snowflakes on the changing-room floor. She shook her head, trying to force the thoughts of snow, of anything to do with that terrible night, from her mind.

Chapter 4

THEN

The night that her parents died, the ground was covered with the first snow of the season.

It had started snowing early that afternoon, just as dusk was falling. The air was chilly and crisp, perfect for the few weeks before Christmas, when everyone rushed off to find their trees and buy their presents. Abi and her parents had been having an early dinner at her grandparents', where she'd be staying the night, as her parents were off to the Mayflower Theatre to watch some reunion show from an eighties band they had been into when they were childhood sweethearts. Her mum and gran waved from the kitchen window while Abi and her dad whirled around the back garden, trying to catch snowflakes on their tongues, seeing how many could fall into their open hands without melting, shrieking with glee at the impromptu fun.

Before they left, her mother checked and double-checked that the roads were OK, and made her dad leave double the time to get there so they wouldn't have to rush on the white roads. Abi then enjoyed the evening watching *The X Factor* with Grannie Annie, trying to explain the intricacies of the backstage gossip, begging to be allowed to call the premium-rate number to vote and finally calling her new friend Georgie to gossip about which of the boyband acts they rated the most highly – for looks *and* talent.

It was a cold night and Abi slept well, as cosy as ever with Grannie Annie's thick Highland blanket on top of the duvet. While she lay there, her parents, singing along to the car radio as they headed home, never saw the Range Rover that ploughed into them. Months later at the inquest, Abi and her grandparents would find out that the driver had been on his way back from the pub after only a pint and a half, but the dark and icy conditions had been enough for him not to spot the Pattersons' car as he'd thundered across one of the many roundabouts on the way out of the city.

Her mum died instantly, the four-wheel drive hitting her side of the car first. Her dad almost made it through the night, but by 9 a.m. the staff at the hospital were trying to figure out who to contact with the bad news. By 11 a.m. Abi had been to her regular tennis lesson, again with her new friend Georgie, and was still waiting for her parents to come and collect her when her grandparents turned into the tennis-club car park, ashen-faced.

Grandad Bob stood by the side of the car, as if leaning on it for strength, his hand over his mouth. Grannie Annie came out and walked round the car towards Abi, giving her such a huge hug that the zip of her winter coat dug into Abi's top lip.

'I'm sorry, darling. I'm so, so sorry,' Abi heard her mumbling into her shoulder. She felt something curdle inside her, some primal part of her understanding what the news would be long before Grannie Annie found the words to tell her.

'Don't say it!' Abi heard her voice begging her grandmother. It sounded like someone else's – strange, high-pitched, far away. 'Grannie, don't say it!'

'Anne...' Her grandfather stepped forward just as Grannie Annie crumpled into tears.

'Oh, my love, it's your parents, I'm so sorry.'

'Don't...' It was only seconds later that Abi realised the wail was coming from herself.

'Abigail, we are both so very sorry, but we had a visit from the police this morning, and your parents were in a car accident during the night...'

Abi either couldn't hear or didn't remember anything after this, until she was back at her grandparents' house, which, while familiar, had, for the last twelve years, just been a much-loved stopover. But it was now her home.

She sat on the edge of the bed, a hand brushing across the Highland blanket that last night had represented nothing but warmth and the cosiness of Christmas to her. It now seemed like a relic from another life.

She never went back to her childhood bedroom – a friend of her parents instead bringing a couple of storage boxes full of her stuff back to her grandparents' later that week. The posters she had once fallen to sleep staring at would never find a place on the walls at her new home. Instead, tournament wall charts would go up as she tracked her idols' progress, dreaming of following in their footsteps.

She was still in her sports kit as she sat on her new bed that first surreal Sunday afternoon. When she looked down, she saw her tennis shoes – the ones she had had to work so hard to persuade her parents to get her. It had only been a month or two earlier that she had finally managed to convince them, after spending countless evenings and even breakfasts before school explaining to them that she absolutely was serious about tennis – not just as a passion or a hobby, but as her *future*.

She had taken to tearing out pages of young tennis stars from glossy magazines, poring over features that detailed the early starts in life and ceaseless parental support that today's champions had been lucky enough to have. When she'd realised that proper, detailed research was what it might take to get her parents on board that she was planning to do this professionally, she'd started recording any televised press conferences and spent hours in the library making thorough notes from as many sports autobiographies as she could find.

Time and again, her mother had fretted about the insecurity of the profession, suggesting half-heartedly that Abi also focus on exams, throwing in very grown-up-sounding terms such as 'job security'. Her dad, meanwhile, had trodden a slim line between the two of them, a gentle arm slung around her mum's shoulder while she spoke, never undermining her, while waiting his turn to tell Abi that recommending backup plans did not mean not believing her – it meant not trusting everyone else. He would remind her how many players had fallen foul of the capricious whims of sponsors, the sheer bad luck of an on-court injury or the weight of the mental toll that international sport – with the constant travel, the insecure finances and the time away from friends and family – could take. As a twelve-year-old, a lot of what he said went straight over her head. All she wanted to do was play tennis at the very top level, and nothing was going to get in her way.

'We believe in you, darling,' he'd tell her. 'We just don't want anyone or anything to take you away from us just yet.'

Little did she know that bad luck and an icy road would take *them* away from her that winter.

Luck cannot be trusted, she told herself that day, and she had never relied on it since.

Chapter 5

NOW

Abi wiped a hot tear from her cheek and sat up, smoothing her hair back with her hands, running her fingers down across the bumps of her fresh French plait, checking for any kinks or stray strands. Twenty years ago, she'd have been happy with a hastily scraped ponytail, but these days she knew not to risk having to fiddle with her hair on court. She loved her long auburn locks – something that never failed to remind her of her mother – but she really, really needed not to have to think about them for the next couple of hours.

1.56 p.m.

She heard the cleaner leave the changing area and, as a strange silence settled over the room, she realised that, for the first time in a long time, she was entirely alone. So often over the last few weeks, as the Wimbledon whirlwind had ripped through her life, it had felt as if she'd been tugged in a zillion different directions at any given moment. The tiny basement flat she'd rented in Wimbledon Village had always felt full of people: Robbie popping in and out with his school friends, Max arriving back from the States and negotiating deals from the galley kitchen, Georgie rushing around with her headset and mobile phone giving carefully curated statements to the press on Abi's behalf. They'd all been there to help her, but from time to time she'd felt as if what would be most helpful of all was an hour or two alone. It's not that she wasn't grateful for them all dropping everything to be with her, but at certain moments, she had longed for a minute to herself for some yoga, or to zone out with a good book or a blast of Coldplay.

Finally, the time had come. Just a couple of minutes, but it felt worth it.

She'd always been a private person who needed to recharge with some quiet alone time. When Robbie was little, she'd guiltily loved that magical moment of calm after he'd fallen asleep and she could slip downstairs and curl up to watch something trashy on the sofa in her pyjamas. Maybe Bradley Cunningham was more spot-on with his comments than he even realised.

At least Georgie had done a brilliant job of constructing an iron-clad wall around her life to protect it from the press. Abi knew the media was an invaluable part of making a name for herself in the game – a strong personality and a bold presence on court could go pretty far in unnerving opponents, and securing sponsorship deals, too.

She knew an almost encyclopaedic amount about virtually everyone she was playing, but barely anyone knew a thing about her. It was just the way she liked it, but she wasn't sure how long it could possibly last.

Just the thought of the papers – or worse, the social media super-fans – pulling at her past to try to find a loose thread sent her heart rate spiralling. She looked at her hands and saw that she had been picking at a tiny bit of skin around her thumbnail.

It was close to bleeding, and she knew she'd be feeling it later if it was a lengthy match and she was gripping the racket for too long. She took a deep breath, forcing herself to rest her hands on her lap for a minute. As she exhaled, she promised herself she would face her future this afternoon, not dwell on her past.

1.58 p.m.

There was a knock on the door and Angela Chadwick-Hall, a member of the championships committee, entered the changing room, her patent leather pumps clack-clack-clacking on the parquet floor.

'Abigail, it's time to make your way to Centre Court.'

Abi smiled up at her, wondering if this sort of moment was as big a deal to Angela as it was to her. It certainly seemed to be, judging by the formality with which she was carrying herself.

She got up off the bench, and followed Angela through the labyrinthine corridors of the All England Club. Today, the route was different – she wasn't headed to one of the far-flung outer courts where she had played the previous week's matches, but to the glass doors that led the way to the hallowed turf of Centre Court itself.

Abi looked up at the Kipling quote inscribed on the wall above them, its reference to meeting triumph and disaster but treating them just the same hitting a nerve.

Well, I've had my fair share of the latter, thought Abi, as she noticed Angela gesticulating that it was time to pass her racket bag to a ballboy. Carly bounced down the stairs from the more opulent seeded-players' dressing room on level one with the confidence of someone who had been there plenty of times before.

Abi smiled cautiously at her, but Carly barely seemed to

notice either her or the smile. A brief nod was all she got, as Carly shook herself, her gaze reaching far into the distance, focus entirely on the match.

They waited at the doorway, the two competitors next to each other, hidden by the frosted glass of the clubhouse doors. Angela, a couple of steps ahead of them, reminded the women what the protocol for the next couple of minutes was. Carly ran a tanned hand through her choppy blonde hair, which stuck up from her head with the sort of effortless chic that would take someone more Abi's age several hours in a salon. Abi patted her plait for reassurance one more time, looked down at her shoes and tried to exhale slowly, calming her racing heartbeat.

The ball kids, the lines judges and the umpire were all in place. Through the glass, the two women heard the players' names announced, immediately followed by the crowd breaking into thunderous applause. Throughout it all, Abi's heart was racing, the weight of all those dreams on her shoulders, as well as a sudden sense of responsibility to do everything she'd always promised her parents that she could. That she would. *This one's for them*, she told herself, swallowing back the lump in her throat.

Then, slowly, the frosted-glass doors opened. Angela led the way, the competitors a couple of steps behind. Seconds later, they rounded the corner onto the most famous tennis court in the world and stepped in front of the crowd of fifteen thousand beaming faces.

The noise felt like an enormous wave crashing over Abi and, despite the sun beating down overhead, she felt a moment of dizzying claustrophobia as she saw the stands rising up around her on all sides. Wave after wave of people. She was grateful to Georgie for making her do a dry run of the court the previous day – it was overwhelming enough without the glaring lenses of a hundred cameras capturing your every move. Out of the corner of her eye, she could see her face livecast onto the big screens, so close up that you could see the flash of her silver necklace.

She remembered Georgie's instructions: stand side by side with Carly and walk eight steps in tandem, turn, count to three and curtsey to the royal box. There they were, as she turned. The royals. Just sitting there, eyes on her. A trickle of sweat crept down her left temple and as her heart thundered away in her chest, she felt sure that even the roaring crowd would be able to hear it beating.

Abi was relieved to make it to her chair next to the umpire's seat before her legs buckled beneath her entirely. Once she was sitting, she let herself take a proper look up at the front row of the players' box, searching out the faces she so desperately wanted to see.

She spotted Barb first – she was actually impossible to miss in her fuchsia-pink trouser suit and a pair of sunglasses almost as wide as the digital scoreboard itself. Next to her was Georgie, who gave her a quick, enthusiastic wave before leaning to whisper something in Robbie's ear, pointing at something in the audience. Robbie's face split into a wide grin and when he locked eyes with Abi, he gave her a thumbs up and mouthed, 'You got this, Mum.'

Her heart lurched again, thinking of the rest of her family who should have been sat beside him, cheering her on. But then, next to Robbie was Max, and he was almost family, wasn't he? Dressed in a smart navy linen suit, Max looked like a different man from the one in casual jeans and jumper that she'd been used to seeing over the last few weeks. He looked like an A-list celeb, she thought, those flutters of electricity shooting through her again. *Must be adrenaline.* They were all there, her tiny, brilliant team. Her whole world.

In comparison, the rest of the box was crammed to the seams with Carly's entourage. Her father, Brad, sat nearest to the central aisle, staring forward with a broad grin, one arm casually slung around his second wife's neck. Abi thought she remembered that she was a Swedish supermodel; she certainly looked like it. A few seats along sat Carly's mother, another ex-tennis pro, although she seemed far more interested in looking daggers at the Swedish supermodel than waving to her daughter on the court. Several more seats were taken by Carly's coach, her trainer and a whole squad of hangers-on in heavily branded sportswear.

Abi unzipped her racket bag, took out two rackets and put on her sweatbands and visor. Then she tenderly removed her silver locket from around her neck, opened it and slipped it into the same pocket where she had earlier hidden Robbie's note.

Breathe. Take a long, deep breath. You've got this.

And then, as the umpire called them to the net, Abi reminded herself of what she always told her students if they were nervous.

Move your feet, swish your racket, make some shadow strokes.

Once they were up at the net, the umpire went over the rules of the match and performed the coin toss. Abi, finally starting to block out the low murmur of the crowd, found herself wishing they could just play Rock, Paper, Scissors like she would with the kids at her club. But she played along with the formality of the coin toss, accepting the umpire decision that she was to call, and called heads.

The coin spun briefly in the air, glinting in the sunlight, before hitting the grass.

Heads.

Without hesitation, she chose to start at the royal box end – partly because that meant playing just one game with the sun in her eyes, but mainly because even though she was relaxing a little, she still wasn't sure if she could comfortably warm up while facing the dual distraction of the Princess of Wales and the fresh-from-rehab Hollywood actor who she'd spotted in the front row.

Carly had barely blinked throughout the whole process. In fact, she seemed utterly oblivious to the crowd, or indeed to Abi. She did some slow stretches, glanced briefly at the players' box and strode off to the other end of the court, in a manner not dissimilar to how Robbie reacted when told to finish his homework.

At eighteen years old, she was already ranked 12 in the world. She was exactly where Abi had dreamed of being at the same age. Travelling the world, playing all the major events. And winning. Yet Abi felt more than a little sorry for her. She'd heard the rumours of how her father would sit on a chair outside her hotel room so that nobody could interrupt or distract her without him knowing. He seemed to control every aspect of her life and, from Abi's perspective, it didn't appear to be a whole lot of fun.

Abi turned towards the baseline, kicking up her heels to warm up her muscles again, and nodding to the ball kid below the players' box to throw her a couple of the bright yellow balls so closely identified with the tournament.

As she deftly caught the balls, checking them over before tucking one into her skirt, it hit her. She was here, at Wimbledon in the quarter-final, on Centre Court. After a lifetime of dreaming and more kinks in the road than she could ever have imagined, her time had finally come. There had been so many days she had believed this chance was far behind her, and so many nights she had sobbed herself to sleep, so many times when she had almost given hope. Almost.

But this was it. The comeback of all comebacks.

Chapter 6

THEN

'It's going to be an absolutely epic comeback,' said Georgie, her mouth full of chocolate buttons. 'And I mean *epic*.'

Georgie was talking about her post-injury return to the junior circuit, as she sat facing Abi and Max on a rickety old cross-country train to a tournament in Cumbria. Barb's frighteningly healthy packed lunches lay untouched on the table in front of them, Georgie choosing to raid the station shop for them all with her pocket money instead.

Georgie had been off with an injured hamstring and, despite seeing Abi almost every day, had barely come up for air in between sentences since they'd boarded the train. It was as if she'd been banned from talking for a month, as well as tennis. Abi saw Max's eyes flick to the headphones of his prized Sony Discman, and knew he was desperate to plug into the new band Coldplay's album, rather than listen to Georgie's breathless recap of the club's latest gossip. She shared a flicker of a smile with him, keen to let him know that she appreciated that sometimes the two girls could be a bit full on. He winked back, conspiratorially.

Abi flushed and returned her focus to her mate – they couldn't be more different, but Georgie was the best friend she'd ever had. The girls had first met at Bracken Lane Tennis Club when their rackets were almost bigger than they were. When Abi's parents had died and she'd moved in with her grandparents, it had been Georgie (and Barb, of course) who'd picked her up for tennis practice every week, treating her just like normal – but giving her the hugs she'd needed in those darker moments.

At school, she'd suddenly become 'the girl whose parents died'. She would hear the other children whispering in the corridors and see them pointing at her in lessons as notes were passed between the desks. It had been almost as if she'd had something contagious, something that had to be avoided. The tennis club had soon become her safe space, where no one mentioned what had happened that snowy night in December, and instead she could drive all her pain into beating her opponents at a sport she loved.

It had been at Bracken Lane that Georgie, and then Max when he moved to the area a few years later, had provided the non-judgemental friendship that by then Abi had been so desperate for. Neither of them had much real context for the Abi who had existed 'before'. Sure, she was quiet, a pretty reserved sort for most of the time that she wasn't on court. But on court was where they spent most of their time and it was where Abi felt joyfully free to express herself. Tennis allowed her to escape from her past.

Nothing got past Georgie, though, least of all the way that the dynamic between Abi and Max had shifted while she had been off with her injury.

'I see you two!' she said. 'Taking the piss just because I'm excited to be back. What did you get up to without me anyway?'

Abi felt a giveaway flush rise up her neck and onto her face. Her freckles were barely visible now, as she gave Georgie a half-smile with eyes wide, as if to say, *Leave it, not in front of him*...

Max suddenly seemed to be preoccupied by his Discman, and just raised his gaze to tell Georgie that nothing had changed. 'In fact, it's just the same as it ever was: Abi is still winning everything.'

The dimple on her right cheek creased as Abi smiled at him, relieved that he had deflected things back to tennis.

'I see,' said Georgie, nonchalantly juggling two apples and an orange, avoiding both their gazes. 'So it's been nothing but tennis, not a hint of flirting, and clubs across the land still fear the mighty Miss Abigail Patterson.'

'That's the long and the short of it,' replied Max, snatching an apple mid-air and taking a bite.

Abi shrugged. 'What can I say, I'm having a lucky streak.' She didn't care which way Georgie took that comment. She had been playing well, after all, and it wasn't as if there wasn't a little flicker of... something... going on between her and Max recently.

'Well, I look forward to seeing this on court,' she said. The three of them looked at each other. A truce. 'The formidable tennis, that is. Nothing else, of course...'

Or perhaps not.

The following evening, it was Max who was proved right. Abi breezed through the tournament, making the rest of the opposition look like primary-school kids. Even Georgie was visibly thrilled to see the improvement in her friend's game, but she still seemed just as interested in the other developments afoot.

As soon as Max stood up from his seat on the return train home, Georgie leant forward across the laminate train table, her face as close to Abi's as she could reach.

'Seriously, though, I'm picking up some ... energy here.' Her finger was jabbing back and forth from Abi to Max's empty seat. 'What's going on? You know he's always had a bit of a' – she waggled her eyebrows up and down – 'thing about you.'

'I don't know,' whispered Abi. 'I mean he's *fit*, but I'm crap with boys. I don't know how to read the situation at all.'

'For God's sake, what more do you need?'

'Do you *really* think he likes me?'

'Let's put it this way. It's not just the junior tennis circuit that thinks you're the hottest thing around right now.'

The way Abi blushed at that comment became a memory that never faded. Max appeared in the aisle behind Georgie a heartbeat later and the conversation went unfinished.

That summer, for a short while, she felt that her path to the top of the tennis ladder looked clear and unimpeded – a straight line forward.

Chapter 7

NOW

There was a gentle hum of crowd chit-chat across the court as the two players sat either side of the umpire, taking the quickest of breaks before the match itself began. Abi resisted the temptation to let her gaze wander round the multitude of faces pointed her way, focusing on steadying her breath and recalling everything she'd studied about Carly's game. Over the last thirty-six hours, she'd pored over match footage and media features sent to her by Max and Georgie: Carly's slightly weak left ankle, which she'd turned a few games back; the way she started flattening her skirt when she felt under pressure; the way she spun the ball high and deep into the left-hand corner of the court.

'We love you, Carly!' came a shout from behind Abi, reminding her how much support her opponent had out there.

She took a quick drink from the first of her three water bottles, each of which Georgie had taken the label off first thing that morning, knowing that they were from a rival brand to the official tournament sponsor. She smiled to herself at the sheer volume of things she had learned in the last few days. A lifetime of tennis and she felt like a total rookie all over again…

Then, almost without realising she was doing it, she reached down to touch her most treasured possession, the silver locket she had dropped into the top of her bag. Pulling it out, she flipped it open with her thumbnail, as she did before every match, and took a glance at the old photograph inside. Baby Robbie, gummily smiling at the camera, with a white, green and purple Wimbledon headband on his tiny bald head. A gift from Barb to cheer her up, just when she had thought everything was over.

The day the photo had been taken felt like both a lifetime ago and yesterday. As Abi closed the locket, she held it tight in her fist, eyes closed, for a couple of seconds. She reminded herself that today was all about love. Love of the game. Love of her family. Love of her friends. And, at last, love of herself. Finally, she kissed the locket and put it safely back in the bag before the cameras managed to zoom in any closer.

'Time, please,' came the call from the umpire, as impassive as they ever were.

Let's do this.

Abi picked up her racket and walked as calmly as possible to the baseline, ready to serve first. She could feel the adrenaline coursing through her body, readying her for a fight. She exhaled slowly, spinning her racket in her hand, and subconsciously tucking invisible strands of hair behind her ears, a habit from a long time ago.

Abi stared down the court at her youthful opponent, who swayed threateningly on the opposite baseline, her features set in a frown. Carly was one of the most talented players of her generation and, Abi realised suddenly, the pressure was really all on her. *She* was the seeded player and had the weight of the media, the fans and an overbearing father on her shoulders, not Abi. *No one* expected a thirty-six-year-old wild card to win this match.

But, Abi thought, as she rolled the ball in her hand, *I have the power to take advantage of the situation.* Carly's game style was one thing, but her mindset was another, and it was important to understand both. Abi had experience on her side. Experience of life and a fierce drive for survival. She knew the young Aussie had a history of cracking when things got tough, especially when her father started bellowing from the sidelines. Just like the coin toss mere minutes earlier, this could go either way. There was a semi-final place up for grabs in the world's biggest tournament, and Abi wanted it to be hers.

The huge clock in the corner of the screen flickered into action. One second. Two seconds. Three. Abi threw the ball high up into the air and served.

She didn't give her opponent any chance to settle into the match. The blustery cross-court wind didn't help Carly either, playing havoc with her ball toss on serve and making it difficult for her to get into the right position to dictate the points with her usually lethal forehand. Abi played smartly in the breeze, with lots of floated sliced backhands deep up the centre of the court, frustrating the teenager with the lack of pace and width. As Carly rushed from point to point, banging her racket in disgust into the manicured grass, she made error after error and became more and more exasperated. As did her father, who came close to being removed from the players' box by the security guards for making wild and angry gestures towards his daughter when she lost the first set 6–2.

As they edged towards the start of the second set, Abi was keenly aware of all the eyes in the royal box trained directly on her as she took the short walk to the baseline. It was only a dozen or so steps there, but it seemed to take longer every time.

As she nodded to the ballboy in the left-hand corner, she caught a glimpse of a young girl waving furiously at her from the front row. Dressed in her tennis whites, Union Jack sweatbands on each wrist and a white cap with *ABI* scribbled on the brim in big red lettering, she was leaning forward with an urgency Abi felt keenly. Resisting the temptation to wave back, she threw the quickest of glances and the tiniest of smiles in her direction as she placed her towel in the court-side tub. The girl looked as if she might pass out with excitement, turning to her mum next to her with an enormous gasp.

Abi managed to hold her nerve – and her serve – to level at 1–1, boosted hugely by the cheering of the crowd, which seemed to have increased in volume during the break. Was their hope feeding hers, or was that just her imagination?

She looked up, scanned the crowd as she fixed her visor, clocking a small group of women around her age. On some sort of girls' day out, they were in smart floral dresses and straw hats, but had undeniably been enjoying the sizeable tumblers of Pimms, as enthusiastically as they had the tennis. Just as Abi caught the eye of one of them, she stood up, clutching her straw hat to her lap, and yelled, 'Go get her, Abi babe!'

Abi couldn't help but smile as the crowd broke into laughter, but Carly was not amused. She was preparing to serve and was once again delayed by what she later called 'deranged fans'. Face frozen, she glowered down the court and threw the ball up into the sunshine.

Double fault.

Some sections of the crowd clapped. Carly dismissed them with a sniff of the air above her head and busied herself wiping sweat off her shiny and youthful forehead. She settled herself to serve once more and began her aggravating ball bouncing. One, two, three, four, five…

A mobile phone rang out, breaking the silence with its decidedly chirpy ringtone. The crowd groaned. Abi's eyes darted up into the stands, where a man in a tan business suit was frantically patting his pockets to find the incriminating device.

Carly threw her racket to the ground and stood, hands on hips, glowering at the umpire, who immediately belted out his customary, 'Quiet, please, ladies and gentlemen. As a courtesy to the players, would you please ensure all mobile phones are switched to silent.'

The crowd applauded, the businessman shrinking back into his seat.

The court fell silent again and Carly readied herself to serve again. Another wayward ball toss. Another miscued serve. She was rattled. Abi sensed it and began to creep closer up the court. This clearly distracted Carly, who caught the next ball toss. She bounced and bounced and bounced the ball before eventually throwing it high into the cloudless sky and whacking it two metres past the service line. Another double fault. 0–30.

Abi could feel something shifting within the crowd. If there was anything she knew, it was that the Wimbledon spectators loved an underdog. With every point she won, the cheers grew louder and the gasps greater, and their growing hope in Abi gave *her* hope, too. *Maybe I can do this.*

And as Carly started to lose her head, Abi knew that all she had to do was keep her head down, stay calm and finish the job. Carly was her own worst enemy.

When Abi broke serve for the fourth time in the match to lead 6–2, 5–2, she headed to her chair knowing that she was just one game away from a place in the final four at Wimbledon. Only a few feet away, Carly grabbed her towel from the waiting steward, pounded the strings on her racket, her face like thunder when she glanced up at her father and her team in the players' box.

Abi stared straight ahead, not really looking at anything. She took a few sips of her water and listened to the sound of the animated crowd chattering during the break, a few spectators squeezing past the rows of people to get back to their seats with fresh drinks. Despite her best efforts, Abi's attention began to wander. *Is that Mary Berry behind George Clooney in the royal box? Has Robbie remembered to put sun cream on – he's starting to look very pink?* She shook her head. This *really* wasn't the time to be worrying about sun cream. She had just a few points to win and she'd be in the semi-finals. *The semi-finals!*

Then, from a far corner of the crowd, came a voice she hadn't heard for twenty years. A voice she had never expected to hear again.

'Let's go, Abi-girl!'

Loud and clear. *Abi-girl.* Her blood ran cold. Could she really have heard that? She couldn't lose focus now, not with seconds to spare. *Mind over matter.* But it was easier said than done when adrenaline was flooding through her body as if someone were pumping poison through her veins. Because there was only one person who had ever called her Abi-girl.

Chapter 8

THEN

She'd heard about him before she met him. Of course she had. The minute she clapped eyes on him, she realised that this was who Barb had been talking about with her friends the other day on the patio at Blackwood Towers. Cole Connolly.

And it was Barb who she saw peering at him over the top of her designer sunglasses that first day when she had dropped the girls off at Bracken Lane Tennis Club for their Saturday morning training session. They'd been oblivious to what she was looking at while they scrambled out of the back seat – tennis bags, lunch boxes, water bottles and the rest of it spilling onto the gravel driveway that formed part of the members' car park. But when Abi turned to thank her for the lift, Barb was transfixed by something in the direction of the old Tudor-style clubhouse. Abi followed Barb's gaze and saw him at the top of the car park. Was he checking himself out in the wing mirror of a Bentley? Abi wasn't sure.

From a distance, he didn't look like anything special. By this point in her teens, Abi had seen hundreds of athletic young men in tennis shorts and wasn't quite as dazzled by bulging biceps or a toned butt as some of Barb's more desperate divorced pals. But the world seemed to shift in focus as they got closer to him and he turned to face them with a grin that would melt the coldest of hearts.

'Morning, ladies,' he said, pushing his sandy blond hair back off his brow and adjusting his shades. Abi noticed that the golden hairs on his muscular, tanned arms were exactly the same colour as those on his head. Glinting in the sun. She was starting to understand what had captured Barb's attention.

'Hi?' replied Georgie, for whom the penny had clearly not yet dropped.

'Heading to the south courts, are we?' he asked.

'Yes, we are,' she replied quizzically.

Abi, meanwhile, felt as if the sun were a little too bright all of a sudden. She was hot and clammy, pinching the front of her shirt to pull it away from her skin.

'Then you'll be with me.' He held out a hand to the girls. Abi swallowed. 'I'm the new head coach here, and you have the pleasure of my company for this morning's session.'

'Oh, I seeeeee,' said Georgie.

Abi glanced over to her friend – strangely, she didn't seem to have noticed that this new coach looked like some sort of Greek god. Georgie stuck out a hand to shake his and her racket bag promptly slid off her shoulder and towards the tarmac. She bent to retrieve it, leaving Abi standing directly in front of him. For a moment, she really did just stare, before remembering to put her hand out too.

Her palm felt cool in his – she had only just stepped out of the extreme air conditioning of Barb's four-by-four, which Abi reckoned was not dissimilar to travelling in a mobile fridge. His skin was already warmed by the morning sun and as he held her hand in his for a second, she could feel the rough skin on his upper palm, hardened by the day-in, day-out grind of hitting tennis balls. She felt his pulse too, pumping in the soft flesh between his thumb and forefinger.

'Connolly. Cole Connolly. But you can call me Cole.'

'Hi. Patterson. Abigail Patterson. But you can call me Abi.'

They were still smiling at each other, Cole's thumb still warm across the cool of the back of Abi's hand, when Georgie stood up again, bag safely reunited with her shoulders.

'And I'm Georgie Blackwood,' she said.

Abi felt her hand suddenly fall as Cole relaxed his grip, letting go and turning towards Georgie.

'I think you know my mum… Barb. She's committee member number nine?'

Cole looked blank.

'Ladies' second-team captain? Bright red hair and a truly horrific backhand?'

Cole threw his head back and roared with laughter.

'Ah, yes, so I do. Are you girls ready to go to the court?'

'I need to go to the bathroom actually. I'll see you out there,' said Georgie, still oblivious to the fact that Abigail felt as if she was seeing the entire world through a fresh lens. What was happening to her? she wondered as she and Cole walked past the immaculately manicured croquet lawn to the far end of the club, her mouth dry with excitement.

'So where has Barb snared you from?' she asked, a sassiness to her tone that startled even her.

'I spent a few years on the circuit, of course,' he replied. 'Left-hander. Counterpuncher. Jimmy Connors style. If you know what I mean.'

She didn't, but she nodded, frowning as if deep in concentration.

'Before that, born and bred in California.'

'I see.' Abi hoped she didn't sound as dazzled as she felt.

'Now. Well, now it's all about the next generation for me. I wanna focus on nurturing talent.'

'So that's what has brought you here?'

'Yeah. What works for me is really getting to *know* people. You can't maximise someone's potential unless you know them back to front,' he said, looking back at her as he opened the gate to the courts.

Abi had never really heard anyone put it like that before. No one had ever suggested that *who she was* might be an integral part of her game. From the minute she had persuaded her family to let her play tennis year-round, paying for as many lessons as they could, she had worked hard and believed that the training was everything. She had lapped it up willingly: every fitness session, every county squad, every hour of drilling and her limited competition schedule.

But no one, in nearly eight years of this, had ever suggested that who she might *be* was every bit as important as what she *did*. Now, here was a man who looked like a Home-Counties Brad Pitt telling her that he wanted to get to know her, and that this might be the key to maximising her undoubted promise.

By the time Abi had started her warm-up routine, Georgie was back. Dumping her racket bag at the side of the court and hanging her hoodie on the net post, she proceeded to do a few token stretches. Abi felt her friend's beady gaze on her, and once again fell prey to her waggling eyebrows. It had apparently not escaped Georgie that this new coach was causing just as much of a stir among his players as he had among the mums. The minute Cole's back was turned, she nodded her head towards him, looked at Abi and pointed a finger, mouthing, 'WOW.' Abi did her best not to giggle.

Georgie was so busy messing about making faces that she didn't spot Cole himself, turning to pick up a hopper of balls and watching her from the corner of his eye. He said nothing. But as he set off to the other side of the court to begin the session, he looked back at Abi with what she thought might have been a wink. She felt herself blush from her heart to the top of her French braid.

That was all it took for a little spark of conspiratorial energy to flicker between Abi and Cole. He had spotted a moment when Georgie had not been paying attention and used it. This jokey 'I'm not one of your teachers' bit was something he said more than once, especially when training got hard. And, as they came to discover, it worked.

From that session on, Cole pushed the girls harder than any coach ever had before, increasing their training schedule to the point where they were training almost every single day and in all weathers. And if there was ever any protest (usually from Georgie, but even then it was usually on behalf of the team), he would put on his matey act, highlighting his cheeky sense of humour and emphasising that he was less of a teacher, more of a *colleague*.

It was addictive, as the more they played, the more they improved. Abi's game in particular came on in leaps and bounds, and with the increase in wins came a huge surge in confidence. She thought about little else beyond tennis – and of course Cole's part in it – watching matches on her grandfather's desktop computer long after her grandparents had gone to bed. She would practise at every opportunity, cramming in her fitness programme before school and hitting against the rebound net – a prize she had won in an early tournament – in the driveway until late in the evening, stopping only when it got too dark to see.

Part of the reason Abi started to get these results was because Cole had proved to be a strict disciplinarian, expecting the squad to show up for additional strength and conditioning training as well as tennis coaching. He had total control over the club's junior programme and was both possessive and demanding of his key players. This meant that the more willing you were to put the hours in, the more attention he paid you. And as praise from him was rare, Abi realised that his attention felt almost as good.

The first time he told her that he was pleased with how she was 'shaping up', he had removed the black wrap-around shades he always wore to protect his eyes against the glare. His cornflower-blue eyes twinkled against his tanned face as he whispered, 'There's something about you, you know.'

She had so desperately wanted there to be 'something about her', but, as the summer had worn on, the line between her and *her game* had become increasingly blurry. She wanted to dazzle Cole with her skilful net play, with the tweaks she was making to her serve and the strength that was developing in her body.

The extra work and the effort she was putting in certainly managed to keep his gaze on her for most of the summer. And that did not go unnoticed by Georgie, who, despite finding him easy company, and falling for his matey act, started to show the first twinges of jealousy. Just the odd 'Oh, what did *Cole* think?' from time to time, but enough to let Abi know that she'd noticed. Noticed the shift beginning – now, when Abi wanted to talk tennis, it was increasingly likely to be Cole rather than

Georgie for whom she saved the insights she wanted to share most.

The days passed and the grass on the Blackwoods' tennis court grew ever paler as a heatwave swept across the south of England. But Abi increasingly chose to play at Bracken Lane rather than at Georgie's house. By late summer, she was starting to wonder if she was imagining things or if the way Cole was treating her was also changing a little. The man who, back in June, had seemed straightforward, interested in her, encouraging – firm but fair, with a hint of fun – was someone that she now saw fewer glimpses of. In turn, she had started to take life – tennis in particular – far more seriously.

Cole's tone had shifted, there was an edge to his observations now. The less Georgie chose to train with them, or even meet Abi at the club, the more Cole's observations started to sound like criticisms. He was definitely pushing for more, yet nothing she did seemed to be quite enough. She needed to be faster, stronger, to reach higher, to add more spin. And to do it while juggling a part-time holiday job at the local corner-shop, helping her grandparents with the household chores and trying to reach her peak of physical fitness.

Abi told herself that this harsh new approach was all part of Cole's plan to toughen her up for life in the dog-eat-dog world of the professional circuit. He had told her time and again that 'only the toughest survive', so she started to accept the little jibes, the short, sharp responses to what she'd thought were reasonable questions, or … just being ignored altogether. Was it her mind playing tricks or was he now giving much more attention to the other players in the squad?

Already pulled in so many different directions, trying to please so many people, Abi felt cold in the shade as praise from Cole started to ease off. She realised that she had come to rely on it as a way to get her through the days when she was pushing herself to the limit in training or fighting a tough opponent in competition. Sure, she was getting stronger physically, but emotionally she felt herself going backwards, constantly questioning herself. She needed his reassurance just as much as she needed his direction and his time.

But tennis was the love of her life, her safe space and her route out of the pain of the last few years. It had always been the case that the more she put in, the more she got out. For so long, in a youth that had proved so wildly unpredictable, she had had a sense that she could control the uncontrollable with diet, exercise and training, find a way to harness the unexpected and forge herself a future. So she kept reminding herself that this opportunity to work with a world-class coach was the key to fulfilling all those childhood dreams *and* to make her grandparents proud – to live the life she had longed for.

On top of that, now that she had experienced the sweet intensity of his smile when she played a great point, his hand on her shoulder as he imparted some of his gold-dust tips, or the warmth of his chest against hers when he hugged her after a match well won, she wanted to impress him too. She hadn't admitted to herself yet, much less Georgie, but part of winning was now about the fact she didn't want to kiss goodbye to that connection to him that they shared when they won – or rather, she won, she'd remind herself. She couldn't afford to lose that golden thread between them. She had felt nothing like it since . . . well, since before the accident. So she *had* to find a way to please him. She *had* to keep winning.

Abi's seventeenth birthday was at the very end of August, and Barb and the Blackwoods were throwing her a party to celebrate.

Georgie's own birthday had been in July, a Wimbledon-themed party with both serving staff and guests all in tennis whites. Confusing, to say the least. Barb, as keen as ever to show off both her garden and her culinary skills, had been delighted to host Abi's birthday too. Knowing that tea and cake at her grandparents' was not going to make for much of a celebration, and pleased to keep things off the radar of friends she knew from school rather than the club, Abi had said yes with great enthusiasm, only to feel sick with nerves on the day of the party itself.

She had spent all her hard-earned cash that summer on tennis kit or fitness equipment. Every penny she had saved from her shifts at Jones the Grocers was spent on whatever Cole had recommended. Grips, shoes, restrings, the very latest skipping rope, a medicine ball and a stopwatch all took priority over fashion fads, so for the party she was left with whichever of last year's summer clothes still fitted her, and that was not much.

In the end, after much deliberation with Georgie (who was bewildered by why Abi was finding it such a big deal to choose an outfit for a relatively low-key party, by Barb's auspicious standards), she decided on some low-waisted, wide-legged jeans and a bright pink vest top with a lace edge around the neckline. After countless hours of practice outside, her arms were almost as tanned and toned as Cole's and, although she knew that the look she had settled on was a poor second-best to a box-fresh strappy dress, she was at least pleased to have the opportunity to show off her tan in something other than tennis kit. It felt like a big deal, the first time Cole was going to see her 'done up', and she wanted to show that she was more than just a schoolgirl. A woman, even. This lacy vest top would fit the bill.

Barb had invited the rest of the training squad, including players who Abi, and indeed Georgie, had barely exchanged a word with all summer, to 'the do', as well as a few of her own friends from the club – and Cole. Abi had heard Barb describe him as 'the club's greatest asset' on more than one occasion now, and felt queasy at the prospect of trying to wrestle his attention away from her formidable hostess. Because while Abi had been working out all summer, so had Barb – and only one of them had a wardrobe full of leopard-print blouses and pony-skin minis that were designed to show off the body of a woman who was both in her prime *and* enthusiastic to showcase that fact.

Abi had been standing in front of the mirror, holding her long auburn hair up and over her face to mimic a fringe – *would she suit bangs?* – when she realised that she was starting to see Barb less as a surrogate mother figure than a potential romantic rival, and in an instant she felt sick with guilt and shame. Apart from anything else, what would Mr Blackwood think?

She stood, barefoot, in her sports bra and tracksuit bottoms and watched the flush of emotion spread, crimson, up her neck and face. She had been telling herself for months that it was impressing Cole on court that was her key focus, but as she let her hand fall slack, her hair falling softly against the top of her back, she knew deep down that it was now more than that.

But what could she do to stop these feelings, and who could she talk to about them? She'd seen much less of Max this summer as training had seemed to become so much more gendered than in previous years. At first, this had felt like a relief, but now Abi found herself sorely missing his friendship at the very least. And Georgie, well, she had made it clear that she was resolutely unfussed by Cole. Sure, she'd take his training advice and laugh when he made a good joke, but it was obvious – thank God – that she didn't see him *like that*. Barb, however, adored him, as did much of her clique. What did she, a naïve teenager who had chosen her first-ever bright lipstick to wear that night, have to offer a real *man* like Cole? Especially when held up alongside the undeniable glamour and worldliness of Barb? Abi pushed the thoughts aside, reminded herself that training was what would lift her out of this life, and tried to focus on her game.

As the party approached, the sky became a pale grey with muggy clouds, an occasional rumble of thunder in the distance threatening to come closer and hurry them all indoors. The whole event had started to feel like a race against time to celebrate the end of summer before summer decided to end itself. By eight o'clock, most of the guests were scattered across the grass, the haze of the day just about giving way to a delicious cool, albeit one that was still forecast to turn to rain before midnight. Abi's grandfather was having a wonderful time chatting to Derek Blackwood on the patio, each clutching a beer dripping with condensation. Georgie was flitting from group to group, trying to keep her mum calm despite a couple of minor canapé catastrophes, as well as dropping in and out of gossip with some of their mates. Barb herself looked stupendous in a backless halter-neck silk blouse and a white leather miniskirt. She knew she looked a million dollars, even if she was in a minor flap about the birthday cake's icing starting to melt in the late summer heat.

But despite the idyllic surroundings, the endless troop of waiting staff continually refilling glasses and the genuine warmth and good humour from everyone who was here – for her! – Abi felt on edge, constantly looking over the shoulder of whoever she was talking to, tugging at her top to straighten it, and sipping from what seemed to be a never-ending glass of Prosecco. She rarely drank, avoiding any of the secret trips to the pub that she knew others in her class made on the weekend, preferring to focus on training. So she'd told herself she'd stop at one glass, only it seemed as if the servers were just going to keep refilling it all night. Then, at last, she heard the crunch of tyres on gravel at the front of the house, and her heart leapt, knowing that there was only one guest still to arrive.

She hurried inside to greet him, but, as she passed through the huge glass doors and into the kitchen, she could see that even in her skyscraper heels, Barb had beaten her to it and was already only a few steps away from the front door. Darting into the bathroom just off the entrance hall, Abi waited, wanting to avoid speaking to both of them at the same time.

'Cole Connolly… Darling, so great that you could come. It will mean a lot to Abigail.'

Abi heard Barb air-kiss Cole.

'Well, you know me, Barbara, anything for the team. And it's important to spend time with your players away from the tennis court.'

Abi could smell the cut-grass freshness of what she recognised as Cole's aftershave from her hiding place in the bathroom. She peered through the crack in the bathroom door and saw Barb's hand run down the length of Cole's back as she greeted him.

'So I hear, my dear.' Abi could see Barb's scarlet mouth open in laughter over Cole's shoulder.

She glanced at herself in the mirror, before checking her own teeth for lipstick with the side of her finger. The colour suddenly looked garish on her, like fancy dress, rather than the big reveal of her womanliness that she had been aiming for.

'Anyway, come in and say hi to everyone. Let's find the birthday girl. You'll have made her day – she could do with a few more of us watching out for her.'

'It's a pleasure to be here – what a beautiful home. And... what's that about needing more of us?'

'Well, you know the poor thing lives with her grandparents, don't you? Her parents died a few years ago under the most dreadful circumstances, a horrible accident. You must meet her grandparents soon, though, they're so hugely grateful for everything you've already done for her.'

With that, Barb took him by the hand and led him back towards the kitchen.

'Look who's here, everyone!' Abi heard her cry as they headed into the party.

She left the bathroom and followed them into the garden. As she did, she saw Cole turn, almost in slow motion, and notice her with a smile. 'Happy birthday,' he mouthed, as Barb continued to lead him by the hand towards the throng of guests.

Like a clap of thunder in the distance, the melancholy that had been threatening to engulf her vanished. No longer was she feeling that tug of grief at wondering what her parents might have thought of her if they could have seen her today. And no longer was she fretting that she was invisible to Cole, lost in the shadows of Barb's radiance. He had noticed her. And he had noticed *her*, Abi, not just her tennis skills.

Time dragged as Barb wheeled Cole around the guests as if he were a championship trophy. Abi felt herself tracking him wherever he was in the garden. Once or twice, she tried to make her way over to the group he was chatting to, but somehow it never quite happened – people went to get more food, to find a cardigan from inside, or to leave. Was he moving away from her? Did he not want to talk to her, or did he not want to be seen talking to her? Or was it Georgie, whose home this was after all, who kept things moving, trying to get her to chat to some of the other tennis squad boys, filling her glass on more than one occasion, doing her very best to shift the mood towards the girlish fun they used to have?

Eventually, Abi headed into the kitchen to try to get something to eat. The serving staff seemed to have been intent on topping everyone's glasses up, but she had been on the wrong side of the garden every time any of them had appeared with trays laden with food. Now, she felt a little light-headed and knew where she could at the very least pilfer an apple from. Taking a breath and steadying herself – as the Prosecco suddenly seemed to have gone to her head – she didn't notice that Cole had followed her until she almost hit him with the fridge door.

'Oh my gosh, I'm so sorry,' she gasped out, startled.

'Hello, birthday girl.' His smile was lupine, his eyebrows raised.

'Hi,' she said quietly.

'Hi. I've been trying to find you to say happy birthday all evening. You're a hard woman to pin down …'

A woman. That was how he saw her. She felt her pulse quicken, the Prosecco moving faster through her veins. 'Well, it's my night, I suppose!' Again, that surge of confidence that came whenever he offered her the smallest of compliments.

'Indeed it is. And a birthday girl needs a birthday present.'

This time, Abi had no quip, no sassy comeback. Instinctively, she glanced around to see if anyone was watching them. Why did she feel furtive, receiving a birthday present on her birthday? But there was something about the air between them that she knew would raise an eyebrow in Georgie, and probably do more than that in Barb.

But no one seemed interested in the slightest. Even the waiters were all in the garden. So Cole pulled a small, wrapped box out of the back pocket of his jeans and was pressing it into her palm. Abi looked up at him, unsure whether to open it now. What if someone came in? They were all so close, just on the other side of the Crittall windows. She knew he hadn't given Georgie a gift at her birthday a few weeks ago. She knew this was a shift between them. At last. She looked down, feeling the telltale slow flush starting to work its way up and across her clavicle. She'd be puce soon.

'Go on then ...' He nodded at the box.

Abi pulled at the ribbon and found herself handing it to Cole, along with the wrapping paper as she peeled it away. Then she lifted the lid and saw inside a delicate silver bracelet, with a tiny silver tennis-ball charm dangling from it.

'I ... I don't know what to say,' she remarked, taken aback by the generosity and thoughtfulness of the gift.

'Then don't say anything.' He was looking at her now, his head slightly dipped to meet her downward gaze. He lifted his hand to her chin and tipped her face up, so they were eye to eye.

But then, in a flash, he let his hand fall, and the mood shifted.

'So, have you got your eye on any of the boys here tonight?' he asked, as if none of the last five minutes had happened.

'No!' she replied, aghast. It would have been an inappropriate question under any circumstances, but now it felt almost like a taunt.

'Sweet sixteen and never been kissed...' His mouth was inches from hers.

'Hey! You don't know that,' she replied, trying to hold her own amid this fast-moving current. But she was pretty sure he did know. How could it not be obvious? She was close to crimson now.

'Well, if you like, perhaps we can do something about that...'

His face seemed closer now. Was it him or her leaning in? In that moment, it didn't seem to matter. Their lips touched.

Chapter 9

NOW

'Time.' The umpire's voice yanked her back into the present.

Abi rubbed her face with her towel, trying to scrub his voice, his face, from her mind. Was he really here? Today? Nobody else had ever called her Abi-girl.

Had it been ninety seconds or nine?

Abigail's thoughts were scrambled, tumbling on top of each other, fighting for space, so many new ones rushing in that she hadn't had the chance to quell the noise, to calm herself.

It couldn't be. Or could it? Was it an unwelcome blast from her past or was her mind playing tricks on her under the weight of the occasion?

Cole.

Or had she misheard? It really had sounded just like him. The soft Californian twang and the way he drew out 'gurrrl'. Or had the wind changed direction as someone had shouted, altering the sound as it had reached her?

The voice had come from behind her chair and over to her left. She was desperate to look, to turn and start scanning the crowd. But she didn't dare. She felt another lurch of nausea deep in the pit of her stomach, closed her eyes and took a deep breath, trying to bring her thoughts back to one clear thread.

Slowly, she removed the towel from her head with the grim realisation that she couldn't hide under there any longer.

Remember who this is for.

She didn't dare look up to the players' box. Had Georgie heard? Was it going to be written on her face? And what about Max?

Instead, Abi reached to pick up her racket, preparing to face both the crowd and the ever more antagonised Carly. She promised herself she would keep her eyes from wandering, scanning faces in the direction of that voice, trying to work out what or who she might have heard.

Don't look. Don't look. Don't look.

An American gentleman in the front row jumped up and called out, 'Marry me, Carly!' in the pause before play started. The crowd laughed and even Carly smiled down at the grass, trying not to let herself get distracted – or give the man any more airtime. The man sat back down, safe in the knowledge that he had captured her attention and achieved a few seconds of global TV coverage, and there was something about Carly's smile that made Abi suspect she had rather enjoyed the outburst. It had broken the tension.

Now, Carly took her time returning to the baseline. Striding slowly with her unwavering confidence, she seemed to be trying to maximise the applause, gleaning as much sympathy as she could from the crowd, using her familiarity to them to her advantage.

Abi was glad it wasn't her serving. Her emotions were in such turmoil that she didn't think she could trust her left arm to throw the ball up straight.

It's only four points.

Keep a cool head; it's what you've got over her.

It might not even be him...

Abi just kept repeating the positive mantras she had rehearsed until mind started to win out over body. She knew that Carly was feeling the pressure. The constant glances towards her father and the endless smoothing of her skirt between points proved that, plus she had a mountain to climb in terms of the scoreboard. The nonchalance Abi had seen in her as she'd trotted down from the dressing room was draining, and fast. If Abi could just keep believing she could win, perhaps Carly would start believing she might not...

And so the mental battle played out on the court, Abi's will to win enabling her to torment her opponent with drop shots, slices and constant forays to the net. The unpredictability of her play had bamboozled her young opponent from the outset and, just as she'd hoped, Carly found neither answers nor consistency.

Her own head in a complete spin, Abi realised that she needed no more than the original game plan, and, against the odds, she found she was more willing to take risks, rather than less. After all, she just needed four more points. All she had to do was keep mixing things up, throwing curveball after curveball in a game of percentage tennis and let Carly continue to self-destruct.

A double fault – two misfired forehands from Carly – gave Abi a 0–40 lead and three match points.

She narrowed her eyes. Breathed in and out slowly and loudly, twirled her racket in her clammy hands and waited for Carly's serve to come crashing down. It came to her backhand and Abi blocked it back deep up the centre of the court and raced to the net. Carly didn't see her coming and played a mediocre forehand cross-court, right onto Abi's racket. A simple stop volley was all she needed to finish the point.

She'd done it.

That spot in the semi-finals was hers.

For a moment, she wondered what the noise was. It was the crowd. On their feet, screaming for her. Was this really happening? In a daze, Abi turned towards the players' box and a grin broke out across her face as she caught sight of her team.

Barb was bobbing up and down, her sunglasses tumbling off her face, which was as pink as her suit. Georgie grabbed Robbie and planted a smacker on his cheek and Max was punching the air and spinning round to shake the hand of a man behind him. As he turned back, she met his eyes and he gave her an almost imperceptible wink, too quick for the cameras to catch. *She'd done it.*

And then she remembered. Abi-girl. Was he here? Had she really heard his voice? Her eyes scanned the crowd, and, as she spun round, the crowd followed her gaze, rising from their seats and bellowing out their applause. She'd never be able to spot him, even if he was here.

She caught sight of her face on the big screens in the corners of the court and, beating down the sense of unease that flooded through her body, did what Georgie would want her to do and waved to the crowd. The noise was deafening.

Carly was starting to head back over to her chair, her face like thunder. Abi ran up to the net and held out her hand to shake it, and as Carly looked up at her, she spotted a tear rolling down her cheek.

'You have an amazing future,' said Abi, making sure she dipped her own head to catch Carly's eye. 'All I had over you was experience, and this will have helped you to build yours.'

Carly didn't reply. But Abi knew it wasn't rudeness: it was that she'd burst into tears if she did. The women smiled at each other, and made their way to their chairs.

Shoving her racket back into the bag and slinging it over her shoulder, Abi stood up to leave the court with Carly. Just as she reached the tunnel that led out of the spotlight, the young girl she'd seen earlier ran up to the barrier, her 'Abi' cap askew, holding out a giant tennis ball for Abi to sign. Abi grabbed the pen and scribbled her name across the surface, the girl looking as if she might pass out. Abi turned round to give the crowd a final wave and couldn't help but smile on seeing so many cheering faces and Union Jack flags, then she disappeared into the shadow of the tunnel.

Carly was a few metres ahead now and so, for a brief moment, Abi was alone. She breathed a huge sigh of relief, desperate to reach the safety of the downstairs dressing rooms and away from the long lenses of the hundreds of cameras. Away from that voice.

'I'm here! Come in!' called out Abi, still slumped on the bench in the dressing room, as she saw her oldest friend walking towards her, grinning.

'You've DONE IT! You're in the semi-finals of bloody WIMBLEDON!' screeched Georgie, safe in the knowledge that they were the only two in there.

'I know, I know, I can't believe it...' Abi was still shaking at the speed with which things seemed to have happened. Final four – she was in the final four.

Georgie gave her an enormous bear hug.

'Urgh, mistake. Now I'm nearly as drenched as you are!' She pulled at her expensive silk top, which was indeed marked with

Abi's sweat. 'Going to fetch a fortune on eBay later, though ...' she said with a wink. 'Give us a smile then! You were fantastic out there. You nailed it.'

Georgie noticed the flutter in her friend's hand, the way she was blinking too fast with the shock of it all.

'Are you all right? Do you need water?' She started to root around in Abi's bag, looking for the rest of the pre-prepared drink that she knew Abi hadn't yet had.

'I'm fine, of course. I'm fine ... It's just ...' Abi sat down again, her hand across her chest.

Georgie lowered her voice. 'What? Do you feel OK?'

'Yeah, it's nothing like that. I think I heard him out there, Georgie, in the crowd.'

'What do you mean? Who?'

Abi turned to look at her friend, grabbing her forearm. 'Cole. I think he was there today.'

'What the ...? Why? Did you see him?'

'I heard someone calling out "Abi-girl" ... "Let's go, Abi-girl." Right at the 6–2 5–2 changeover.'

Georgie took a deep breath and exhaled slowly, her lips pursed as if she were blowing out candles on a birthday cake. She took a moment before saying anything.

'Oh, Jesus. Are you sure?' Georgie was standing again now, pacing in front of her friend.

'Well, I can't be one hundred per cent. But no one else has ever called me that. What if it's him? What do I do?' Abi put her head in her hands.

'Listen.' Georgie was standing over Abi now. 'You don't do anything. This is your moment. You are through to the god-damn semi-finals of the Wimbledon Championships. There were thousands of people in that stadium and they were there for you. We don't know if he was there. We don't care if he was there. We have *significantly* more important things to be thinking about right now.'

Abi raised her head slowly, unconvinced.

'I'm serious, Abi. Do not let him take this moment from you; he's already taken enough. Max is waiting for you. He's off to watch Carly's press conference for me – I wanted to get straight here, but one of us needs to brief you before you do yours. Get yourself showered, I'll order you some food, and then you can speak to Max. He's not going to let you speak to the media before he's talked to you. And I'm going to go and find out where I can get a recording of the match so we can check out the crowd and that voice. Just to be sure . . .'

'What about Robbie?'

'He's fine – he's bloody *thrilled* for you! – but Max and I told him you'd be wrapped up with press for a bit, so he said he was going to have a wander around the grounds to soak it all up, then walk back to the flat and chill.'

Relieved to hear that Robbie was away from the chaos, away from *him*, Abi stood up.

'Listen, Abi. It's going to be fine. You've got this far without him – he can't mess anything up for you now. His power is long gone.'

Abi wished that she felt as certain as her friend, and buried her head in Georgie's shoulder. She couldn't let this man back in to her life, not now. Not ever. Not again.

Chapter 10

THEN

'Billie! For heaven's sake! Give it a rest!'

Barb's voice rang out across the kitchen as she rounded the corner, chasing after Billie the bichon frise. The dog ran straight past them with what looked like a half-eaten chicken satay in his mouth as Abi and Cole stood a foot apart, Abi having leapt back as if she'd been electrocuted at the sound of Barb's voice. Cole kept his cool, immediately focusing on Barb, and in the commotion that followed, Abi dropped her gift under the kitchen island. By the time she had scrabbled on the floor to retrieve it, Cole had followed Barb in the hunt for the dog and the moment had slipped through her fingers like sand. Abi was left stunned, wondering what on earth that moment between them – and the gift – could have meant. Memories immediately began to scramble, scenes she had imagined in the small hours so many times tumbling across what she thought might have just taken place. Hope clashed with reality and the lines between each were now blurry, fragments floating across her mind for the rest of the evening and beyond.

There were no answers forthcoming that evening, though.

For the rest of the night, Cole was playing the social butterfly and when the storm finally broke, the remaining guests running inside to hide from the rain, the party came to a rather abrupt end. Abi pinned her hopes on some sort of sign from him when they said goodbye. Was that a quick happy birthday peck that she was already misremembering or was it a kiss? But people were now standing in the hallway, leaving at the same time, a throng of damp chaos she couldn't see past, let alone reach through. Instead, she got nothing more than a cheery wave and a 'See you Monday', while Barb was lavished with effusive thanks and a conspiratorial whisper in her ear.

Ten minutes later, Abi was in the back of her grandparents' car, the side of her head resting on the window as rain lashed down outside. Her grandfather was focused entirely on navigating the country lanes through the storm, but after a while, Grannie Annie's soft, sweet voice reached her in the back seat.

'So, did you have a lovely birthday, darling? Was it everything you'd hoped for?'

Abi's hand clasped the small jewellery box tightly, not quite sure if she was hiding it or keeping it safe, while she said a quiet, 'Yes, it was wonderful.'

But the Prosecco seemed to be curdling inside her, acid sloshing in the pit of her stomach as the car negotiated the turns of the road, while she thought over and over about what else she could have done differently. Had Barb noticed anything? What did the gift mean? Could she even wear it in public or should she keep it a secret? Or would being secretive about it imply she had something to hide? Hadn't Cole given it to her right there, in the Blackwoods' house, without seeming embarrassed in the slightest?

And, most of all, what did the kiss mean? And how on earth could she ever find out?

Then she'd flash back to earlier in the night: Barb, trying to be kind, but inadvertently reinforcing one of her biggest anxieties.

'The poor thing'... 'taken in'... 'dreadful circumstances'...

Abi had fought so hard at the tennis club to be more than just the girl whose parents had died. Bracken Lane had been her safe space, away from the glares and whispers she had put up with for so long at school. Now someone she had always trusted had told Cole about it?

But had Cole cared at all? He'd kissed her regardless, hadn't he? And he'd even asked her permission first. The way he had handed over the gift, encouraging her to open it. The way he had leant in (hadn't he?). He hadn't seemed to be thinking about her being an orphan at all, in any of these moments. Surely?

Abi barely slept that night, their shared moments running through her mind again and again like an old movie, while she tried to eke out every last bit of meaning from them. The next morning, she felt queasy – her first hangover. Anxiety about what might happen next gnawed at the edges of her confidence, endlessly suggesting she had imagined the whole thing. And even if she hadn't, would people understand? Had anyone seen? And why was she worrying about getting her 'story straight' if she'd done nothing wrong. She hadn't, had she?

She saw the bracelet in her knicker drawer. Tucked away at the back by her tampons, just where she knew her grandparents would never dare go looking. She thought about it again as she headed off to training, the silver charm letting her confidence grow a little, convincing her that all was not lost. Nothing that was, except the fact that she now seemed to be keeping a secret from people she loved.

Later that morning, it was as if her birthday had never happened. She'd been awake all night trying to work out what various signs from Cole might mean, but what she hadn't anticipated was that they meant nothing. As she stood at the side of the court chatting to Georgie about the gossip she had missed out on last night, he interrupted them with a brusque, 'Party's over, ladies. We're back at training now. Eyes on me, please.'

'Sorry,' said Georgie, with a hint of surliness, but Abi was too shocked to reply at all.

'Hangovers are no excuse for a sloppy performance. If anything, I want to see more commitment than ever today.'

Abi did her best, but she was exhausted, and now she was dejected. If she didn't have the proof right there in her drawer, she might have imagined the whole party, the whole kiss, had been a dream. She was paired against a player two years younger than her who Cole clearly knew hadn't been at the party and had probably never had a sip of booze in her life. She seemed to be springing around the court like a gazelle and when Abi stumbled while merely walking to the baseline to serve, she heard Cole calling out, audible to everyone, 'Next time, strategise, Patterson. Either more water before bed or don't drink more than you can handle.'

There was a ripple of giggles across the surrounding courts. Her peers seemed shocked, even a little impressed, that Cole wasn't reprimanding her about the drinking but about how she'd handled it. Classic 'I'm not a real teacher' behaviour. Abi pretended to be focusing on her shoelace, but inside she was shrivelling with shame; his words of wisdom were like silver bullets in her side, delivered from the opposite side of the court, eye contact entirely absent, physical contact similarly so.

Then, when the new school term began a couple of weeks later, just as her hope seemed to be fading for good, Abi's grandmother was late picking her up from training one evening. Abi was starting to wonder if she had forgotten entirely. Moments earlier, she had been ushered out of the clubhouse, as juniors so often were when one of the club's regular social events was being set up. Barb, resplendent in gaudy, low-cut silk and drowning in a heady waft of expensive scent, was in her element – stringing up fairy lights, tweaking floral displays and barking orders at the poor teenagers who had been roped in to clear tables and keep glasses topped up all night.

On his way out, Cole spotted Abi waiting by the car park, looking more than a little anxious. The sun was vanishing beneath the horizon and her arms were starting to prickle with goosebumps as a breeze kicked in. He'd been cold and critical with her for a couple of weeks now and they hadn't been alone for just as long. Maybe she had been oversensitive and had read too much into the situation? It was just a kiss after all. But it had felt like more than that. She wanted it to be more than that. She didn't understand why he was treating her so harshly, but she had no doubt the fault somehow lay with her.

As he pulled out of the car park, he slowed his car to stop alongside her and reached over to open the passenger door. As he leant towards her, she saw hair curling from the unbuttoned top of his pale pink polo shirt.

'Need a lift, Abi-girl?'

The excitement left Abi feeling as if she'd been winded, but she still somehow replied, 'It's OK. Grannie Ann— my grandmother is coming to get me in a bit.'

'Don't be silly, I'll drop you. Hop in. We'll call her.'

How could she resist?

The car was warm and smelled of expensive leather.

'There's a jumper in the back if you need it,' he said.

She leant around to grab it and as she did, her right breast brushed against his left arm. Flustered, she tried to focus on putting the elegant cotton jumper on over her tennis top. But she still saw the corner of his mouth curl, a twinkle in his eye.

'Get yourself covered, Abi-girl – you know how you make me feel.' His smile was wolfish.

Abi didn't know what to reply, and simply apologised, muttering something about how she was worried about Grannie Annie, cursing herself for using the childish nickname.

'No need to get your panties in a twist. Like I said, we'll call her,' he replied.

Moments later, the car pulled up to the side of the country lane they were on, and Cole whipped his mobile phone out of his pocket. Abi dictated the number to him and he got through to her grandmother immediately – it turned out she was in a terrible flap as her car had a flat tyre and no one was answering at Bracken Lane amid all the party hubbub.

'Don't you worry, Grannie Annie,' he said into the phone, winking at Abi. 'I'm bringing her home safely right now. We won't be long.' He slammed the clam-shaped mobile shut with a flourish and grinned at her. 'You see? No need to worry – you're safe with me.'

With that, he reached over to open the glovebox in front

of her and chucked the phone in before shutting it and slowly raising his face until it was barely an inch from hers.

'Unless you don't want to be?'

Abi froze. She could smell his shampoo, and feel the warmth of his breath on her face. He raised a hand and stroked the side of her face.

'I'm only kidding,' he whispered. 'I've told you before you're safe with me.'

And that was all the lonely teenager needed to hear. She turned her mouth to his, and within a second there was no going back.

The next month or so marked their longest unbroken spell of intimacy. Kissing in his car, on the now frequent lifts he gave her through the Hampshire countryside. Grannie Annie was relieved not to be driving in the dark and raised no objection. And Georgie, who seemed to have a new group of friends with little or no interest in boys – or men – didn't seem to care much. So, time after time, they would find themselves pulled into a lay-by beneath some beech trees, on the way home, gasping with the excitement of it all.

At first, Cole's behaviour on the court barely changed at all. If anything, he was even harder on her. But Abi took it, satisfied with his explanation that it would help keep things secret, that the finger of suspicion would never be pointed at them if he continued to be so dismissive of her in public. But she couldn't help but change her behaviour. On the days she knew she'd be getting a lift home, she would think about it all day, then throw herself into her training in order to try to impress him, while simultaneously feeling more self-conscious than ever about her own body. She was waking up ever earlier to make sure that she arrived at training, legs shaved, body moisturised, fully deodorised. She was easily distracted, snapping at anyone who wasn't Cole, then flustered around him in public, ashamed of the slightest stumble or mishit. The stakes always seemed so high, all of the time.

And then Cole raised them.

Chapter 11

NOW

Abi stood in the changing-room shower, the hot, powerful jets pummelling her shoulders and neck, trying to rinse all thoughts of Cole from her mind. And as the last suds of the expensive club body wash bubbled onto the shower floor, a strange sense of calm settled over her. He didn't deserve to take up any more space in her head. She was older now, more worldly-wise. The match against Carly had proved it.

She pulled an enormous fluffy Wimbledon towel from the cubicle shelf and stepped out of the shower. She only had another ten minutes or so before she needed to get to the press conference, and while she knew Max wouldn't barge into the dressing room in the same way Georgie had, she didn't want to keep him waiting.

As she quickly moisturised her legs and brushed her damp hair, she absent-mindedly watched the tennis playing silently from the television on the dressing-room wall. The internal channel, Wimbledon Live, allowed players to watch every court, press conference and all the news programmes. On the screen, one of the men's doubles matches had just finished on Court 2, with Todd Fitzgerald triumphantly high-fiving his partner. Abi was a big fan of the fiery Australian with the old-school serve-volley tactics and effortless slice backhand that had been honed to perfection on the grass courts of the exclusive Kooyong Club in Melbourne. He was one of the few players in the men's draw whose game was perfectly suited to the conditions at Wimbledon and Abi liked to think her game mirrored his in lots of ways.

She wiped the excess body cream off her hand and flicked through the channels, catching a powerful serve from bookies' favourite, Renate van Cutsem, who was warming up on another court, in preparation for her own quarter-final match. Abi switched it over. There was no need to wind herself up now, and she knew that Georgie and Max would have hours of footage for her to study of whoever her next opponent was. But judging by that serve, it looked like the bookies might just be right about Renate.

On the next channel, Abi instantly recognised the steps leading down from Gangway 211, where the guests exited the Centre Court players' box. Sarah Jones, the reporter for London TV, was interviewing a man wrapped in a huge England flag, who was grinning and waving wildly at the camera at every opportunity. The camera angle shifted suddenly, as Sarah spotted Bradley Cunningham storming down the steps and tried desperately to catch him for a comment. Bradley's usual broad smile seemed to have slipped off his face over the last hour and he stormed past the reporter without a second glance. Abi caught sight of Georgie's chic blow-dry in the background of the shot as she dashed in the opposite direction, presumably to brief her social media team on the content and timings of posts leading up to the semi-final match and to ensure they kept on top of any adverse commentary coming Abi's way – including the inevitable death threats that came from gamblers who had lost big money by backing the wrong player. Abi smiled. That woman never walked anywhere, she thought – Abi was forever jogging alongside her to keep up.

The camera panned out slightly and her heart leapt as she spotted Robbie on the left of the screen, gazing up at a giant venue map – was he trying to work out the best route out of the grounds? She leant towards the TV, wanting to reach out and tell him, *I wouldn't be here if it wasn't for you*!

Clearly working out his bearings, he turned away from the board and started to follow the throngs of people streaming away from the court. Which just happened to be towards the camera. And as the angle swung once more, Abi realised she wasn't the only one who had recognised him. Sarah dashed out into the crowd again, microphone in hand, and Abi's heart plummeted.

She scrabbled for the remote, managing to unmute the sound just as Sarah reached Robbie and thrust the microphone under his nose.

'Robbie Patterson! We're live on London TV. What an amazing match – you must be thrilled for your mum! How are you feeling?' she asked with a smile, slightly leaning in towards him to avoid the crowds passing behind her.

Just say a few words and walk away, Robbie. That's all you need to do. Abi's heart was pounding.

'Of course, really thrilled. Couldn't be prouder,' he replied, a slightly startled look on his face.

He started to step away, but Sarah moved with him, like a

fisherman, knowing she just had to hold on and she might reel something in.

'I bet you are! What a moment...'

Two women swept past, their arms laden with strawberry punnets, and Abi saw Robbie's eyes follow them, desperate for an escape.

'And will you be back on Thursday for the semi-finals?'

'Of course! It's not every day your mum reaches the semi-finals of Wimbledon, is it?' he replied, raising an eyebrow at Sarah Jones.

Abi laughed. She needn't have worried; Robbie had this under control.

'It's certainly caught us all by surprise,' Sarah said, not missing a beat. 'And do you play tennis yourself, Robbie?'

'Oh, a bit. But not like her, I didn't get those genes!'

Sarah laughed. 'More like your dad, then? Was he here today, too?'

Abi gasped. A shadow flickered across Robbie's face. It might have been imperceptible to anyone else, and at first even Abi thought that perhaps he had seen something behind the woman. Was it Cole? Then she realised – it was the question itself. Robbie's worst nightmare.

'I've got to go,' he was saying, panic now etched on his forehead for all to see. 'Sorry, I'm really sorry. But thanks!' He waved at the camera, then twisted away from Sarah's grip and melted into the crowd.

Sarah Jones turned back and looked directly into the camera. Abi felt as if her own eyes were locked with the reporter's. Her heart thundered in her chest. She had to find Robbie.

'Well, an exclusive interview there for you. A lot of you will only have heard Abigail Patterson's name for the first time this last week and now we're all desperate to find out more about her. And with such a handsome son, I'm sure it won't just be Abigail who comes away from today with a few more fans ...'

Abi muted the television and sank onto the seat behind her.

What had she done? She'd spent the last twenty years keeping Robbie away from the tennis world and now, selfishly chasing after a childhood dream, she'd put his face on the map. Yes, she had exposed him, but now, with that evasive interview, he had made himself interesting. Between them, they had created the suggestion of a mystery around him. As Georgie had told Abi so many times in the past, there was nothing the press liked more than the sniff of a story. And that's what they'd just given them.

Abi finished dressing hurriedly and rammed her belongings into her bag, haphazard in a way that was the exact opposite of how she'd started the match. She needed to find Georgie and Max. She needed to keep Robbie's face out of the papers, or at the very least get their stories straight. Dashing out of the changing room, she almost crashed straight into Max, who was striding down the corridor towards her.

For a second, the beaming smile on his face reminded her of sixteen-year-old Max, lolloping off court in the summer sunshine. But the smartly dressed man heading towards her was a world away from the teenage boy she was used to seeing in his tracksuit and trainers. But as he put his arms out towards her and she fell into them, she realised how little had really changed.

'Abigail Patterson. Wimbledon semi-finalist,' he said as he hugged her tightly, before grabbing her by the tops of her arms and holding her in front of him, grinning. 'Let me look at you.'

They hugged again, and Abi felt for a moment as if she could stay there for ever. But even Max couldn't calm the sense of unease that was coiling in her stomach.

'Max, I need to find Robbie,' she said, pulling back from him. 'I just saw him being interviewed on London TV and I'm worried that it's upset him.'

'Why? What did they say?' The smiled had vanished from Max's face.

'They asked about his dad,' she replied, chewing her lip.

Max looked directly at her, a river of unanswered questions roaring between them.

'I'll call Georgie,' he said. 'And as soon as the press conference is over, we'll go straight back to the flat, OK? But we've got to get you over there now. Carly's already done her piece.'

Abi breathed a sigh of relief. 'OK. Good plan. How did Carly seem?'

'To be honest, she seemed fine. A little sulky, but she said all the polite stuff too: that you were a great opponent, that she's thrilled for you, that you had the crowd behind you. But then Brad got hold of the microphone – and, well … he's livid.' Max laughed.

'I saw him leaving the stands.' Abi nodded. 'He looked like he was ready to explode.'

'That wasn't even the half of it! Ridiculously controlling man. Horribly sore loser. He went on and on about Carly being the future and you being past it. Putting your win down to luck – and the wind! – saying the crowd were disrespectful to his daughter. It's nonsense, but when you go in, be careful about being drawn into responding to his comments. You've got to stick to talking about you. Your game. Your next match. She's not tomorrow's headlines like he hoped she would be, but whatever you say is going to be plastered all over the papers.'

Abi felt sick and it must have shown on her face, because Max continued, 'Hey, it's all part of the game, remember. You're the country's darling right now – their wild card that's come out fighting! You played like a winner and you won. That's all that counts. And you heard the cheers yourself. Come on, let's get this over with. We don't want to keep the hounds waiting.'

He took her bags, then slung his arm around her shoulders and guided her back down the corridor out towards the All England Club interview room. How had she forgotten over the years how good Max always made her feel. How safe he made her feel. But also how alive. When she was with him, she felt like she could do anything. How had she let his friendship slip through her fingers?

Chapter 12

THEN

Max handed Abi a bottle of water as they stood by the side of the track, breathless. She took a long swig and wiped her mouth with the back of her hand.

'How many miles have we done?'

'Just under five.'

'OK, so maybe three, three and a bit left? But the hills…'

'You know it…'

They were doing one of their favourite runs, through some woods and along a stretch of beach on the south coast, by the Solent. It was about half an hour away from Max's house, a route he knew like the back of his hand from dog walks with his family as a young teen, but now he and Abi had taken to doing it on a Monday after school from time to time.

It had been Max's idea about six months ago. 'Something more for endurance, less about the endless effing winning,' he had explained at the time. And Abi adored it. Without siblings or a battered car that had once been his mum's like Max had, she often felt a little constrained between school, home and the tennis club, shuttling endlessly between the three.

Abi often found the strategy, the mental gymnastics required for tennis an effective way of blocking the rest of the world out. If she were playing, zoning in on what her opponent was thinking, what she might do next, and how she could counteract it, she didn't have time for fretting about boys, school, body image. She felt free on court – she felt *herself.* And she was gaining quite a reputation up and down the country for this combination of having a smart game and some real speed on grass. Once or twice, she had caught the eye of scouts on the junior circuit. They'd only been casual chats, but Cole had noticed every time, dragging her away, insisting she wasn't ready for 'all that' yet. Moments like that left her feeling as if she'd had her wings clipped.

Even before Cole had come on the scene, she had sometimes found herself itching for a bit of spontaneity, something a little closer to wildness, freedom, nature, away from the courts, the club and the gym, away from the routine, discipline and rigidity of her training programme.

And it had been Max who had sensed that she might like the route and enjoy the run.

It took them just over an hour, and covered farm tracks, woodland and beach, and each time they did it, Abi felt not just closer to Max but also to herself. She didn't have to worry about exactly where she put her feet, she didn't have to worry about exactly how long she took, she didn't have to worry about how she performed. And no one cared what she looked like – especially Max, who seemed to take her how she was, regardless, and do nothing but heap her with praise about how she was doing. While looking pretty good in running kit himself.

Towards the end of today's run, Abi fell a little behind him, but neither was bothered by it. She enjoyed letting her mind wander as she watched the sun set, a milky pink and orange settling across the skyline to the west of the sea. And she enjoyed watching Max lollop across the beach, his stride effortless, his curls bouncing as he went. He seemed so content in himself, so happy with who he was, that he made intoxicating company.

So often she had found herself having to second-guess what people were thinking about her, how they were treating her. She had grown up wary of the sort of girls who pitied her, who sensed a weakness in her parentless state. And now, as girls in class started to discuss 'doing it' more and more, she found herself wondering if any of that would ever mean anything concrete to her. She'd looked things up on the little computer in the hallway at her grandparents', but lived in fear of her grandad finding out what search items she'd been using on there.

But Max, perhaps because his mum had the straightforward honesty of a nurse, seemed more relaxed about everything to do with bodies. He had grown up with sisters, and never batted an eyelid if Georgie asked to borrow a tampon, where others on the squad would squeal and squirm at the very mention of the topic. But, above all, he genuinely seemed to like himself. When he complimented Abi on her times, or how her workouts were doing, he seemed to really mean it, rather than having an agenda. Nevertheless, this often left Abi confused – wondering if he was flirting, or simply so at home with himself that he wasn't trying to make any point at all.

As they reached the eight-mile part of their run, Abi knew that there was one last sprint before the car park by the beach and did her very best to catch Max up. He heard her behind him and yelled back, 'You'll never get me, Patterson! You'll never pin me down!'

Was he making a point? Or was he really just talking about the run? Either way, ninety seconds later, instead of taking a right off the beach and towards the car park, he took a left, heading down the beach and towards the sea. He took his running top off, whirling it around his head before flinging it onto the shingle and pegging it into the sea.

Whooping at the cold of the water and the sheer glee of feeling the waves on his tired legs, he begged Abi to join him, splashing her with sea foam until she did, her top clinging to her sports bra. They laughed till their sides ached, Abi all the while wondering if he was like this with everyone, or if she was the only one who saw this side to him.

As they headed back into town, an old swimming towel from the back of the car round her shoulders, she wasn't sure if she wanted that to be the case or not. After all, she had Cole now. Didn't she?

Chapter 13

NOW

'You've got this,' said Max, his hand in the small of Abi's back as he led her the final few steps towards the Wimbledon media room. Abi didn't want him to remove it, and he seemed in no hurry to. 'I'll be in there too, and there's a moderator – it'll be a member of the All England Club, night of their year, looking forward to their moment on BBC One tonight.'

The press conference went almost exactly as Max had predicted. He stood at the side of the room out of shot of the cameras, as did the All England Club moderator. The first few questions were celebratory, congratulating her on her incredible run to the semi-finals, asking if she'd ever imagined such a turn of events, what she might do to prepare, how she felt about each of her two potential opponents in the last four. Then, as expected, came a sly little query about what Brad Cunningham had said.

'Bradley Cunningham seemed to be putting a lot about your win down to luck when we spoke to him earlier. How do you feel about that, Abigail? Was there a lot of luck out there this afternoon?'

She saw Max's shoulders stiffen in her peripheral gaze. 'Some twerp from the blogosphere', he'd call the journalist later, but the question didn't bother her nearly as much as it did him. She only had to tell the truth, and so she did.

'Well, yeah, to Mr Cunningham, I am a relative unknown. And I was able to use that to my advantage to a certain degree. I am completely new to this level of event and I have an unusual style that you don't often find on the women's tour these days, so I can be tough to read, harder to predict. But, also, we all ride that combination of having to make our own luck, our own opportunities when it gets tough on court – and getting some lucky breaks. And I guess today I had both.'

A quick glance across at Max, who, safe in the knowledge that he wasn't on camera, shot her a subtle thumbs up.

'I can't really speak about Carly's career, though,' she continued. 'All I can do is focus on my own – I've had long enough to think about it after all!'

A ripple of laughter made its way across the room. She was on a roll now. She could sense Max grinning.

'So, yeah, I'm focusing on my own game. I'm playing really well, I have a lot of variety, and I'm comfortable playing on grass courts because I was brought up on them. Very few players can say that nowadays and I have the added advantage that the other players here don't really know me. I am a proper wild card.'

The room broke into more raucous laughter now, and Abi felt relief wash over her that the press conference must surely be coming to a close. She snuck a glance over to Max, who was laughing with the room.

'There's time for one last question,' said the moderator,

nodding at a blonde woman right at the back of the room. It was Sarah Jones. The woman was everywhere!

'Hi, Abigail, it's Sarah Jones from London TV here. Congratulations on your win today. I was wondering if you could talk us through your team in the players' box today. We know your agent Max Chamberlain, of course, and we saw a woman in there too?'

'Yes, that's my press agent,' Abi replied carefully. 'Georgie Blackwood. A familiar face to a few of you, I'm sure. I think she's on the phone out there right now actually. And next to her was her mum, Barb ...'

The journalists were scribbling, pencils scratching on paper and tablets being tap-tap-tapped on.

'And I saw your son up there too. He told me earlier he's incredibly proud of how well you've done today. He seemed very modest about his own game, but I think we're all wondering whether this same sporting talent might run in the family?'

Abi felt as if someone had thrown a bucket of cold water down her back. How could she have thought she'd be able to keep the press's noses out of digging into her business. Into Robbie's business.

'Oh no, he's not much of a player. More into cricket!' She tried to laugh, but a strange, strangled noise came out.

'Is his dad a player then ...? Will he be supporting you in the semi-final?'

What was with this woman? Abi was sure her face was now flushed. She reached for her glass, hoping that taking a sip would give her a moment before she had to reply, but her jerky movement ended up sending the glass flying and the water spilling out over the table.

'Tennis questions only, please.' Max had stepped forward,

almost within range of the cameras as he tried to stand between Abi and the journalists. But he'd done it too fast. The whole of the room had seen his desperation to stop this line of questioning. He'd given himself away just as much as she had with her water spillage.

'No, he won't be there,' Abi said, looking directly at Sarah Jones. Almost daring her to ask another question.

But the problem was, Abi didn't know if that was true or not.

Chapter 14

THEN

This week, Cole had specifically told Abi that he didn't want her doing any endurance training. The focus was to be on weight-bearing exercise to build strength and 'mental toughness. Abi accepted that that was what was needed, until she was in the dressing rooms scraping her hair back into her plait when Georgie came over and asked, 'What was all that about?'

'What do you mean?'

'No endurance training. Is he just pissed off that you still go running with Max?'

'Why would he be?'

Georgie looked at her. It was that look again. The one that said, *Do I really need to tell you?* without using a single word.

'What?' said Abi. 'We literally go running – you know the bloody route we take!'

'Uh-huh. So how come he's told me about naked sea-swimming with such relish?'

'Well, first of all, it was NOT naked. And, second of all, why was he telling you about what we get up to after our runs anyway?'

'So it's not just running.'

'It was *part* of the run. We ended up in the sea. It's good for our legs!'

'I think I've made my point. You guys have far too much fun. And there isn't a single person in this club with eyes in their head who hasn't seen the way Max looks at you.'

'Don't be daft. He's just . . . my friend.'

'Keep telling yourself that . . .' said Georgie as she headed out, her patience clearly worn thin by trying to show Abi what she didn't seem to be able to see.

Abi herself wasn't sure why she was so reluctant to accept that there might be more than matey team-spiritedness between her and Max. Perhaps it seemed too good to be true, that girls like her – brooding, ambitious, over-anxious – simply didn't end up with guys like him. He could have his pick of the squad, so Georgie's insistence that it was her who he wanted seemed unlikely in the extreme. She had a face full of freckles and hair that was far from the Kournikova blonde that most guys on the squad seemed interested in.

Or perhaps it was just that Cole's animal magnetism was too good to say no to. He could have anyone at the club – anyone! From the raunchy divorcées to the yummy mummies, and beyond. He was gorgeous, charismatic and he seemed to know exactly what Abi's body needed. He was unlocking the potential that could realise the dreams Abi had had all her life – playing tennis on the pro tour and winning. He was almost impossible to please, but he was doing this, with his detailed training plans, his well-researched tournament schedules, his nit-picking attention to detail, his insistence that nothing less than one hundred per cent effort and commitment would do. So no wonder Max's happy-go-lucky, sunshine-and-smiles approach to life felt a little too easy to Abi, who had only ever really known how to do things the hard way.

But as Abi left the changing room and headed to the clubhouse for something to eat, she saw Cole talking to Max in the distance. The older man was leaning in, clearly imposing himself into Max's space. But instead of squaring up to him, looking threatened or concerned, Max was simply standing his ground. His hands were in his pockets, not defiant, but there was certainly no deference there either.

Abi approached, hoping they wouldn't notice her and she could hear what they were saying. The shadows were long now, the criss-cross patterns of the wire fence around the court dancing on the tarmac where the sun was hitting it.

'It's cool,' she heard Max saying. 'But then, it's not my choice, is it?'

'You're right. It's mine. It's me who's her coach, it's me who's running her schedule, it's me who knows what she needs. And I don't need you messing it up.'

They couldn't be, could they?

'I get it, you know best. But what I'm saying is that it's Abi's choice.'

They were. They *were* talking about her.

Cole inhaled, ready to carry on talking, but Max just continued. 'I'm not trying to tell you I know more about VO_2 max or whatever, I'm just saying that Abi is the one who chooses, not me. I don't force her to run with me, so I can't force her not to. It's just something we enjoy. You know, *enjoy*?'

Abi had never heard anyone at the club talk back to Cole like that. Even Georgie's backchat was done behind his back, or as an aside. Yet, somehow, Max was being so bold, but also so charming about it. Not losing his cool, not actually telling him no. It was impressive. But it also left her conflicted.

How dare Max interfere with what Cole thought was best for her training. Had Cole asked before? Or was this the first time he had spoken to Max? But also – how dare Cole reach into the areas of her life that had up to now felt safe. And fun. And Max was one of her very few friends. Running had for so long been a release, a simple pleasure, a bit of time away from it all, and now Cole wanted to influence that too? Both of them, and especially the conflict between the two, left her suffocated, short of breath.

She had been just about to walk up to the court when she turned away. She was her own woman, she wouldn't get involved, she told herself. She'd make her own decision next week. But making a decision never quite seemed to happen. There were different training sessions in her schedule the next weekend, and the one after that. And before long, so much else had changed that no one seemed to mention running ever again.

Chapter 15

NOW

Abi watched the crowds unseen as the car eased its way out of the club, tinted windows protecting her from prying eyes at last. She stared at the houses en route to the flat, and noticed that the same woman was out front, still half-heartedly tackling her roses with her elegant secateurs. As she watched the woman's gaze follow the blacked-out courtesy car, Abi found herself surprised that there were any blooms left in the garden at all.

She reached for her phone, which had been buzzing away on the seat next to her. She silenced the myriad notifications piling in and brought up Robbie's name.

You OK? I saw the interview when you were leaving? Hope it didn't freak you out?

She held the phone in her hand, willing it to buzz right back. She seemed to be hearing from everyone she'd ever met, but there was really only one response she wanted. And then it came.

Yeah, I mean weird. That woman was nosy. But it's cool, just wanna do what's right for you this week. Headed out for a beer. Felix and Al want to celebrate your win! Xo

Abi exhaled. Relief that he sounded OK – but where was he off to now?

'He's eighteen,' Georgie said from the seat next to her, having seen Robbie's name flash up on Abi's screen. 'He'll be fine. He's thrilled for you. And I'm pretty sure he won't be buying any drinks tonight after that win.'

She was right. Abi rested her head on the soft leather headrest and stared up through the skylight of the sleek electric car.

When they arrived back at the flat, Max was waiting for them. As they went inside, Georgie immediately started turning on lights, plumping up cushions and generally tidying the large open-plan kitchen. Abi went to put her bags in her room, and came back to find her friend still trying to make things cosy for a much-needed evening of rest and relaxation. As Georgie ran a cloth across the kitchen island where Robbie had clearly started making a sandwich on his return, she picked up a note, turning it over in her hand and reading it out loud.

'"Gone out for a bit. Back later. R *xx.*" You see, he even left you a note before he left… Such a well-brought-up boy!' she called after Abi, who was now crouched in the utility room, emptying her kitbag, separating things for the wash, taking out shoes that just needed a bit of a wipe down and carefully putting sentimental items and her notes to herself to one side.

Her head was buzzing, though. She felt like a teenager all over again – back in the perilous position she had been in before, with men holding undue influence over her and her life, when all she wanted to do was play tennis without distraction. As today had proved, she told herself, huffily.

'Good for him!' said Max as he dumped his own bags and peered at the row of serving trays on the kitchen counter. Peeling back the cling film on one of them, he stuck a finger in to taste the tabouleh, an impish grin on his face.

'Yessss!' said Georgie, when she noticed what he was doing. 'Mum's delivery is here!'

'Oh, fantastic, how kind!' said Abi, deciding to shift her mood for the time being and deal with the other issues once she had eaten and watched the rest of her next opponent's match.

In the chaos and rush of the weeks running up to Wimbledon, as it had started to look like Abi actually might get a place in the main draw, when Max had been frantically booking flights from Miami and Georgie had been clearing her diary, Abi had accepted Barb's very kind offer of providing food for the duration of the tournament.

A decade or so ago, Barb had graduated from simply arranging the catering at Bracken Lane parties and taken an actual qualification. She was now a well-respected sports nutritionist and chef, very big on the fitness scene, with a surprisingly impressive business acumen and an increasingly healthy online presence. Now, like a fairy godmother, she had swept in and taken care of what might otherwise have been a bit of a grind for Abi.

They hadn't spoken for quite a while when Barb had called her a couple of weeks ago, taking care of things just like she'd always done. Part of Abi had wanted to resist Barb's kindness, to stand on her own two feet more, but then, part of her knew that resisting Barb was futile. Largely because now that Abi was older she knew that there was no doubt that Barb's enthusiasm was rooted in kindness above all else.

'It's not a business thing, sweetie,' she'd explained. 'Just think how much time you'll all save if I can just bring the food for the duration and you can focus on *winning*.'

'Barb, you're quite right,' Abi had said, knowing how happy it would make Barb. Because, yes, it was rooted in kindness, but she knew as well as Barb did that it was also about excitement, about being part of a Wimbledon player's entourage and, well, that it might all have been worth it after all.

And, thus far, they'd both been right. Abi, Georgie, Max and (usually) Robbie had been feasting on Barb's finest since the tournament had begun, and it had worked a treat, grounding them all at the end of the day, rebooting friendships in a way that none of them might have been able to if they'd simply spent the evening texting Abi in the small basement flat. Instead, it had become a de facto HQ, and an effective one. As ever, Barb knew best.

Georgie set about laying the food out on the coffee table in front of the enormous TV in the living room, all of them trying to move around the flat while keeping their eyes on the match that was going to determine who Abi would face next.

The fearsome six-foot Renate van Cutsem was obliterating her opponent in straight sets. Not surprising, Abi thought, when her serve was that terrifying – and her long legs meant she could make it across the court in a couple of strides.

Max, meanwhile, was on his phone, scrolling busily through his emails with a notepad to one side, which he seemed to be making a list on. 'Is it naïve of me to ask if we actually have any idea when Robbie might be back, Abi? I think I'd like to give him a bit of a heads-up about that question.'

'Please, let's just leave it for now.' Abi felt her maternal hackles rising, but she also didn't want to return to the discussion about Robbie's father. Today had been enough. 'He deserves a bit of time and space after traipsing around after me the last few days. I hope he's found a decent pub and some fun with his mates.'

'Fair enough,' replied Max. 'Not been much of an end-of-exams treat for him, has it?'

'Exactly,' said Abi. 'We've been meaning to talk about his plans for the next year for weeks – I've sat down so many times to have the big "what comes after college; are you really serious about becoming a physio; what about all that talk about travelling?" and then someone's phone goes. He deserves my full attention, he really does, but—'

'It's fine. We get it,' said Georgie, putting a hand on her shoulder. 'You've waited a very long time for this. You deserve to experience it to the full. But we've got Robbie's back too. It's going to be a delicate balance for the next few days, but it is only going to be a few days.'

Max and Georgie shared a glance across the kitchen. There was so much to celebrate tonight, but there was also so much dangerous ground that they needed to avoid treading on. Abi pulled up a chair at the kitchen island beside Max and put her head on his shoulder.

'Thanks, guys. I know you're giving a lot of yourselves too.'

'Yeah, it's a real nightmare for me to have a sudden Wimbledon star on my books,' replied Georgie. 'And I imagine it's the same for you, Maxie. I mean, the woman's a nightmare, isn't she?'

'Worst client ever. So demanding,' he said as he put his arm round Abi. 'Gets a bit hangry before dinner, though.'

Abi gave him a shove. 'OK, okaaay. Point made. Eyes on the prize, best team in the business, et cetera, et cetera.'

'You know it,' said Max, tapping his phone screen to dark and lobbing it into his briefcase.

Georgie pulled two bottles of fancy organic kombucha out of the fridge, slamming the door behind her with her hip as she turned round. 'Bubbles, anyone?'

Abi smiled at Max. 'We thought you'd never ask.'

'If you can't have a glass of fizz after a big win, when can you?' said Max with a grin, ambling over to the coffee table.

Georgie found some champagne glasses in the cupboard and began to pour the pale fizzy drink. The three of them clinked glasses, congratulating Abi on the achievements of the day as if they were sipping the finest champagne from their flutes.

Enjoying their kombucha and digging into the feast that Barb had sent over, Georgie, Max and Abi finally let themselves relax a little, laughing about the wackier moments of today's match, from the rugby-shirted quartet who stood up and shouted 'ABI DABI DOOOO!' whenever she broke serve, to the irritating bloke who had yelled 'Come on, Tim!' just as Carly had tossed the ball up to serve. Georgie in particular had enjoyed seeing a mishit shot from Carly bounce off the frame and into the crowd, caught by an uber-enthusiastic super-fan who'd inadvertently infuriated his idol by refusing to throw the ball back when she'd been itching to keep the momentum going.

It had been over a decade since the three of them had sat around like this so regularly, luxuriating in their own highly specific brand of post-match analysis – part silly, part fastidious, part scattered with throwbacks to their youthful experiences. Before things had changed, they'd spent hours on trains, lounging on the grass outside the Bracken Lane clubhouse or in the TV room at the Blackwoods' home, analysing the playing styles, psychological weaknesses and kit choices of their opponents. As Max leant across them to refill their glasses and Georgie stole the last snippet of halloumi from his plate, it was as if time was temporarily suspended, their childhood dreams becoming a reality.

When the second quarter-final reached its predicted result, with Renate van Cutsem confirmed as Abi's next opponent, Max and Georgie immediately swung into action, looking up potential hitters with a comparable style to practise with tomorrow, and tentatively mentioning a press strategy for the next few days.

Abi felt relieved all over again that these two were here for her as, within minutes of the match ending, her phone had started to buzz with news alerts announcing the four semi-finalists. Moments later came the attached news stories, pinging up like cicadas chirping from her phone. She tried not to look, wondering if she would ever get used to seeing her own name in the BBC Breaking News ticker tape. She hadn't really taken on board that she was one of the biggest stories of the day until now, so she caved and clicked on a link.

She hadn't really had the chance to stop and think about what she might read before she saw that *WHO IS ABIGAIL PATTERSON?* was one of the subheadings and her stomach lurched anew. It all seemed fairly standard, if slightly odd seeing her own life story in that familiar layout. But further down were a few embedded tweets from journalists, one of which was next to the face of the same journalist she had seen twice already today – Sarah Jones. Her bland smile was only thumbnail-sized, but her post made Abigail shiver.

Intrigued to see Abigail Patterson had her son in the box today – anyone got any info on him? His dad? Timings there are interesting given her story. My DMs are, as ever, open . . .

Chapter 16

THEN

As far as her grandparents were concerned, Abigail was simply working harder than ever. But appearances were starting to prove deceptive.

So far, it had only been Georgie's eagle eye that had spotted the increased focus Abi had on her diet – one she was following for 'maximum training efficiency'. But her grandparents had noticed that Abi hadn't had her mates round for weeks.

'You don't seem to have spent any time with them lately. How about I cook a nice Sunday roast for the gang?' offered Grannie Annie one Friday evening on the way back from the club. Abi was silently frustrated that Cole had pulled out of an evening training session, which she had hoped might turn into something more, but Grannie was only trying to be kind, so she tried to focus on that.

'I think I'll have training,' she replied, hoping it sounded believable.

'That Cole needs to give you a bit of time off, though,' her grandmother said softly. 'He's got you training all hours, on this strict diet – you've barely had time to yourself lately. And you look exhausted.'

'I know, Grannie, it's tough, but I *am* seeing Georgie tonight, and I might sleep over.' Abi hoped she sounded convincing. It *was* tough, the level of training she was now engaged in, but perhaps not in the way that her grandmother meant. She was exhausted. Not just from the training, and fretting, but from trying to keep up with the little white lies she was now peppering throughout her life. A couple here to Grannie, a couple to Georgie, and even one or two to Max. 'Anyway, Cole says it's the price that has to be paid if my talent is going to reach its full potential,' she continued. 'So I'm hoping by spring I'll start to see some real results.'

'Well, my love, as long as you know that we love you regardless. And we always will. We are behind you, all the way.'

There was part of Abi that wanted to curl up on the sofa the minute they got in and let Grannie Annie stroke her hair until she fell asleep. But she had a bigger plan that night. One that had been tying her stomach in larger knots than ever. No wonder she had barely been able to get her dinner down the last couple of days. And it was nothing to do with a sleepover at Georgie's.

Instead, she had hatched a plan to meet up with Cole, who had suggested she needed some 'extra physio' and it would be best done at his place. He had suggested it earlier in the week and she had barely grasped what he was getting at. She could have kicked herself. For weeks now, she had been desperate for his approval, training harder than ever in order to impress him on court, while leaving these half-truths like crumbs behind her – telling Georgie she had been with Max, telling Max she'd been home, telling her grandparents she was in group training when it was one-to-one. Then Cole had been in front of her, suggesting time at his flat, and her mind had gone blank, barely able to remember what she had told to whom, or why she was lying at all.

By now, as far as Abi was concerned, they were in a relationship, just one that she sensed people might 'be a bit funny about'. Georgie, she told herself, would probably be jealous at her being given the upper hand where training was concerned. Sometimes, at 3 a.m., as she lay there thinking about how she hadn't had a proper chat with her friend for a while, there was a small voice whispering that she hadn't told her because she knew she wouldn't approve of the relationship.

As for Max, Abi put any objections he might have down to jealousy on account of the crush Georgie was convinced he had on her. He was nice enough, and, yeah, that same small voice had pointed out that he was kind of hotter than Cole. But Cole, well, Cole held the keys to her future. He was the one who told her she could become exactly the person, the player, she always dreamed of being, so long as she did what he told her. So, again, she ignored the voice inside.

In fact, she was starting to get good at silencing that voice. 'Commitment is everything,' she'd whisper back to herself in the dead of night, when she thought she might lose her nerve altogether.

Because, by now, Cole had total control over her dreams, her every chance of success, and her sense of self, so whatever he declared a distraction, she was finding easier to ignore. Even if it was her closest friends.

Abi had made sure she knew exactly what Georgie was doing tonight (she was having a sleepover, but it was not with tennis friends) and had told her grandmother only that she might be staying. Then she'd arranged with Cole to pick her up on the corner, rather than in full view of the house, 'as it's easier to turn there'.

Her hamstring *had* been sore that week, and as she slung her sports bag into the boot of his car, her freshly washed hair flicking across her shoulders as she turned to let herself into the now familiar passenger seat, she really was hoping that he could help her with it.

Either way, as the car pulled out, it was impossible to tell if the spark she immediately felt deep in the pit of her stomach was fear or excitement. The two had come to feel so similar as she rode her daily rollercoaster of emotions that they were all but indistinguishable. One thing was for sure, though: there was no chance she was going to say no to whatever was on the cards.

When she first walked into the dark living room, Abi was a little surprised that someone who loomed so large on court, at the club and in her emotions lived so simply. There was barely a picture on the walls, and a simple dark leather modular sofa took up most of the room. The kitchen had as many protein powders as actual ingredients, and the main piece of equipment seemed to be an enormous juice maker. The bedroom, she supposed, was off the hallway. She didn't dare think about it.

By the time she had removed her coat and placed it over one of the bleached-pine dining chairs on the other side of the room, Cole was back, with a folding massage table under his arm. So little time seemed to pass between him encouraging her to take off her tracksuit bottoms and 'hop on' while he warmed his hands with some massage oil. To her relief, he knew exactly what he was doing when he started to massage her. His hands felt like velvet on her thighs and her muscles relaxed in minutes under his touch. She was mortified at the huge sigh she let out as he worked on the exact muscles she had needed help with, but couldn't hide how good it felt to have his undivided attention on her, with no chance of prying eyes appearing.

She felt limp with relaxation, like honey, when he lifted her off the massage table a little later, gently laying her on the huge leather sofa.

'Oh, Abi-girl,' he muttered, as he took his own trousers off, pressing his warm skin against hers, before reaching into a nearby table drawer for a condom. Moments later, he was on top of her, his face pressed right up against her ear, speaking through her now messy hair as her face burrowed into the rough fabric of his sofa cushion. The avalanche of emotions was so enormous that it was only once he'd finished, and went to the bathroom to clean himself up, that she realised he hadn't kissed her once. In fact, he barely spoke to her for the whole of the ride home.

Abi felt chilly after so long spent half naked. Cole had never taken her top off, just shoving his hands up beneath her Bracken Lane hoodie instead. She still had her arms wrapped around herself as Cole's car pulled up on the same corner where he'd picked her up only a couple of hours earlier. As she walked up the street, she could see Grannie Annie waving at her from the window-facing kitchen sink, washing-up gloves still on as she looked out onto the driveway. The house looked so cosy, she thought, shocked to find herself wanting to cry.

'Now then, my little superstar . . .' She heard Cole's last words ringing in her head as she waved back at Grannie Annie. 'Let's not go bragging to the rest of the team about your extra massages, shall we. We don't want them getting jealous.'

Abi had nodded at him and closed the car door behind her. A few hours later, as she stared up at her bedroom ceiling, a dull ache inside her – nowhere near her hamstring – she thought about how much she wanted to tell Georgie, to see what she thought. Was that it? Was that what it was meant to feel like? She had imagined more . . . fireworks, and she was sure that Georgie would know. Or at least know where to find out. But telling her seemed impossible. If she mentioned a word to her friend, quite frankly she may as well tell Barb herself!

So Abi decided to stay quiet. And she still stayed quiet when it happened again. And again. By late spring, it was just a part of training that was 'sometimes needed'.

'A useful outlet', Cole once called it, although she was never quite sure who for.

'Commitment is everything,' she would tell her grandparents if they ever commented that she was spending so long training, with hours getting later and later. If they suggested she accepted an invitation to one of her friend's parties, offered to drive her to the cinema for a night off or even proposed a training-free weekend, she would repeat her mantra. 'Commitment is everything.'

The words would rattle around her head at night, when she tried to figure out a way she might connect with Georgie, to bridge the distance between them. Because that distance was growing almost daily. Yes, there was the undeniable fact that Abi's tennis was now reaching a far higher standard than her friend's. But she knew that Georgie couldn't *really* be jealous about just that – she had never cared too much about it before – she enjoyed the actual playing of the game much more than the winning. Was it, deep down, that Georgie knew her friend was keeping secrets from her? It must be. But how could Abi even begin to tell her what was going on without the whole house of cards collapsing?

She knew Georgie wouldn't approve of her relationship with Cole. At best, she'd laugh at it. At worst, she'd tell Barb, and who knew where that would end. How could she get Georgie to understand that, yes, maybe the Cole situation was now feeling a little bit outside of her control, but she *needed* him? It wasn't just about the emotional dependence she could now reluctantly admit she had on him, but as far as the tennis was concerned, she was still convinced that he was the key to her long-term success. She just needed to get through the next match, the next competition, the next rankings run, and telling Georgie would never allow for that. Maybe in a week, a month, a season, she could tell her? When she was just a little older? When she'd won just a couple more tournaments? And maybe then things could get back to normal?

Instead, normal was edging into the past, out of their grasp. Afternoons that were once spent playing Wannabe Wimbledon in the sunshine, or lying on their stomachs in front of the Blackwoods' huge flat-screen TV, watching iconic matches, were now spent training or at Cole's. Abi never knew when it might happen or what might prompt it. Her nerves were constantly frayed, kept eternally busy by the twin responsibilities to work hard, get results, do better and also to look good, seem womanly, play the pliant but discreet girlfriend.

She kept things up for a while, but then one evening when she was particularly tired after a bad match, and wishing she could just call her mates and have a good old bitch about it, she did something that surprised even her. Just as Cole was laying her down on the sofa (never the bedroom, where the door remained resolutely shut), she said that perhaps she'd just like to go home instead.

'Babe,' came the response, as he brushed her hair back off her face, his thigh rubbing up against her on the dark leather. 'You want to leave me like this?'

'Oh, Cole, of course not,' she replied, suddenly panicking that she might be shutting the whole relationship down instead of opening it up. 'It's just . . . I'm tired. All the sneaking around . . .'

'It kills me too that we have to live like this,' he mumbled, trying to get the physical side of things back on track.

For a moment, Abi felt the words she had been psyching herself up to say evaporate from her mouth. She sat, feeling a little defeated, as Cole started to stroke her face, then her throat, then her clavicle, and below. She was so tired, it was easier just to lie down and imagine that what was happening was closer to what she'd dreamed of. But in doing that, as he thrust away, a bubble of rage boiled up inside her, something she had no idea how to manage.

So she sat up, trying to push him off her, and said, 'But why do we have to live like this? I'm going to be eighteen in a few months, and you're not even my school teacher. I could just leave school now, start on the tour, why are we wasting time?'

Visibly shocked by her momentary rejection, Cole leapt back as if he'd been slapped. 'Don't you know how much I'm risking with this, with you?' he said, his voice louder than she'd ever heard off court.

'What do you mean? I thought you wanted to be with me?'

'Of course I do, but, bloody hell, I'm putting more into your training than any other single player at that club – the last thing I need is accusations of favouritism. People chucking around the idea that I'm only putting the hours in if there's something more to it.'

'I would never let anyone think that!' Abi protested, grabbing for her clothes to cover her naked chest.

'It's not you they'd be listening to, though, is it, once they'd got hold of a story…'

'But, Cole, we mean so much to each other, don't we? And my game is the best it's ever been! How could anyone mind?'

Cole threw his hands in the air in frustration. Even as the words had been leaving her mouth, she'd known how silly they sounded. Of course Barb would be furious, of course Georgie would be vindicated, of course her grandparents would be worried. She was a fool to have believed otherwise.

Minutes later, Cole was back to cooing, promising her that as soon as she started to move onto bigger tournaments they'd be able to travel together, they could be open with each other in public, they could even book hotel rooms together. But the petulance, the self-interest he had just displayed meant that these scenarios – ones Abi had spent the whole winter daydreaming of sacrificing so much else for – now didn't seem entirely appealing.

Later that week, Cole's cousin came to London for a few days and, as Cole had some visa business to tie up, he reluctantly headed there for a couple of nights, leaving a gap in the training schedule that was entirely unfamiliar to Abi. At first, she decided to try to spend some time in the gym at the tennis club, to watch some of the senior team's matches and to just hang around in case Cole checked in with anyone, making sure she had maintained her focus. But the looming figure of Barb in a pair of low-slung faded jeans, vertiginous heels and a hip-width belt with an enormous turquoise buckle put paid to that.

'Darling, you look shattered. Please come over to ours tomorrow night – Georgie misses you, even if she's too proud to tell you.'

Abi was flattered at the thought that her friend had let slip she was missing her, but she was keener to make sure that she didn't have to spend too much time with either of the Blackwood women right now. Not until things were clearer with Cole. Just in case either of them saw straight through her.

'Oh, thank you, Barb, but I think I should spend the evening with my grandparents. I have a mountain of schoolwork to catch up on too.'

Barb smiled like a chess player several moves ahead. 'Nonsense, I've cleared it with Annie already.'

And that was that.

What Abi hadn't banked on was arriving the next evening to Georgie opening the front door with a smile, clearly trying her best. The house behind her was deadly quiet, though. Eerily so. Abi felt her shoulders drop an inch.

'So where are your mum and dad then?' she asked, peering round, beyond the hallway.

'Oh God, as if Barb would have a weekend night in. They're at some awards ceremony on a yacht somewhere on the Solent. I mean, literally vom.'

Abi chuckled. Perhaps there was enough of the old friendship left there after all.

'Come on in,' said Georgie, cheerier than Abi had seen her for weeks. 'Mum has left us an absolute mountain of lasagne, and I found Ben and Jerry's in the freezer.'

'Wow, thanks,' said Abi, stepping into the once-familiar

hallway. Everything looked exactly the same – the family portraits climbing the wall up the stairs, parquet flooring she had skidded over in tennis socks so many times, the warm hum of the kitchen just a few metres away. She tried her best to exude the same casualness with which she had entered so many times, to smooth over the fact that she was rippling with anxiety. Could they find a way back to those times? Could she find a path through the maze of lies she'd built for herself? Could Georgie forgive her if she fessed up now? Abi missed her friend, she missed those times, and yet… would she have to sacrifice everything with Cole – and possibly forgo her tennis dream – to get them back? Was there a way to have both?

Georgie walked ahead and into the kitchen, her own fluffy socks gliding across the polished floors.

'Anything to drink?' she asked.

'Oh, whatever you're having,' said Abi, expecting a glass of elderflower pressé, which was what Barb – conscious not to fill them with fizzy drinks, but mindful not to seem so tight as to serve merely water – often gave her.

'Sure,' replied Georgie, her head inside the fridge. A second later, she emerged with a bottle of cold white wine in her hand, jabbing the end of a corkscrew into the top without unpeeling the foil from around it first.

'I—' Abi felt her stomach tighten. The girls had never drunk alcohol together, not like this. There had been the odd glass of Prosecco at her party, and perhaps with family at Christmas. But this was new. And it felt like a challenge.

Georgie turned, one eyebrow raised. 'Not for you?' she asked. Definitely a challenge.

'Oh no, I mean, yes. Yes, I'd love some… not too much, though… you know, training…' The truth was that Abi had

had next to nothing to eat all day and was worried that her nerves, worn paper-thin by trying to keep up appearances on so many fronts all at the same time, might get the better of her.

'Ah, yes. Training.' Georgie's lips became a thin line.

Abi wasn't sure what she was supposed to say next. She could see the lasagne starting to bubble in the oven. Its smell was overwhelming. She realised she was starving; she always was these days. *It's those that really have the hunger who become winners*, she remembered Cole telling her.

Georgie pulled the cork and poured each of them a generous glass of Gavi.

'Cheers!' she said, in a tone no less adversarial than before.

Abi took a sip. The wine felt deliciously cool as it slid down her throat, and she felt it hit her stomach almost immediately. 'It's so lovely to see you. Thank you for having me over.'

'You know Barb when she's got an idea into her head . . .' Georgie shrugged.

'Ha ha, yes, I do know – where would we be without some of your mum's plans . . . ?' Abi tried to steer the conversation onto safer ground, joking about Barb. She trusted that Georgie wouldn't have tired of that sport yet, and she was right. Before long, Georgie was regaling her with tales of Barb getting ready for this awards do.

'She was literally shrieking at my dad, accusing him of having done something with her hair extensions . . .'

'But, Georgie, he's entirely bald. What the HELL did she think he was planning to attach them to?'

'Turned out Billie had them, and was running around literally chasing her tail – only it wasn't her tail, it was Barb's bloody clip-on ponytail!'

Within half an hour, the girls were crying with laughter,

their plates scraped clean and the bottle of wine more than half empty. Abi felt light-headed with relief that there was still such fun to be had with this friend who she had let become so distant. She didn't even mind when Georgie started grilling her about Max, unaware that she'd only seen half as much of him as she'd told her she had. The lies suddenly caught her by surprise, a riptide almost knocking her off her feet.

Keen to cover her tracks as fast as possible, she turned the conversation back to Georgie, who was wearing a pair of dark grey skinny jeans and a white ribbed vest. Abi could see her shoulders flex as she reached a high shelf to get down a second bottle of wine. God, she just looked so confident, even the way she moved across the kitchen, she seemed to know exactly what she was doing, exactly what she was *meant* to be doing. Abi felt sick with envy. Envy and half a bottle of Gavi.

'You look great,' said Abi, trying a fresh approach at chat. 'I really like your jeans.'

Georgie smirked.

'What's so funny? They're great! I am so hopeless at shopping, unless it's sports kit. I was hoping I would have found my style, or whatever it is they say in magazines. I just get overwhelmed and leave most of the time.'

'Barb hates these jeans so much. She says they're too manly.'

'Ha ha, oh yeah, I can see how she might not be keen.' Abi was pleased to have at last found some common ground to giggle about.

'She'd love your skirt, though – she's quite the boho queen these days.'

Abi was wearing a long prairie skirt with a big fluffy jumper over it. Boho skirts were the one trend she was embracing that summer as Cole had been quite clear, on more than one occasion, that he preferred to see her covered up when she wasn't in training kit. 'Your body is a tool built for winning,' he had told her. 'It's not for display.'

'Thank you,' she replied to Georgie. 'That means a lot. Your mum always looks so glam.'

Georgie gave a quiet smile as she picked up the two chic white plates and began to clear away dinner. Abi felt hopeful. Perhaps the friendship was still there, dormant, waiting for them. So Abi kept the conversation safe – on the international tour, what TV they had both been enjoying lately and even the recent football championships. Georgie kept their glasses topped up while the conversation actually continued to flow, later taking a tub of ice cream out of the freezer and putting it on the side next to two small bowls and spoons to warm up a little. Abi sat there, grateful, passive, submissive even. She was just happy to feel safe, to feel something close to how she used to.

Again, she noticed the slow, deliberate confidence with which Georgie seemed to do everything, never jumping when cutlery clanked on a plate or she knocked the jug of dressing with her chunky silver bangle as she reached to pick it up. Only this time, with a couple of glasses of wine inside her, it started to look a little different. There was a thread of jealousy running through her now – prompted by the wine? Abi wondered if perhaps Georgie was showing off, trying to be purposefully adult to make a point. To keep Abi in her place? Two could play at that game, she thought, her earlier anxiety being replaced with a queasy new false confidence in herself.

It wasn't just Georgie who had grown up recently, she found herself thinking. After all, she was in a proper adult relationship these days, while Georgie never seemed to want to talk about boys at all.

'So, come on then, have you been seeing anyone? Got your eye on any blokes?' Abi ventured.

'What do you mean?'

'Well, there are all those new guys who have started training at Bracken Lane, and I've seen you hanging out a lot with the whole theatre-studies lot at school...'

It used to be so easy, the casual chatter about who they might fancy. Now Georgie was the one who seemed guarded, for the first time all evening.

'What's that supposed to mean – about the theatre-studies lot?'

'Nothing! Just that I've seen you together a lot and I wondered. Come on... tell me.' Abi noticed that her voice was starting to sound a little different, a little distant. The ice cream was starting to drip on the side, condensation pooling on the countertop. She felt bleary, out of control, unsure what she was reaching for.

'How come you're suddenly poking around in my love life when yours has been off-limits for so long?'

'What love life!' protested Abi, stuttering like an outraged vicar. 'I haven't got one!'

Her body was vibrating with the memory of that leather sofa, Cole's breath in her ear, all of it. Suddenly, she saw with every fibre of her being that this was no time to start confiding in Georgie.

'Abi, I might be a virgin, but I'm not a moron.'

Abi felt her face flush, even her neck was pulsating with heat. 'What do you mean?' She could have kicked herself. What a stupid, stupid question.

'What do I mean? I've seen the way you look at Cole.'

'Oh, it's nothing like that,' she replied sharply. 'I am just giving everything I've got to training. He is the one who holds the keys to my future now; he's got it all mapped out for me. I just have to trust him and put in the hours to give myself the best chance.'

'Get over yourself, Abi. You've still got a phone, haven't you? Or does training leave you too tired to text your mates back.'

Abi stared, realising that Georgie might actually have been missing *her*.

'When was the last time you even asked how I was?' Georgie seemed huge now, standing over Abi, her eyes flickering with fury. But it was a confused fury, flecked with genuine hurt. Abi could tell this, but she couldn't reach for the words she needed to acknowledge it, to try to explain herself, to articulate that she honestly didn't think Georgie would ever have missed her. She had everything, and all Abi had was Cole.

'Honestly, I have been working so hard . . . it means so much to me . . .'

'If only it was just the tennis that we were talking about.'

'It is! I *need* Cole. I have to keep him happy to keep my—'

'*You have to keep him happy?*'

Sweat was gathering on Abi's skin. She was reaching for words that would never come, the acid of the wine at the back of her throat as she swallowed, trying to stay calm.

'*Whatever*, Abi, you've made yourself very clear. I really don't recognise you any more. As you've said yourself, your priority is keeping Cole happy these days. Of course, I of all people couldn't *possibly* be expected to understand how important tennis is to you.'

'It's not that! That's not how I meant it... God, it's so difficult...'

'What's difficult, Abi? You have made your choice, you're not really interested in hanging out with me, or any of us any more. You think you're above the lot of us, and that's fine. I can't try any more, I really can't.'

'Georgie! That's not true!' Abi stood up and the room lurched with her. Things seemed to be spinning horribly out of control.

'It is, Abi. You can try to explain all you like, but just seeing you here, dressed like a surrendered wife, not listening to anything I'm saying – you couldn't make your priorities any clearer. I barely recognise you.'

While she'd been speaking, Georgie had been rummaging in her bag for what Abi now realised was a packet of cigarettes. Abi tried to conceal the shock on her face, determined not to look judgemental when she was already under such attack. But there wasn't time anyway: Georgie stormed out of the kitchen and out of the house, saying she was going for a walk.

The house was deadly silent. Abi assumed Georgie was just going for a cigarette in the woods beyond the garden and busied herself putting dishes in the dishwasher, wiping down the table and replacing the now soft tub of ice cream, condensation dripping off its sides as she tried to slot it upright in the freezer drawer. She poured herself a huge glass of water and downed it, then sat, waiting for her friend.

But she never came. At first, Abi told herself she'd wait twenty minutes, then forty, then an hour. But the house remained silent and Abi started to worry that the Blackwoods would come home and find her alone, then demand to know what had gone on. So she dialled the pre-programmed number in the landline handset and called a cab.

As she stood in the kitchen, leaning on the counter waiting for the taxi, she was no longer thinking about when Georgie might come back. She was looking at the spot where she had stood several months ago for that first kiss. The moment that had changed everything. She had thought she'd been really at the beginning of something back then, but now it just felt as if door after door was being slammed in her face.

Chapter 17

NOW

Abi slammed her phone down on the kitchen counter on seeing mention of her son in print, and busied herself with helping Max and Georgie to clear up dinner.

'You OK?'

'Yeah, I just looked online, though. The Robbie thing... I think people really are going to take an interest.'

'For God's sake. It's no one's business,' muttered Max.

'It's very much your business if you run a newspaper, though,' Georgie reminded him.

'Right. Social media's coming off this phone for starters,' said Max. 'I'm just sorry I didn't make sure you'd done it sooner.' He held the phone up at Abi's face to unlock it, a cheeky grin on his face. Abi didn't protest as he started swiping and deleting.

Seconds later, the front door slammed and Robbie himself walked in. Despite the warmth of the evening, he had a navy-blue hoodie on, and was yanking the hood down from his face as he kicked his high-tops off and shoved them to the side of the hallway.

'Hi!' said Abi, standing up, trying to look relaxed and achieving nothing close to it. 'We thought you'd gone out for the night!'

'Hey,' he said, running a hand through his dark curls, one of them springing down over his forehead, almost meeting his eyebrows.

'What's up?' asked Georgie, as she headed towards him and gave him what she had long referred to as an 'auntie-cuddle'.

'Weird out there...'

This time, it was Max that Abi exchanged a worried glance with.

'What do you mean?' Max asked.

'I dunno.' Robbie sighed. 'It's probably stupid. I think someone took my picture when I was on my way to the pub. It was rammed in Wimbledon Village. I just felt weirded out and went for a walk, didn't feel like being out out.'

'Oh, sweetheart...' began Georgie.

'Then, when I was coming back down this road, someone was following me. Asking me shit.'

'Oh, Robbie. I'm so sor—'

He shrugged. 'Whatever. I mean, I didn't tell them anything.'

Abi moved towards him, putting a hand out to stroke his forearm. 'Hey – that interview – are you really OK about it?'

Robbie shrugged again. 'Why wouldn't I be?' He tried to make his way past her and towards the bedrooms at the other end of the flat.

'Robbie, darling. I know we have a lot to talk about. We haven't discussed your father that much.'

'No, *you* haven't discussed him that much...' He was turning back to look at her now, his face heavy with... she wasn't quite sure what. Rage? Sadness? Worry?

For so long, the question of his father was not one that she'd ever wanted to discuss. The first time that he'd asked her outright, she had got away with simply telling him that his father was 'not someone he needed to worry about', but it had left her guts churning for days in case he pressed her for further details. Back then, when he was still in primary school, they both simply got used to telling his friends that he didn't have a dad.

He had pressed her on it again the summer before he'd started secondary school, but that time she had been firmer, insisting that he 'wasn't a great guy', then adding that it was not something he should worry about, or feel guilty about. Again, she'd thought for a while that she had got away with leaving it at that, but for months afterwards she had suspected that this answer had done little to diminish his curiosity, only leaving him awake for nights on end, wondering, as she so often did, whether there was a part of him that 'wasn't a great guy' too.

Time and again, she had found herself checking, trying to figure out whether any and all behaviour was perfectly normal or a sign of something darker. Was his cheekiness at five a sign of confidence with his new school friends or the beginning of a manipulative trait? Was that confidence on the golf course at only thirteen, or a bit of a swagger? Where did the line lie? And now that he was on the threshold of adulthood, dating, talking about girls and doing Lord knows what with them, had she told him enough about consent, consideration, connection? And what if she had and he'd chosen to ignore her, preferring to emulate an imagined father figure – or, worse still, one found online?

When might this part of him reveal itself? When might it come into play? Should she try to keep it at bay? Or prepare for it? And were these simply the anxieties of a single mother, or of a woman who had gone through too much, too young?

In the end, she had decided on the latter. Robbie was his own person; he had grown up entirely untouched by the influence of his dad. She mustn't project her fears onto him, she told herself, time and again. He'd be fine. And, on the whole, he was. Better than that, he thrived. Or so she'd thought.

'You always shut the conversation down. And now it feels as if the whole world is about to find out who he is before I do.'

'I would never let that happen. I won't, I just won't. Look, shall I drop out? That will surely put a stop to things.'

Abi glanced behind her to see if Max and Georgie could hear what she was suggesting, but at the other end of the flat they seemed to be busy talking to each other.

'Of course I don't want that for you. Don't be ridiculous! It was me who put you here in the first place, wasn't it? I just don't want to be left… answering questions I can't.'

'OK, OK. It's just this week. Just a few days, really, at most. And we will talk. We'll talk properly.' She was playing for time now, hoping she could lay the track out in front of her as fast as this train seemed to be moving.

'Sure, Mum.'

The bedroom door slammed. Abi's shoulders slumped. Max appeared at her side.

'Come on, Patterson, he's a teenage boy who's just left school. Of course he's frustrated that this summer hasn't worked out for him the way he'd hoped.'

It was true. He had only finished his exams a couple of weeks ago and had originally planned to go travelling with mates before their results arrived, but then changed his mind to be around for Wimbledon and his mum. But if only Max knew how much more pressure the boy was under.

'I know,' whispered Abi. 'I guess I always imagined him being more pleased for me.'

'Of course he is,' said Georgie, now joining the two of them. 'He can be *thrilled* for you *and* at the same be pissed off that there are some pillocks from the press following him around.'

'Suppose so.' Still, it wasn't the evening Abi had envisaged.

'Look,' said Max. 'I need to get back to mine. I have work to do, and I need fresh clothes and stuff for tomorrow. But I'll be on the phone whenever you need me, and I'll be back super early. Take another look at Renate's match if you can, and I'll see you first thing.'

The women hugged him goodbye, Abi wishing the place was big enough for him to stay over. As promised, Georgie started watching a re-run of Renate's quarter-final, while Abi went to her room and tried to do some stretching and breathing exercises.

A while later, Georgie knocked quietly on Abi's door, before letting herself in to see her friend sitting on the side of the bed, rubbing peppermint cooling cream into her feet. She plonked herself down on the bed next to her with a sigh. It was as if they were sixteen again, sharing a twin room in some cheap and cheerful B&B on the junior circuit.

'I watched a bit of Renate's match. But I also just watched most of yours back. I really scanned the footage, the bit you mentioned – as well as twenty minutes or so either side of it.'

Abi turned to look at Georgie, her face as open and anxious as it had been in those early days, whenever she had been taken out of her comfort zone.

'Yes?' she asked.

Georgie sighed. 'I don't know. I really can't be sure.'

Abi continued to rub the cream into her foot, working the heel more vigorously, no longer looking up at her friend.

'I've listened back and I can hear the voice in the crowd – there definitely is one,' continued Georgie. 'I just can't be certain it's his. But then it's impossible to scan every single face in the crowd. Which you'd have to do, allowing for the acoustics of that place.'

'Did you hear him say "Abi-girl", though?'

'I think so, but I can't be sure.'

'It's what he said. It's what he *always* said when he watched me play. "Let's go, Abi-girl." And he's the only one who ever called me that…'

Georgie turned to face her full on, sitting cross-legged on the bed opposite her. It felt like yesterday that they had been discussing this man, and yet a thousand years ago.

'Look, I think we have to prepare for the fact that we have no way of *knowing* if it was him or not, so we have to work with that.'

But Abi was ignoring her. 'Oh God. I just *know* he is going to crawl out of the woodwork.'

'We don't know. That's what I'm trying to say – we can't know for sure about any of this.'

'Do you think he might contact the media? Start talking about me? About *us*?'

Abi suspected that this might have been running through Georgie's mind too, given her experience with the press. Could Cole make his presence felt by speaking with the media, thereby exposing their relationship, or worse, misrepresenting it? It happened time and time again when a player had a big breakthrough. Every man and his dog with even the most spurious involvement came out of the woodwork to highlight their role in that success.

'Abi, Abi, hold on a minute, your mind is galloping. Remember, it might not have been him. It's hardly a dazzlingly original name – I mean he was hardly creative, was he?'

'Yeah, yeah, yeah, I know you always loathed him.' Abi was bristling.

'It's not about that. I'm just saying. You've seen the fans out there – they do all sorts. It might just have been a name someone else shouted out. It might have been an unfamiliar accent that we misheard. And if it wasn't, we can't do anything about that either.'

'So I'm supposed to just forget about it? To just pretend it never happened? It's freaking me out thinking that he might be there. Not knowing what he might do. And what about Robbie? With the mood he's in ...'

Georgie pushed her hair back off her face, trying to stay calm despite Abi's obviously increasing agitation. 'Babe, I'm not trying to pretend that this shouldn't freak you out a bit. I'm just saying that we can't *know* it was him, so we need to get our heads round that.'

'You mean, *I* need to. I can't bear it ... trying to get his fifteen minutes of fame on the back of mine, working out how to make a few quid ...'

'We can't say that for sure.'

The trouble was, it was highly likely that the man Cole had become would be trying to boost his own profile given half the chance. After all, having disgraced himself in the UK, he had resurfaced online in the dawn of social media, making a pretty decent fist of life as a YouTuber. He had got in early and used his good looks and easy charm to good effect, offering coaching and fitness tips, which were often demonstrated on what seemed to be a conveyor belt of perky young women eager for their moment to shine on the internet.

'Look, there is no wrong answer here,' said Georgie, her hands extended, palms raised to show that the forthcoming question wasn't an accusation, 'but have you googled him recently? Obviously we know he resurfaced at some point, but do we know what he's doing now?'

'Arrgh,' said Abi into her hands, rubbing her palms over her hair in despair. 'Of course I have. Well, I hadn't for ages, but then a couple of years ago – around the time Robbie turned sixteen, when he was asking a lot of questions – I had a good rummage. It was not a great evening, seeing his face leap out of my laptop again while Robbie was upstairs asleep. That public charm he had, all smiles, all willingness to gift the ladies his insider knowledge, it made my insides churn.'

'No judgement here. You don't ever want to see my Google Images search history, mate. But that was a couple of years ago. Do we know what he's doing now, like this week? Any Insta Lives from Henman Hill type of thing?'

'Oh God, just thinking about it is making me sweat. Of course I have kept some sort of tabs on him. I'll do what we all do: log on when I'm feeling down, when I'm feeling nostalgic—'

'Maaaate.'

'Not for him, just for those days, what might have been, that sort of thing. You know what it's like. The three o'clock in the mornings when you question all your choices. It's like picking a scab, isn't it?'

'It sure is. More scar tissue than most in your case.'

'It's weird, though, isn't it. The informality of the internet. You spend a decade wondering what on earth became of someone

– what they look like now, who they turned out to be – and then a tiny box on your bedside tells you in three seconds. He's right there, blending a protein shake at his kitchen island and babbling on about hemp seeds. At first, it was impossible to look away, but I got it in hand after a while, deleted all my search histories, retrained my fingers not to type his name into the search bar any more.'

'And you didn't want to go back. Again.'

'Exactly. So what I'm saying is that I haven't looked. In fact, I was quite bloody proud of not even having had a peek this week. Not even one little spite-google to see how unkind all those years in the sun have been to his skin. You know, sometimes his ring lamp would catch the thinning hair on the top of his head and it would really make the worst part of me chuckle. He was even a bit paunchy last time I checked. A little bit desperate. It cheered me up, made me feel rather strong that I hadn't even needed to look lately. It had started to feel quite easy to forget about him. Until now.'

'Until now. Which is a good job you have me, because I'll have a sniff around the internet for you. Your phone, madam, will remain social-media-free.'

'Oh, G, the rewards that will await you in heaven.'

'Don't sweat it – you should see some of the things I've had to do online for my sports stars.'

Abi roared with laughter, thrilled to momentarily consider someone else's dilemmas.

'Look,' said Georgie, pulling her focus back to the present. 'Regardless of where he is, we need to prioritise accepting that, yes, it's a bit of a nightmare that he might be around. Then we are in with a chance of him not getting in your head on Thursday. That is our priority. Him not affecting your game.'

'I just don't know if I can.'

'OK, let's look at it differently. Worst-case scenario, he gives some crappy interview to the press about how your success is all down to him. So bloody what? It's not him who has made it to the Wimbledon semi-final, is it? It's you! Your success! His playing days are long gone, so who cares if he makes a quick buck—'

'Georgie, please. You know that is not the worst thing he could say. And what if he finds out...' Abi's voice faded away, unable to express what she feared the most. Now facing Georgie on the bed, her eyes were glassy with tears.

Georgie knew she was seconds from floods of tears. And couldn't blame her for it. 'I get it. I do. I know I'm being the infuriatingly pragmatic one, but it's because I care.'

Abi put her head in her hands, and Georgie leant forward to wrap her arms around her friend's back. She felt the sobs as Abi finally let go.

'Just when I thought things were finally looking up for me.'

'They are, though! They *are*! Don't let him have you thinking otherwise – *you* did this! He's been out of your life for nineteen years, don't let him back in. You got here, it's *your* championships now, and you deserve it! Don't let Mr Boot-Cuts-and-Wrap-arounds get in your head!'

Abi looked up and laughed, and within seconds, the two of them were giggling.

'Oh God, he was the worrrst,' said Abi. 'What was I thinking?'

Georgie threw her hands in the air and they laughed some more. Then, as they both settled a little, Georgie pulled her friend's face close to hers and said softly, 'It doesn't matter what you were thinking, because you were still a child. Never forget that. Not tonight, not tomorrow and certainly not on Thursday.'

Abi blinked, her eyelashes wet with tears. 'I know,' she whispered. 'And thank you.'

'Now get to sleep, goddammit!' said Georgie as she stood up and put her slippers back on. 'Alarm for 7 a.m. please and I'm in charge of breakfast. It's run-through day. You know, run-through for being a Wimbledon semi-finalist … in case you'd forgotten?'

'Ha ha,' replied her friend. 'Thanks for reminding me …'

The women hugged, as fiercely as only women who have shared lifelong experience and the secrets that go with that can do, and Georgie softly closed the door behind her.

Twenty minutes later, as she reached to turn off her bedside light, Abi hoped Robbie was OK in his room. He hadn't answered when she'd knocked on his door. She turned her phone back on quickly and dropped him a text to say goodnight.

I promise we'll talk properly tomorrow. I love you. Xxx

It was time. She had put this conversation off for long enough. And now she couldn't risk someone else telling him the truth.

Chapter 18

THEN

For a few days after her disastrous evening at the Blackwoods' with Georgie, Abi had thought that that would be the end of it with her friend. The ultimate teen friendship gone sour. She swung between grief for the friendship and relief at having one less person to keep her secret from. Cole returned from London and things picked up where they had left off.

The following Saturday morning, she was packing her bag for the weekend's competition when Grannie Annie peered round the door of her room.

'Good news, sweetie. Barb's going to take you to Manor Park.'

Abi looked up sharply. 'But Georgie isn't even playing this weekend.'

'I know, but Barb says she has some networking that needs doing, so she's arranged meetings in their clubhouse while your match is on, and it makes sense for her to take you. You'll have a much more comfortable drive down all those country roads in her four-by-four than you would in my banger anyway!'

Abi gave her gran the smile she always used when she was

just trying to keep everyone happy, and started to look for Max's old Discman, which he had lent her for long train journeys. Today, she wanted it to hand in case Barb wanted to make calls on her hi-tech car phone and she could tune out to some music.

No such luck. The drive to Manor Park was fifty minutes and they had been driving for a mere five before Barb reached to turn her phone off entirely, then, as they pulled up to some red lights, turned to face Abi and asked, quite simply, 'What on earth is going on with you, darling? You've become a stranger.'

'I'm just so busy with traini—'

'Please, Abigail. Don't patronise me. I am well aware of the time and dedication you are devoting to your tennis, and of how necessary it is. But I am also more than aware that that is not the heart of the issue.'

The lights changed to amber, and, as Barb reached for the gearstick, she turned again to Abi, this time peering over the top of her enormous shades, making eye contact. Abi, stunned by the directness of the intervention, could not think of a single thing to say.

'You are wise not to deny your crush, but let me warn you, you'd be highly unwise to act on it. Tash is extremely fond of Mr Connolly, and as I understand it, that fondness is more than reciprocated...'

Tash. One of Barb's friends from the club. Abi felt sick, desperate to open a window, but she was both flummoxed by the panel of buttons on the door and panicked that gasping for air might give her away. So Cole *had* been doing what he had long sworn he wasn't: dating one of the chic divorcées of Bracken Lane. Someone he didn't have to keep secret. Someone who was allowed into his bedroom.

The thought that Cole had been cheating on Abi did not

cross her mind at first. As the car pulled away from the lights at speed and she pressed her head into the plush leather headrest of the passenger seat, she could only see that she and Cole had been having an affair behind Tash's back. She had to protect him, to make sure that he didn't incur the wrath of Barb, or his job would be on the line – along with her future.

'Barb, honestly, I might have had a bit of a crush to begin with, I mean, who wouldn't . . .' she let out a weird strangled laugh, rather than the chummy chuckle she had hoped to hide behind. 'But things are very professional with C— Mr Connolly, he just has my absolute best interests at heart, and I just want to keep improving, and to give myself the best chance to turn pro. I'm prepared to do whatever it takes to achieve that.'

A pause, as Barb took a left turn that nearly left an imprint of Abi's face on the window.

'Very well,' replied Barb. And she left it at that.

Abi would probably have got away with it, if not for the match that followed. While Barb was inside the clubhouse, air-kissing the chairman and taking sneaky sideways glances at his head coach from behind her shades, Abi went to pieces.

Minutes before the match, she rushed to the bathroom with cramps, sure that her period – erratic for so long now – was here at last. She felt clammy, exhausted, her bowels threatening to betray her at any minute, but knew that she couldn't bail on the game.

Her game bailed on her, though. She lost the first set in twenty-five minutes and the second in even fewer. She struggled to keep her eye on the ball, she slipped on grass at the front of the net and embarrassed herself by trying to fall in a discreet way, convinced that her period might yet still have arrived. Her opponent, a plain public schoolgirl who had clearly not expected to come even close to winning, was gobsmacked, squawking with delight as Abi missed her final shot, handing her victory.

Devastated, Abi hoped to get herself a sandwich and have a long shower before heading home, but it turned out Barb was already done with her networking and had seen the last ten minutes of the match. As Abi walked off court, Barb told her to have a shower and meet her in the car park in fifteen minutes, as she had already bought her some food for the way home.

The warm leather of the Range Rover, exhaustion that had reached her very bones, and the visceral desire not to meet Barb's eye meant that within five minutes of them setting off for home, Abi fell sound asleep for at least half an hour. When she first woke up, the engine purring as only Barb's top-notch vehicle could, she felt for a moment or two as if she were made of honey. Then, with a start, the state of deep relaxation left her as she remembered where she was, and what had just happened.

She gasped and sat up, lifting her head away from the head-rest and looking around. The sun was low in the sky and Barb was listening to her favourite David Grey album.

'Welcome back, Abigail,' she said with a smile. 'How are you feeling?'

'Great, thanks!' Abi tried her best to sound chirpy.

'So what happened on the court then? That performance was very unlike you.'

'I don't know. I didn't feel great and I had no energy. I think I'm just really tired.'

'Abi, I understand how tiring training at this level can be. But I'm afraid to say that after seeing your absolute lack of concentration and total lethargy this afternoon, I'm certain that the real issue lies elsewhere.'

'I—'

Barb raised her fingers up and off the grip of the steering wheel to silence Abi. '*Please.* Let me finish.'

'Sorry,' Abi whispered.

'I am going to be keeping a very close eye on you from now on. It is going to take some convincing that this training relationship is entirely healthy. I take my responsibilities at Bracken Lane very seriously, and I don't want to be accused of being neglectful of the well-being of my girls. So watch your step.'

Chapter 19

NOW

Abi yanked the memory-foam eye-mask off and rubbed at her eyes. They stung as if she'd been out clubbing all night. She appreciated the cool of the wooden floor by the side of the bed as she pressed her feet into the ground and stretched. Her shoulders were stiff, a grim combination of yesterday's match and a night spent tossing and turning. She reckoned she'd had a few decent hours after dawn had broken, but far from enough. There was little she could do to avoid today, though, she reminded herself as she pulled on a pair of tracksuit bottoms and headed across the flat towards the kitchen.

Georgie was already up, ponytail high and chic black leggings glistening in the morning sun. Breakfast was laid out – chopped fruit, seeds and nuts in little bowls ready for her to take her pick from, a tub of expensive-looking kefir next to them. To the right of the induction hob was a bowl full of eggs, next to some chopped ham and finely sliced basil.

'Coffee? Omelette?' asked her friend with a smile. Yes, it was a smile, but Abi recognised the flinty determination behind it. This wasn't a smile that said, *Tell me everything*... but one that said, *We're getting on with things today. And we're doing it with a smile.* Abi knew what her role was, and for now she was happy to play it.

'Fantastic, thank you. No milk for me, though.'

Georgie carried the cafetière towards the boiling kettle and filled it, the hiss of the hot liquid giving the women a pause before the chat began.

'Get any sleep?'

Abi grimaced, but said nothing as Georgie pushed a mug and the brewing coffee towards her.

'You can nap this afternoon,' said Georgie with a swish of her ponytail. 'Good news is, I think I've found us a great hitter for this morning.'

'You're the boss. Who is it?' asked Abi, raising her steaming mug at her.

'Dominic Drysdale – that Irish kid who Max signed up after spotting him in the boys singles here last year. He was knocked out of the junior event a couple of days ago and Max encouraged him to stay on and work as a practice partner. There's no better way to learn. As you well know…'

'God, it feels like only yesterday that it was me doing that job,' said Abi, scooping some raspberries, cashews and chia seeds onto a dollop of yoghurt. In the small yard on the other side of the patio doors, she could see Max, sleeves rolled up, his back turned as he paced on his phone. Even from behind, she could see that his glossy dark hair was sticking straight up at the front where he had been running a hand through it.

'Well, let me remind you that it's not your job today. You're the star of the show now.'

'I know…' Abi was grateful for the fact that Georgie was determined that she treat herself like a finalist, even if she wasn't sure she ever would be. She watched her friend for a second, busying herself at the stove, and thought how much like her mother, Barb, she was behaving. When they were teens, Georgie had found Barb's relentless positivity and ambition on her behalf utterly stifling. Today, she seemed to be manifesting the same breed of relentless 'positive energy' herself. Abi tried to remind herself that, as had always been the case with Barb, Georgie's intentions might sometimes nudge towards overbearing, but they were always entirely well-meaning.

Nevertheless, she felt caught between frustration at Georgie's refusal to let her air her genuine anxiety, and momentary distraction as Max turned around to reveal that he was in a very tight running top, leaving the contours of his chest rippling like a cartoon superhero. And... was he wearing novelty Arsenal sliders over his running socks?

Georgie poured an egg into a frying pan that was bubbling with melted butter. The way she spoke, it was as if holding her nerve under these conditions would be a walk in the park. Her face had obviously fallen, as a moment later Georgie was repeating her mantra from last night.

'You know I'm right. You can do this. You always could. You just had to wait longer than some.'

'I'm just going to have to take your word for it!' Abi licked her lips in gratitude as Georgie slid the omelette across the kitchen island towards her.

'Exactly. And don't look to him for reassurance, because he thinks exactly the same as I do.' Georgie waved a hand in the direction of the courtyard, where Max was still on the phone, albeit facing them now, giving Abi a cheery wave. *That running top...*

Moments later, as Abi was polishing off her food and pouring herself a second coffee, Max slid open the French door and headed back inside, wishing the women good morning, and giving each of them a brief kiss. Abi could feel his stubble against her cheek and the warmth of his hand on her shoulders as he did so.

'Morning, morning. All set, are we?' he asked.

'Yes, we're off shortly for practice and a timing run-through.'

'Great stuff.' He lobbed a blueberry from the bowl into the air and caught it in his mouth. 'Any sign of his lordship?'

'I haven't heard a thing – must still be in his pit,' said Abi, referring to the tiny second room Robbie had been sleeping in all week.

'Fair enough …' replied Max.

'I texted him last night that we'll have a proper chat later today. It's time.'

'Are you sure?' said Max. 'This morning? I'm about to go for a run, but I can be on hand for you if you need me around. Moral support and all that?'

'I'll never be sure. But I can't avoid it any longer. We have this morning all planned. This afternoon is all about Robbie.'

'You're the boss …' said Max, smiling as he looked up from tying his trainers.

As soon as he was out of earshot, Georgie leant over the island, her voice low. 'And how are you feeling about this chat?'

Abi shrugged at first, sensing that the truth wasn't what Georgie wanted to hear.

Equally, she was unsure that she could maintain any further secrets. The gnawing in the pit of her stomach was still there, and to pretend otherwise wasn't going to make it go away any faster. She had tried all night – mindfulness apps, breathing exercises, senseless scrolling through the last few websites her mobile would actually access, looking for something, someone who could ease the itch in her mind – but she had failed spectacularly to park thoughts of 'that voice'.

'Oh, you know, it was all buzzing through my brain at all hours. Memories flashing through my mind every time I closed my eyes.'

'Babe, this is a lot. Tell me what you need. You know that when you're ready, I want to sit down and talk about this properly. I want to really hear what you went through – if you want to tell me, that is. I don't want anything that needs airing to be left unsaid.'

'But not today…'

'Of course not today, you maniac!'

'Oh, Georgie, I bloody love you.'

'I love you too. And I know how many sacrifices you've made for me. A win for me would be a win for all of us. I didn't get here on my own, and even though I might look alone out there tomorrow, I know I won't be. Right?'

'Damn straight.'

Georgie fished a tissue out of her bag and handed it to Abi, who wiped her eyes.

'I'm going to head to the club, meet this hitter, get him briefed on what you need and I'll see you there, OK? Your car's booked and will be here in less than an hour. I'm going to walk as I want to get some bits in the village en route.'

The women embraced again, and Abi headed into her room, feeling unburdened in a way she hadn't been for eighteen years. For half an hour, she lay on a yoga mat, flat on her bedroom floor, noise-blocking headphones on, trying breathing exercises as she ran through what she needed to discuss with Robbie.

*

She heard the shower running when she walked into the kitchen for her kitbag and realised with a smile that Robbie was up at last. If he hurried up, she'd get to give him a hug before she left, she thought as she finished packing her bag, removing things she had shoved in earlier and replacing them with the bits that she now noticed Georgie had carefully laid out that morning. On top of her second pair of tennis shoes was a piece of paper she recognised as being ripped from Georgie's ever-present notepad, with *DRINKS!!* written in black marker pen on it.

Abi grinned at how their system could be both seamless and lo-fi at the same time, and opened the fridge to find the three cold bottles of pre-prepared electrolyte drinks in there waiting for her. She grabbed them and turned to close the fridge, noting as she did that the noise from the shower had stopped.

Hooray, she thought, as the fridge door swung shut to reveal not Robbie but Max, apparently back from his run, dripping wet and barely managing to get the towel he was rubbing his hair with down to his groin in time.

'Max!'

'I thought you guys had gone!'

'I thought it was Robbie in the shower!'

'Well, it wasn't!'

The two of them spoke over each other for a few seconds, offering excuses the other could neither hear nor care about. Then, a moment's silence. Each of them was slightly winded by the unexpected sight of one another. Abi was holding the bottles to her chest in front of her, but Max, with nothing but some dark curls on his, was more obviously breathing heavily. Water was starting to pool on the kitchen tiles by his feet, which Abi now noticed were tanned with distinctive slider-strap stripes. Just as they both opened their mouths to speak again, the doorbell rang.

'My car...' said Abi.

'Go, go!' said Max as his face broke into an enormous smile. 'Go and be your brilliant self!'

Abi shoved the bottles into her bag and slung it over her shoulder, then leant in to give Max a quick peck on the cheek as she said goodbye. She headed towards the door before calling, 'So is Robbie still asleep, or has he gone out?' behind her.

'Text him! I've got to get dressed!' she heard Max say, and as she snuck a look over her shoulder, she saw him waving as he walked away towards his room, his buttocks entirely naked.

'The All England Club, please,' she said as she dumped her bag onto the back seat and reached for her seat belt.

'Yes, Miss Patterson,' said the driver, looking at her in the rear-view mirror as if to say, *Where else did you think we'd be going?*

She smiled, unsure how to respond, then took a deep breath, trying to clear her mind of the now mounting heap of distractions she had to contend with. She couldn't do anything about her game until she got on court. She trusted that Georgie would do what she could to find out about whether Cole was in town as soon as she had time. She knew Robbie was safe in bed. And as for Max... Suddenly her train of thought snagged on the image of him, his dark curls flopping over his face, the towel barely covering his dignity, that smile as he wished her good luck.

It had been so long since they had shared the sort of closeness that they'd all had while hanging out over the last couple of weeks. Chucking each other pieces of fruit across the kitchen, padding around in cosy clothes as they analysed matches, wishing each other goodnight. It had all been so reminiscent of their days on tour, sharing family rooms, sharing food on trains, in minibuses, across laps. And sharing hope, ambition, and most of all, laughter.

There was a still a niggle, though, the sort of ringing at the back of her mind that she knew Georgie and Max were trying to eliminate for her. Robbie. Was he avoiding her? Still angry, resentful?

She picked up her phone from where it had been lying, lifeless with most of its apps removed, and texted him.

> Hey – didn't want to wake you before I left, but hope you're OK. Thinking of you today. And we will talk. Love you the most, Mum xx

The reply was fast.

> Mum! I left a couple of hours ago – couldn't sleep – went for walk while it was quieter after yesterday 🤯 Meeting Felix and Al for coffee and food in a bit.

Then another.

> And I hope YOU are OK. I'm all good. So proud of you. Go do your thing and don't wait up. Xo

Abi exhaled. Maybe her luck was changing after all.

Chapter 20

THEN

The afternoon that Abi finally confronted Cole about Tash, she felt as if she were going into battle. She had chosen to put her question at him in the car, where he couldn't simply remove himself from the situation or start talking to a nearby adult as if she didn't exist. Both of which were things he had done in the recent past when she had tried to push for a little more clarity from him about her situation.

She had rehearsed a couple of times in the bathroom mirror at home, her face a picture of poised nonchalance, then defiance, then simply innocent curiosity. She didn't know which one she'd use as she got in his car for the drive back to her grandparents', but when she eventually started talking, it felt as if she'd lobbed a grenade at him.

'Do you know Tash, from the club, much?'

A pause. He stared straight ahead at the road.

'One of Barb's lot?'

'Yeah, dark hair. One of her glam mates.'

'I know who you mean… she comes to some of the ladies morning sessions…'

Now it was Abi's turn to stare straight ahead. She took a breath. 'But you're not, like, a couple?'

She watched his hands grip the steering wheel tight, his knuckles whitening. 'What the hell gave you that idea?'

'Barb. She told me the other day.'

'What on God's green earth made you start talking to *Barb* of all people, about *me*? Are you dumb?'

Abi felt sick. Trapped. He was rattled, driving quite fast now. '*I* didn't talk to her, she told *me*.' Her voice was quiet. The road ahead zooming towards them, fast. The conversation even faster.

'Told you what?'

'That you and Tash are ... a thing.'

'Ridiculous. Bloody ridiculous.'

'So you're not?' She couldn't believe she was still going, needling away at him. But she could see she was close to home now, just a couple of streets away.

'No, we bloody well aren't. Any more than I am with *anyone*.'

'Oh, right, including me?'

'No, no, you know things are more complicated than that with us. You know it. But, honestly, Abigail, it's a bit much for you to be making these demands of me for a more open relationship while simultaneously behaving like a child about how I spend my time when I'm not with you.'

'So you do spend time with her?'

'I spend time with lots of people, Abigail. It's kind of my job. In case you hadn't noticed, a huge part of my role at Bracken Lane is keeping the members happy and that includes Barb and her cronies. My job literally depends on it. So thanks for blabbing to her. Thanks very much.'

The car pulled up at the end of Abi's road. Cole flicked the hazard lights on to show that he wasn't driving any further, then walked round to the boot, got Abi's bag out and dumped it on the grass verge while she sheepishly got out.

What had she done? She had no idea. But she had seen a side to Cole that had never been on show before, and she had been left shaken, as if she were in a hall of mirrors. Everything seemed out of proportion. And nothing seemed quite real any more. The ground felt unstable beneath her as she walked to the front door.

She just longed for the safety, the simple pleasure of her old life. But she wasn't sure if she had now left it too far behind her, burning too many bridges along the way.

There was only one way to find out, so later that night she called Barb and accepted the invitation she had made to play tennis at the Blackwoods' that weekend with a group of friends. Even if she couldn't talk to Georgie about everything, she could at least try to rebuild some bridges with her, and playing some low-stakes tennis at the Blackwoods' would be a good place to start.

When Abi arrived, she felt breathless with anxiety, her head buzzing with the pressure of keeping breezy, but letting Georgie sincerely know that she missed her. A good first sign was the broad grin on Barb's face when she opened the door.

'Abigail! It is so good to see you. Come in and get settled – you know where everything is.'

Abi took her jacket off and hung it on one of the hall pegs, before tentatively heading into the kitchen. On the other side of the island, she could see Georgie with Max, peering into a laptop, watching what looked like a DVD recording of a recent match. Her emotions were churning as if on spin dry. Max! She hadn't seen him for a few weeks, and there he was, his broad shoulders hunched over the laptop, Barb having to step over his long legs as he sat next to Georgie at the kitchen island. Would he be an ally? Or was his presence next to her friend an indication that he'd already chosen a side, ready for more confrontation?

How wrong she was to doubt him.

'Well, if it isn't Abigail Patterson,' he said with a smile, as he stood up and stretched out his arms. 'Nice of you to grace us with your company.'

'You know me,' she replied, accepting his hug gladly, barely daring to look at Georgie's response. 'I just love tennis. And the Blackwoods,' she added with a shy smile in Barb's direction. 'How's your dad?' she asked, knowing that he'd been ill recently.

Max waved his hand, to show he was not doing too badly, nor too well. They hugged again, silently.

'Now, come on, crew, no more clogging up my kitchen – go and get playing. The others are out there.' As Barb led them out of the kitchen, she had a gentle hand on both Georgie's and Abi's backs, letting them know that whatever they had to say to each other could be said in the relative privacy of the garden.

By the time they reached the grass, Max had walked on ahead a bit, somehow managing to juggle three tennis balls at the same time as striding towards the court. As soon as he was out of earshot, Abi turned to her friend, her face all but begging for reconciliation, even if her words were cautious.

'Georgie, I'm sorry about the other week.'

'It's fine. I snapped. I guess I missed you, got jealous and shit.'

'I've been a really crappy friend, though.'

'Well …' The first whispers of a smile appeared on Georgie's face. 'I didn't want to say …'

'Well, you kinda did say. But I'm glad you did, and you were right. Everything got on top of me – the training, the pressure, all of it. I guess I lost sight of the important stuff, maybe.'

'I get it. I know I have a lot of support.'

'You shouldn't apologise for that. It's not as if you don't share!' The girls laughed at last, as Abi extended a hand as if showing Georgie her own home – the tennis courts, Mr Blackwood pootling back and forth between the kitchen and the big outdoor barbecue, Barb waving from the patio – for the first time. 'I know I can, sort of, clam up when I'm stressed. I don't find it the easiest to talk.'

'We're all good, Abi,' said her friend. 'Now let's play some tennis.'

Abi felt a lightness to her, knowing that a bridge was being rebuilt. But she knew that she was still keeping so much back, even if her friend was understanding about how she sometimes struggled to chat openly.

Thank God for tennis, she thought, as they and their friends goofed around with some mixed doubles. Georgie made her belly-laugh in a way that left her feeling as if she'd had a proper shoulder massage and Max's quiet confidence and ease around her seemed to leave space for her to feel a little of the sparkle she long ago thought had been sacrificed in the name of hard work and dedication.

While Abi had been desperate for the freedom of leaving school to go into full-time training, this evening cast a different light on things. Georgie was saying she wanted to head to London to intern at a big PR agency as soon as she could. They all knew she'd be back every weekend, knocking around Blackwood Towers, enjoying Barb's food for at least three nights a week and getting her laundry done, but her lust to go and find herself away from the gaze of her parents was obvious.

And Max had been offered an incredible opportunity to study on a scholarship at Miami University – and it looked as if he might be on the cusp of finding the funding to go. When he offered her a lift home that night, an overwhelming sense of melancholy came over Abi when she realised that this might be one of the last occasions she spent time with him like that.

Pulling out of the Blackwoods' drive, Max grinned. 'Thank God all that crap with you and Georgie is over, then.'

'Yeah, we had a good chat. I hated it when we weren't speaking.'

'Me too – the universe feels all wobbly when you two aren't your usual sparkly selves.'

Abi laughed, close to tears with relief that her friends were still there for her, even after the way she'd been lately. The journey home went by in a blur, the two of them feeling as if they were in a little bubble of their own as the light faded and the country roads meandered by.

Max explained that he was keen to get the three of them together as often as possible in the coming weeks if he actually did get the much-longed-for Miami funding. Then he chatted away about anything and everything, occasionally glancing across to smile at her in the passenger seat, while Abi looked at his tanned hand on the gearstick and realised how much she'd miss him when he was gone. Ten minutes later, when he pulled up outside her grandparents' and opened her door on his beloved navy-blue Ford Fiesta, she began to accept that he had really grown up. Yes, as his shirt lifted to reveal the line of his boxer shorts when he bent to tie his shoelace, there was a small voice insisting that Max really had Got Hot.

He kissed her goodbye at the door, waving to Grannie Annie, who was mouthing, 'Hello!' from the kitchen window. He ran a hand through his hair, and as his curls sprang back into place, Abi found herself wanting to touch them. They seemed so much healthier than what repeated close-up views had by now revealed were Cole's rather thinning sandy locks.

Later that night, as Abi lay on her bed, running through that chat on the way home over and again, she heard the beep of a text arriving on her phone.

We might need to train late tomorrow, Abi-girl

Abi sighed, wondering if Tash was there with Cole right now. The leaden feeling that had been gone from her all day suddenly returned, and before she could stop herself, she typed back, keeping it deliberately brief, aloof, even.

Sorry, can't. Have plans

For a while, she lay there, muscles clenched, desperate for sleep but waiting for the rage that would surely follow her message. She had never defied him like this, ever. But nothing came. Silence. Which was almost worse, leaving adrenaline pumping through her body like treacle. She had no idea what to do now, feeling suspended, unsure how to move forward, but increasingly convinced that she couldn't go back.

Chapter 21

NOW

The car pulled up outside the players' security check, but it had taken its time winding through the congestion in the roads around the club. Press and fans alike were hovering at the Somerset Road entrance, peering through the hedges to see who was inside the car as Abi got out. Abi knew exactly where in the clubhouse she was due to meet Georgie, but she had not anticipated it taking her so long to get there, in between signing autographs, smiling at phone cameras and politely saying, 'No, thank you,' to offers of interviews and requests to lean in for a selfie. Faces blurred into one as they approached her, phones out, grins wide, each one asking for something from her.

Making her way through the club was an almost surreal experience – there were so few matches on the schedule now that the whole venue was noticeably emptier than earlier in the week, but so many of the other things that made Wimbledon *Wimbledon* were still in place: there were clusters of die-hard spectators juggling multiple cups of Pimm's towards Murray Mound, there were brands filming promo videos in brightly coloured, strawberry-emblazoned T-shirts, and there were the cameras on dolly mounts, looming high above everyone, capturing it all. And, it dawned on her in between glimpses of all this, that she was the biggest story of the tournament so far.

But everything else slid out of focus once Abi was back on court – bouncing up and down on the baseline, pounding forehands and backhands and moving effortlessly around the freshly prepared grass. The doubts that had been dogging her all night had disappeared. As promised, Georgie really had found the perfect hitter in Dominic Drysdale. Better known as Double D, he sported a man bun and had both ears pierced – not the usual preppy style that a lot of the players tended to stick to. He was loud and a little over-familiar, but Georgie knew it would be worth tolerating his frat-boy attitude as he knew Renate and her game well from years of playing the international junior circuit together. Renate's meteoric rise to the top of the women's game had taken him by surprise, but he could still replicate her playing style with uncanny accuracy, and Abi was grateful for the insight.

She let her game fill her thoughts, allowing the buzz around the grounds to stop feeling intimidating and instead to become a fuel she could feed off. She had spent a lifetime dreaming of being here, and she knew she mustn't blow her biggest chance yet. So many teenage bedtimes had been devoted to imagining that walk onto Centre Court as a finalist, so many late-night chats with Georgie about how it would feel if she got here. Now she was here, she knew she had to capitalise on this belated opportunity. She wanted to prove right everyone who had ever had faith in her – her teachers, her friends, her grandparents, all the juniors she had taught, and, above all, Robbie.

As they moved into a second hour of practice, Abi was feeling increasingly comfortable with her game. She felt good

– confident and relaxed. This morning, she had seen this emotional thawing that seemed to have taken over her as something to fear, but the tension had gone now and she felt energised again, inspired by the environment and the occasion. At last, she was where she had always wanted to be. She even found herself smiling as she leant down to pick up a ball. Then, looking up at the clear blue sky above the practice courts, she allowed herself a few minutes to soak it all in.

Georgie was courtside watching the two of them, pacing the tramlines, her eyes on every ball, fully in the moment and offering surprisingly helpful feedback considering that her own tennis was these days confined to the occasional corporate clinic and a weekly drilling session with her club pro. But she knew Abi better than anyone else did and that was worth its weight in gold. Abi saw Georgie glance down to her own bag, the familiar glow of a ringing phone having caught her friend's eye.

'Nice work!' Georgie called out as Abi floated a perfectly timed backhand drop shot to within an inch of the tramline.

Abi let out a, 'Whoop!' as she skipped back to her chair, noticing as she did that Georgie was leaning into her bag, looking at her phone again, and that Dom was silently applauding the winning shot. She realised, to her satisfaction, that she really was giving him a decent run-around, and the two of them high-fived as they changed ends.

'Thank you so much for this,' said Abi as she passed.

Georgie was squinting at her phone again.

'We keeping you?' called out Abi.

'It's just Max; he keeps calling me. Hang on.'

Abi shrugged at Dom with a smile, relieved that it was just Max, probably calling to ask if they needed anything before he headed to the club.

'I've got seven missed calls, and he knows we're training. Let me just call him back so I can turn this thing off,' said Georgie over her shoulder, one hand trying to shade the phone from the sunlight while she looked at the screen.

Abi held a hand up to Dom, telling him to pause before serving again. Her eyes were on Georgie, whose face had visibly fallen. 'What's up?' she mouthed at her friend.

'Abi,' called Georgie, her phone still in her hand, her arm now slack at her side. 'It's Robbie.'

'Oh God, what does he want?' Frustration was coursing through her now. How could he not know she was meant to be practising? She'd already promised him the afternoon. 'Doesn't he know we're kind of busy?'

'No, sorry, it was Max calling. But calling about Robbie. He's in hospital.'

'What? Since when?' Abi felt the sides of her hands tingle, panic dripping from her fingertips.

'An hour or so. He's not come round yet. They called Max as there were texts from him on his home screen.'

'What do you mean? He's unconscious?'

Abi had dropped her racket on the grass and was striding towards Georgie, reaching for the phone. Her arms felt limp, bloodless, her legs unstable beneath her. *Robbie.*

She grabbed the phone from Georgie.

'Max, what's going on? What's happened to him?' As she spoke, she noticed that her voice sounded strange, strangled, not her own.

'Don't panic—'

'Bit late for that.'

'OK, OK, I'm heading to the hospital now and they are

expecting Robbie to wake up before too long. He's had surgery, he lost a lot of blood—'

'How? What's happened? Where is he?'

'St George's, only down the road. Listen, I've called you a car. I knew you'd want to get there as soon as possible. Get over to Gate 16, the car's waiting, and call me once you're on your way. I'll explain more then.'

Abi felt as if the ground was moving beneath her feet, plates shifting and sliding, reality suddenly too slippery to grasp. Daydreams were indistinguishable from nightmares, each happening within seconds of one another, memories overlapping now, the truth slithering away from her time and again.

So she had lain in bed all night, fretful about Cole, then, once she had got here and finally relaxed, Robbie had been in danger? Of all the worries she'd had when she'd got up, not one of them had been that he'd be somewhere, bleeding, alone. Barely an hour ago, she'd been joking that he wasn't awake yet, and now she was waiting for him to come to in a hospital bed? How was this happening?

She felt Georgie's hand on her shoulder, steadying her. Her friend took the huge designer shades off her own face and handed them to Abi, along with Dom's cap.

'Dom is going to carry your bags to the car. Put these on and let's try to get you out of here as fast as possible.'

The women began the same route Abi had taken not so long before, this time with Georgie's hand around her, propelling her forward. Dom followed a few steps behind, carrying the women's bags, lanyards and any other overtly identifying items.

The car pulled up just as they were arriving at the gate and Georgie bundled Abi into the back seat before directing Dom to shove their kit in the boot. Abi felt the movement of the car as it left the club, but it was as if she wasn't inside it. Instead, she seemed to have floated up and out of herself, watching the two of them in the back seat from somewhere high above.

The car felt as if it was crawling along at an impossibly slow pace. *Why was it taking so long?* She couldn't bear the thought of Robbie waking up on a busy hospital ward, alone and frightened, wondering why she wasn't there. Flashes of memories darted through her mind: the tiny baby with wisps of dark hair she'd brought home from hospital; the quiet middle of the nights spent feeding him; the feeling of his tiny fist curling around her index finger; the first steps he'd taken as a toddler on their kitchen floor; the hours spent watching him learn to play cricket at primary school; and the broken look on his face last night. He'd made her dreams possible, but while she'd been chasing those dreams, she hadn't been able to protect him.

What had she been thinking? He was the only thing that mattered. Her whole world.

Chapter 22

THEN

'I can't believe you're slacking off training today!' Georgie exclaimed, as they climbed into Max's car. 'I thought it was your whole world. I'm still not *quite* convinced you haven't forgotten about us.'

'Guysss, we've been through this. It's my, like, work–life battle.' Abi slid into the back seat, glad that her friends couldn't see her flushed face. 'I missed you both, and I'm so glad things are cool again. For real.'

'Well, whatever happened, we're glad you're back,' Georgie said, beaming back at her as she turned round to look at her from the front passenger seat. 'And we need to make the most of it, because when Max gets his scholarship to Miami, it's going to be the end of an era.'

'*If* I get the scholarship,' Max interrupted, twisting the key in the ignition.

'WHEN,' the girls retorted in unison, then breaking into laughter.

'Although, I must say, donating blood on our "fun day out" is hardly my idea of fun.' Georgie grimaced. 'Even if it *does* help sick people like your dad. Sorry, that was blunt. How is he doing, anyway?'

'He was feeling a bit better this morning, actually. Cheered him right up when I told him that we were coming here first.'

'Oh God, now I feel guilty. Any chance we can just pretend we went?'

Max laughed. 'No such luck. Mum's volunteering there all weekend. But she *did* say there's a whole load of free snacks to choose from afterwards. And *then* we're going out for burgers – on me. I saved up!'

'You and your wacky plans, Max. It's lucky we love you.'

Abi watched her friends bantering in the front of the car and wondered how she could have spent so much time away from them over the last few months. How she could ever have put Cole first or believed anything that he had told her. Apparently, Tash and Cole were 'official' now – an item. Everyone at the club was talking about it. It felt as if he'd twisted a knife into her stomach, but the pain was starting to subside – helped by Max and Georgie being back in her life.

Over the last week, her time spent with Cole had only been during her coaching sessions, and even then he barely spoke to her – only barking criticisms and telling her how he was shocked at how badly she was now playing, when he'd only been away for a short while.

Instead, Barb had been there to meet her as each session ended, taking her straight back to the clubhouse and not letting her out of her sight. But Abi was surprised at how grateful she felt. It was almost a relief not to be spending so much time with him.

'I think we'll have to look after Abi,' Georgie said, laughing. 'She's already looking unwell. You've always been terrible with blood. Do you remember how you nearly fainted that time Max cut his head, falling down the club stairs? He was the one with the injury and it was you we ended up looking after – you went completely green!'

Abi smiled weakly back at her. 'I'll be fine.'

'Don't worry, I'm sure Max will hold your hand, won't you?'

'Er, if you want me to . . .' Max gulped, his eyes firmly on the road ahead of him. Abi noticed a flush of red creeping up the back of his neck.

Abi giggled. 'You don't need to hold my hand, Max. But I'll hold yours if you think you might fall down any stairs . . .'

Ten minutes later, Max pulled in outside a church hall, a gigantic arrow on a sandwich board on the stone path signposting the temporary blood-donor site.

Inside, Abi looked around the room and saw a station with a display of water jugs and packets of crisps and biscuits. She saw a nurse behind a desk, checking people in. And further back in the room, she could see people lying on blue medical beds, many with their feet propped up, each with a recognisable dark red stripe running from the crook of their arm to under the beds. In the distance, Max's mum waved at them all, giving Max thumbs-up with her blue-gloved hand.

Abi could barely wave back, though, because as soon as she had caught sight of the blood, she felt light-headed and reached for Max's arm.

'Are you all right?' he asked, his voice gentle, his head bent down towards hers. 'You don't have to do it, honestly.'

'Hey, if she's not doing it, I'm not doing it,' Georgie said. 'I'm sure I feel absolutely awful. It's come on very suddenly. In fact, I think it might be a fever.'

Abi giggled at the dramatic swoon Georgie was now performing. 'I'll be fine, honestly. I want to.'

And she did feel stronger. Because, despite the sight of blood leaving her reeling, the warmth of Max's hand on the small of her back made Abi feel safer than she had done in a while. Apart from the fact that out of the corner of her eye she could see Georgie looking down at Max's hand, one eyebrow raised. Abi looked away, avoiding eye contact.

The nurse at the desk guided the girls through the registration process, helping them to fill in the requisite forms alongside Max, who joked with her as he handed over his own paperwork.

'Ah, I see you've been here before,' the nurse said, reaching across for his clipboard with a smile. She glanced at the form, then looked up at him again. 'And you're one of our AB-negative superstars . . .'

Max grinned at her, glancing briefly at his friends to see if they had clocked what the nurse had said.

Georgie rolled her eyes. 'Medical marvel, is he? How typical.'

'It's literally the only negative thing about me!' declared Max, his grin even cheesier than ever. Then to Abi, 'I am one of the lucky few with the rarest blood type in the country.'

'I always knew there was something a bit extra about you,' she said with a laugh, starting to relax into the good-natured mood in the room. After all, everyone here had chosen to donate blood rather than doing something else with their Friday night.

As the three of them lay there, on adjacent beds, they were quiet for a moment, listening to the hum of the blood machines at work. Abi had her feet raised on a handful of pillows in case she fainted, and stared up at the ceiling, clenching and unclenching her fist as the nurse had instructed her to do. Cole seemed a million miles away. He would never approve – she couldn't imagine him ever doing something like this. Perhaps if he was paid, or maybe if he was told it was part of an important research project. Either way, this trip spoke to the essential goodness of Max – something Abi was no longer sure she'd ever seen in Cole.

She felt a hand brush against her arm, then take her hand. She quickly turned her head on the pillow, expecting to see the nurse, but instead it was Max.

She felt herself flicker inside. But this time, no second hit of anxiety. Something she was so used to by now.

'I told you I didn't need you to hold my hand!' she mouthed at him, careful not to alert Georgie to what was happening. Although she was pretty sure Georgie wouldn't have noticed – she was interrogating the nurse attending her donation, asking the slightly intimidated woman how quickly she could find out if she had special blood, too.

'I wanted to,' he whispered back firmly.

Once they were done, they sat as instructed and had a pint of cool water and a mini pack of custard creams each, Georgie and Max fighting over the last packet of salt and vinegar crisps like primary-school kids sharing snacks in the playground.

At last, they headed out of the hall, and into the summer mugginess that heralded a storm. Abi could see the pavement was becoming speckled where rain was falling beyond the gable of the church hall.

Georgie dropped behind them, her phone ringing.

'Oh God, it's my mum. Damn, I'm going to have to call her back. With you in a sec.'

Halfway down the path, Abi felt her peripheral vision blur. A loud ringing was in her ears and she swayed on the spot.

'Woah, there. Are you OK?' Max immediately put his arm round her, warmth spreading through her body.

Abi shut her eyes; everything was spinning.

'Oh my God, Abi!' Georgie had chucked her phone in her bag and grabbed Abi's other arm.

'I think I need to sit down for a second,' she murmured.

'Abi, did you have lunch?'

'Yeah, but not that much, I guess.'

'Oh man, this is completely my fault,' Max said. 'I didn't think to check. You should never have donated if you hadn't eaten properly.'

Together, they half carried her to the car, helping her into the back seat.

'I'll go and grab your mum, Max.'

'No, don't!' Abi said, embarrassed, the feeling already beginning to pass. 'I'll be fine in a second; it was a bit of a first-timer's wobble, that's all... I'm fine, honestly.'

'Your grandparents would, like, fully murder me if I brought you home in this state.'

'Oh, for sure, Grandad Bob would have you for dinner,' said Georgie, looming over Max's shoulder. 'Are you really OK, Abi?'

'Yeah, I'll be grand once we've had our burgers...'

'Actually, you guys are going to have to go on without me.' Georgie grimaced. 'Listen to this.'

She replayed the voicemail she'd just been listening to and Barb's voice shrieked out from the speaker.

'As you can hear, apparently I have double-booked myself. I'm going to have to bail, sorry. Any chance you can drop me back first, Max?'

'Of course, hop in and I'll drive you home before we go to Barr's. Do you want me to drive you home, too, Abi?'

'No way, man. I only did this for the burger!'

'Shit, shit, shit. I'm sorry, guys,' said Georgie, bundling herself into the back seat, her head popping up between their shoulders as she carried on chatting while Max pulled away. 'But a lift is great. Look, Abs, I'd say I'll call you later to check you're OK, but you've got Maxie to take care of you. We good?'

'Of course we are,' said Abi, although her stomach was feeling not just empty – but filling with butterflies. It was going to be just her and Max for dinner all of a sudden … almost like a date.

When Max pulled up at the Blackwoods' drive, Georgie hopped out, then ran round to kiss Max goodbye through his window before scuttling round to do the same to Abi. As she hugged her, she muttered in her ear, 'Enjoy the alone time …' Abi didn't know what to say, so she just played innocent. Something Georgie was apparently immune to, given the huge wink she gave her as she looked behind to see her friend waving.

Half an hour later, it was just Max and Abi arriving at Barr's, Max giving Abi a reassuring cuddle as they walked up to the door.

The inside of Barr's diner was warm, fairy lights twinkling around the vintage fifties-style bar. The red leather of the banquettes was glowing in the soft light, and the whole room smelled of fried food. As soon as they walked in, a smiley-eyed waiter showed them to a booth towards the quieter far end of the room. As they slid into their seats across the chrome-edged, fixed tabletop, their knees bashed against each other. It was something that had happened a thousand times on busy, crowded trains up and down the country, but today it felt different. No Georgie. Soft lighting. So date-y.

'Sorry, sorry!' mumbled Abi awkwardly.

'Don't worry about it.' Max reached under the table and patted her knee. She wasn't quite sure if he was teasing her or just seizing a chance to touch her. He was definitely holding something back, and so was she, but was that what they actually wanted?

She didn't have time to think about it too much as the conversation and the food kept her distracted better than she had been by anything for weeks. It was the best burger Abi had ever had. The meat was juicy and the fries crispy, and Max even remembered how much she hated gherkins and whipped hers off the side of her plate before it had had the chance to hit the table.

'Thank you,' she said, mock-courteous, as she watched him eat it. 'You have saved me from my greatest enemy.'

'Anything for you, sweet princess,' he replied. 'Especially if it means me getting more of the tastiest thing on earth.'

'I refuse to believe that you actually think that!'

'That I'd do anything for you?'

'No... well, I... No, I mean that anyone actually likes bloody gherkins!'

'Can't both be true?' he said, looking at her, his gaze steady.

In the cosiness of that diner, as Abi felt the food – and the flirting – warm her up, she let herself imagine that this could become a regular thing. That she could become the sort of young woman who didn't sneak around in lay-bys and on leather sofas, taking whatever scraps of her boyfriend's time he could throw her way. That she might just be able to go out for a burger and fries with sweet, hot boys like Max, who remembered what food she liked and actually encouraged her to eat it. Yes, for an hour or two, it seemed possible that this sort of simple happiness could be hers, if only she reached for it. Then she remembered that Max was probably going to leave the country by the end of the month, and Cole was still barely speaking to her.

As they walked back to Max's car, he put an arm around her shoulder, in a manner that lay flatly between matey and intimate. The butterflies were going crazy inside her.

'D'you wanna come back and watch a movie? It's such a grey evening, and I can't really have a drink if I'm driving. But we could have a cheeky beer and watch something at mine?'

'Yeah, go on,' she said, trying to match her tone to his. She didn't want to read into it too much ... but nor did she want to miss anything. 'It's early.'

'And I might be gone soon. Wanna be able to hang out while we still can.'

The thought of Max leaving the country suddenly made Abi feel absolutely bereft. Could she put these heightened feelings down to blood donation? she wondered.

'My folks will be there, but they love you anyway,' he said. 'We probably won't even have time to watch anything once my mum's finished grilling you for all the Bracken Lane gossip.'

'As if I have any ...' said Abi, her guts tightening at the thought of Cole being a subject of gossip at the Chamberlains' house.

It turned out Max wasn't too far wrong, as Mrs Chamberlain was thrilled to see them both, offering each of them heartfelt congratulations and profuse thanks for coming to her blood-donor drive. By way of saying thank you, she made them each a hot chocolate with mini marshmallows, despite Max's protestations that, 'We're not, like, ten any more, Mum.'

Mrs Chamberlain busied herself in the kitchen warming milk in a little pan on the hob while Abi sat at the table and told her how training was going, what the plans for the forthcoming year were and filled her in on how her grandparents were doing. Again, she felt herself dreaming that this was the kind of normal, safe life she might one day be able to lead. A lad's nice mum treating her with a bit of respect, her being welcome in someone else's home, being thought of kindly by the family. Then, like a stain that she just couldn't quite scrub away, thoughts of Cole and how he might be spending his evening crept back up on her. It took a good half-hour of watching *Moulin Rouge* curled up on the Chamberlains' cosy sofa for those thoughts to recede again.

As Max swung round and plonked his legs on her lap, playfully telling her he needed the rest because of his blood donation, Abi felt calm in a way she hadn't in months.

It was just after eleven when Mrs Chamberlain reappeared in her dressing gown and said that Abi was welcome to stay the night.

'It's still bucketing with rain out there, and you must both be exhausted. The spare room's all made up; you know where everything is. And you can use the phone in the hall to call your grandmother if you want to.'

'Thank you, Mrs Chamberlain,' said Abi, glancing at Max to make sure it would be OK with him too. He smiled a conspiratorial smile at her, then looked up at his mum as if butter wouldn't melt. What was he trying to tell her with that dimpled grin? Either way, his mum seemed not to have noticed and carried on regardless.

'Max can lend you a T-shirt to sleep in, I'm sure, and I've got a spare toothbrush out of the drawer for you. There's that dressing gown on the back of the door if you need it!' And off she went.

As the film reached its last twenty minutes or so, Abi started to feel almost as if she were at sea. Familiar feelings of longing, desire, even, but in an entirely unfamiliar context. She never wanted to move from the cosy position she had ended up in on the sofa, her head on Max's lap as he softly stroked her hair. They had been like that for over an hour, dancing along the line of him 'taking care of her' after her funny turn and something much, much more. Did she want more? Suddenly she thought she did – but what if she overstepped the mark, misunderstood? Her instincts, blunted by Cole's unpredictable treatment of her, felt unreliable. Could she risk losing a friend all over again?

As the credits rolled, she was primed for a romantic move, but none came. Instead, Max was being silly – lost his nerve? – whispering like a kid trying to hide a midnight feast from his parents. He turned all the downstairs lights off as they headed up, leaving them shuffling around the small upstairs landing, finding door handles in the dark.

'Watch out for the creaky floor there!' he whispered, trying to stifle giggles. He put his hand out to steady Abi, only to brush against her boob. 'Shit! Sorry!'

'Max, it's fine,' she whispered back, starting to feel crestfallen that perhaps she had misunderstood, that there was no move coming after all.

They brushed their teeth together, nearly knocking heads as they leant into the basin at the same time. Then, a moment later, under the full glare of the bathroom light, the tension burst. Max reached to wipe his mouth on his towel and, as he did, stood barely an inch from Abi's face. At last, they surrendered to the feelings that each of them had for so long been too shy to acknowledge. Slowly, then urgently, they kissed, toothbrushes still in their hands, hearts inches away from each other, fresh blood coursing through their bodies. Abi, suddenly shy, rested her head on Max's shoulder for a second.

'I've wanted this for so long,' he whispered into her ear.

'I wish you had told me sooner,' she replied. Oh, how she wished.

'I thought you knew.'

Part of her wanted to cry. But a larger part knew that what she had now was too precious to let go of. She took his hand and said simply, 'Let's go to bed.'

When Max came into the spare room with an old, soft, T-shirt for her, he was wearing only his boxer shorts. Abi took her jeans off and stood quietly facing him, not sure if to trust what their actions might actually mean. Wordlessly, Max reached forwards and took off her sweatshirt, lifting it gently over her head. The two of them stood chest to chest for a minute, the white plasters from the blood bank on their arms.

Max put his hand under Abi's chin and lifted her face to his. 'I think I should sleep in here, in case you have another one of your funny turns,' he whispered. 'Unless you don't want me to?'

'No, I would love that.' And, for the first time in so long, she was telling the whole truth.

The two of them spent the night entwined, waking up every couple of hours to kiss, to stroke each other's hair and to reaffirm to each other how much they really did mean this. In the moments of quiet between them, Abi lay stunned, almost unable to process how different every part of this felt in comparison to the time she had spent with Cole. For longer than she'd dared to admit, her body had been tense, closed to emotion when she sensed him coming near. She had come to dread the moment the 'massage' turned to something more. With Max, however, every single touch seemed intimate, intense, a deepening of a connection that had always been there, waiting. Yes, there was sex, but this was so much more than that – less a clashing of body parts, more an entwining of two hearts.

And yet, as the sun crept in around the edges of the curtains, the intensity of the pleasure Abi had finally experienced was replaced by a shame of equal intensity. Was this what she should have been doing all along? Had she been so stupid as to believe that what she had had before was special, worth something? The realisation that she had been strung along, taken advantage of, was profound, but so was the mortification that she had let it happen.

She sat up, trying to hide her naked body with the duvet, and dressed as fast as she could. She had to get home. She had to work out how she was going to find a way through this mess. But just as she was reaching for her shoes, Max woke up, stretched out a languid arm towards her, and pulled her in for another kiss.

'Hey, you,' he said softly. 'Do you have to go so early? I feel like I've only just got you here.'

Like an oyster now opened, she knew in an instant that she couldn't say no to him. That she couldn't lose a second of the time she had left with him. That she could stay another hour or two.

Nuzzling into his chest, she groaned and muttered, 'I guess I can stay a bit longer…'

As he pulled the duvet up and over them again, they giggled, trying to hush each other as the rain continued to batter down outside.

*

If Mrs Chamberlain had noticed that Max's bed had not been slept in, she never said anything. Conversation over breakfast was breezy, the family passing Marmite and cereal to each other as if Abi had been one of them all along. The only time she felt the familiar lurch of anxiety in her guts was when Mr Chamberlain asked Max when he was expecting to hear back from the coach in Florida who was handling his scholarship. Max simply said he wasn't sure, and avoided Abi's gaze.

But as tiredness and the reality of the muddle ahead of her set in, Abi fell silent in the car as Max drove her home, avoiding eye contact, all traces of the night's closeness draining away. It wasn't him, or what had happened between then, but the thoughts of Cole, the encroaching fear of defying him and risking her entire career, now coursing through Abi's veins, as well as fresh terror that Max might find out what had gone on between them. By the time she arrived home, she was almost breathless with panic, a whole spectrum of new and intense feelings now swirling, whirling within.

When Max texted her later that evening, thanking her for such a special night, she stared at her phone for what felt like an hour, paralysed by dread at typing a reply that could lose her something she had never realised meant so much to her. In the end, she sent an emoji, and regretted it within seconds. That Max didn't reply straight away spoke volumes about how much more of a reply he'd hoped for. Abi curled up beneath her duvet, wishing she didn't have to see Cole the following morning, but knowing that if she were to keep Max, she *had* to do something.

Because it was now Max who she wanted to keep, but saying that to him, to anyone, even to herself, meant risking Cole's anger *and* his influence over her tennis career. In fact, it might mean risking her tennis career altogether. Who else could guide her to the top? The stakes felt impossibly high. Doing nothing was no longer an option. Silently, she realised that only the truth could set her free now.

Later that evening, as she came off court at the club, Abi texted Max. She did it quickly, before she'd even returned her racket to its bag, almost as if having Georgie around while she typed into her phone would give her the courage she needed. Because she was determined to tell the truth at last. But it had to start with Max now, especially after the state she'd been in when they'd said goodbye.

> Hey. Wanna chat later?

The reply was terse.

> Not around. Been invited on that Swiss training camp thing. X

It was impossible to tell what was hurt and what was rage. Either way, Abi realised that by prevaricating for so long, she had let him start to slip through her fingers. And when the follow-up text arrived, she wondered if he had already slipped altogether.

> Got Florida scholarship btw

Abi stood blinking at her screen. Had she blown it completely? At least, she told herself, she still had Georgie.

'Oh God,' she whispered, almost under her breath.

'What?' asked Georgie, pulling open a protein bar with her teeth as she spoke.

'It's Max – he's got that Florida funding.'

'You're kidding me! Now that is effing brilliant.' Georgie punched the air, before returning her gaze to Abi, who still looked stunned. 'What? Hang on, *what*? He didn't want it?'

'No, it's not that...'

'Wait – *you* didn't want it? For him?'

'No, I did. Of course I did! It's just...'

'Oh my God. Has something happened?' Georgie grabbed Abi by the shoulders. 'It has, hasn't it? What, what, what, what?'

'It's complicated...'

'Well, yeah, I guess it is if he's going away. But you like him? You really like him? Bloody hell, mate, it's only taken you a year to admit it.'

'To myself as much as anything else.'

'I hear you. Listen, come round to mine for dinner and we can talk game plans. Oh my days, FINALLY! I am so excited for you guys. Not in a creepy way, though... I mean... Well, you know what I mean.' And Abi did.

But when they got to the Blackwoods', the mood was frosty. Georgie opened the door wide-eyed, nodding her head towards the dining room, where Barb was at the huge dark-wood table on the cordless phone. Her conversation sounded intense. Georgie headed in for a minute, before joining Abi in the cosy TV room on the other side of the kitchen.

'It's Cole,' mouthed Georgie. 'He's gone.'

'What do you mean?' whispered Abi in response, her guts immediately churning.

'Apparently he tried to snog one of the junior team and they told their mum, who told mine. Shit has seriously hit the fan.'

The blood was draining from Abi's face. It felt as if it were draining from her entire body. How could this be happening? Did anyone know about them? If not, would they find out? Could they? Where was Cole going? And what did this mean for the unburdening she had spent the last twenty-four hours psyching herself up for?

'Woah,' she mouthed, otherwise speechless. 'What about Tash? I thought they were a thing?'

'So did she, apparently. Mum was speaking to her earlier. She's devastated. But he's got to go or the club is in all kinds of trouble.'

And Barb stayed true to her word. Cole was never seen at the club again. His replacement was Rosie Forbes, a mum of two small young boys with no interest in impressing the club's social scene and a Scottish accent not dissimilar to Abi's grandparents'. Barb took less than twenty-four hours to work out that the girls had heard what was going on, and asked them for their utmost discretion, explaining that she just wanted the best for both the girls concerned and the club itself.

Girls? thought Abi. There had been more than one? And her? What she thought had been her reality for several months was now rendered porous, fresh versions of the truth sliding in where she had thought she'd known so much. She had known barely anything, she now saw. And what a fool, what a heartbroken fool she felt.

Abi was left breathless at the speed with which things

changed. Feelings she had barely had the chance to acknowledge were swept under the carpet as she realised that she had nothing to gain by telling the truth about Cole now. All she would achieve was a grubby reputation for herself. If he was gone, he was gone. At least she didn't have to speak the things he had done out loud, she told herself.

But it was more than that. Because she had never had the chance to tell Georgie – or Max – what had happened on her own terms, and now it seemed like a can of worms no longer worth opening. A week or two later, Max left for Florida and shortly after that Georgie left for London to start her own career. At which point, the secret started to calcify. Becoming harder, tougher to talk about with every month that passed, until it felt impenetrable.

Once Max was on the other side of the world, Abi found it impossible to speak openly to him about the last few weeks and what she had been through. She tried. She wrote countless emails, staying up late, but the words never came. Nothing sounded right, or even close to convincing. Abi found it hard to believe her own story, so why should she expect Max to?

She told herself she would tell him face to face when he came home for his mum's birthday in the autumn. She had to at least honour that one magical night. To give it one last shot. But by the time Max landed at Heathrow, Abi had had the news that would change the rest of her life.

Chapter 23

NOW

Georgie's phone buzzed in the handbag between them. She grabbed it, saw it was Max and immediately held up the handset on speakerphone.

'Hi, we're in the car.'

'OK, I'm at the hospital. Spoken to the ward and waiting to go to Robbie's bed. He cut a big artery on his leg, nasty injury, but the surgery seems to have been a success.'

Abi's stomach lurched.

'How did he do that? Where was he?' Georgie asked.

'There seems to have been some sort of altercation.'

'What the ...? A fight?'

'Well, they're not sure till he comes round. But someone at the scene said to the ambulance crew that he was trying to run away from someone, then tripped and fell. On broken glass.'

'Jeez. Do you think it was the press?' Georgie exhaled in shock.

'Is he going to be OK?' Abi interrupted.

'I don't know. They can't tell me too much because I'm not next of kin, I'm just the guy who came up first on his phone. They could see I was legit – if not a relative.'

Abi lifted a bottle of chilled water from the side of the car door and took a slow sip. Her heart swelled as she realised Max had been checking in on Robbie.

'Abi?' Max's voice was gentle.

'Yes.' Abi's was barely more than a croak. She felt as if pieces of her body might start breaking off. Very far from the global tennis sensation that the media pack only a mile away was raving about.

'Don't panic. I'm here, he'll see a friendly face when he wakes up. And you'll be here soon. We've got this.'

'Thank you,' she whispered.

'Max,' said Georgie, leaning into the handset. 'Do we know if the press know anything about this?'

'I honestly haven't had a chance to check, but it sounds like there were a few people on Wimbledon Common who saw what happened.'

'So there might be stuff on socials already?'

Abi instinctively reached for her phone to start searching, before remembering that Max had taken all social media and news apps off her phone. To think he'd been worried about her being distracted by headlines!

'There might be,' he said. 'National press is not impossible. But it's not a situation we can do anything about right now. Let's just wait until Robbie wakes up and can give us a smile, OK?'

'Quite right,' said Georgie, reaching out to stroke Abi's arm. 'We're nearly here – see you shortly.'

Abi felt the whoosh of air from the double doors to the ward swinging behind her. Until that moment, she had always thought that those performative entrances were something reserved for soaps, the sort of overdramatic scene that usually had her rolling her eyes. But when she and Georgie had burst out of the lift and stomped towards the ward, each of them reaching their hands out to push one half of the doors open, she had realised that, yes, it really happened.

The doors still swinging behind them, they found a nurse at the ward desk and walked behind her, the stiffness of her scrubs rustling as they paced the length of the ward in silence. Then, finally, they reached Robbie's bed, the nurse pulling back a curtain to reveal him lying there, white as a sheet, his thigh heavily bandaged. And on the chair next to him was Max.

Max stood up as the three women entered, gesturing at the chair for Abi. But she barely acknowledged him, rushing towards Robbie, her arms outstretched. He reached his arms towards her, his face crumpled, his hair a mess, the little boy in whom she had invested her heart and soul for so long.

'Mum …'

'Oh, Robbie … what's happened?'

'I'm so sorry, Mum.'

'Why on earth are you apologising – are you OK? Have they looked after you?'

Abi ruffled his hair, then smoothed down his bed sheets, tidying the little tray over his bed as the others arranged themselves as best they could in the limited space available. Georgie filled up Robbie's water from the plastic tub by his bedside, while Max drew the curtain around them.

'Yes, but, Mum, I'm just so sorry.'

Robbie started to sob.

'You've nothing to be sorry for, my darling, it was an accident. Sounds like you had a nasty fall.' Abi stroked the side of his face, startled by how cool he felt despite the airlessness of the ward. She pushed his hair back from his eyes and wiped beneath them.

'I do, though, Mum, I do.'

'Come on, Robbie,' said Max, leaning in. 'You've had a serious injury and what sounds like some big surgery – you don't need to apologise for that.'

'He's right,' chipped in Georgie.

'Shit, shit, shit. Please hear me out. I'm so sorry.' Robbie was serious. 'It was the press. I just lost it with the press.'

'What do you mean? We were told you fell on the common?' Abi's face was almost as ashen as Robbie's.

'I did. But, well, it was kind of a bit of a rumble.' Tears were streaming down his face now.

'What are you talking about, Robbie?' Max asked. They were all listening closely now, the hubbub of the ward beyond the curtain fading away.

'I thought we'd found somewhere quiet, but there were people who recognised me.'

Abi remembered seeing that tweet last night, asking for information about Robbie's dad.

'That kind of thing happens when you get this level of exposure, sweetie, there's no need for you to worry about it,' Georgie tried to reassure him.

'Yeah, but I was so angry. So tired of not knowing about my own life.'

Abi started to hear a ringing in her ears as she realised what Robbie was about to say. There was nothing she could do now but listen. Talking to her son had taken a back seat for too long.

'The thought of some random online knowing more about my own father than me – it was too much. I snapped.'

'OK.' Abi's voice was soft now. Hadn't she longed for a

trusted adult to talk to at the same age? Hadn't having no one to confide in been the cause of so much of her pain back then? How could she have let the same thing happen to her own son?

'So I just kind of lost it when the second or third person was being weird.'

'What kind of weird?' asked Georgie, clearly primed, in professional mode.

'I could see people looking…'

'Where were you?'

'Just in the village. Should have gone further.'

Abi and Georgie exchanged glances. Of course, a high proportion of people in Wimbledon Village would have an idea who he was – it had been the biggest breaking story of yesterday. A mile or two further and he might have been fine.

'Did something happen?'

'Some guy came over, wanting to know if I was hiding something, you know, about my dad.'

'And what did you do?'

'I was trying to keep my cool, but Al was trying to protect me, made it worse, and it all got well out of hand.'

'So what did you say, darling? You can tell me; I won't be angry.' And Abi meant it. This time, she really, really meant it.

'I swear I didn't say anything! What could I say?'

'OK, OK. Robbie, we don't have to do this now.' Max was trying to bring the temperature down.

Beads of sweat started to form along Abi's hairline as she realised the pain her son must have been in. Exposed to these questions. Shut out from his own history.

He put his hand up to his face, rubbing his eyes like a toddler who had just woken up. Abi was sitting in the chair next to his bed now, holding one of his hands, stroking the back of it as if he were a baby she was trying to get to sleep.

'Robbie, darling, what are you trying to tell me?'

'It got loud, we left, and then they followed us, towards the common. Felix was still inside the coffee shop, I think, but Al was so angry for me, for us. He got hit, so I hit back, then I realised there were photographers around, so I just ran. I just wanted to get out of there, away from everything, the questions, the noise, all of it. And that's when I fell. I tried to climb those railings at the Common to take the short cut round the back from the village and fell, gouged my leg.'

Abi nodded, horrified that things had escalated this way. Leaving Robbie with such a lack of agency over his own identity had left him so exposed. It couldn't go on. A grim inevitability about what was coming next washed over her.

Chapter 24

THEN

Abi would never have taken the pregnancy test if not for the fall. It was a couple of months after Cole had vanished from Bracken Lane without ever having said goodbye, and Max and Georgie had gone too. There had been so much change in such a short space of time, but Abi had coped by using it as a chance to focus even harder on her training. She had suffered grief before: the experience of being surrounded by those you love one minute and then finding them gone the next was not new to her. Yes, she had cried when Georgie had left for a flat-share in London. And yes, she missed Max like a constant dull ache.

In the immediate aftermath of Cole's discreet dismissal from Bracken Lane, she had tried to call him once or twice, to try to find out if the rumours Barb had heard really were true – but she only ever reached a voicemail service. A few weeks later, there hadn't even been a dial tone. Instead, a pre-recorded message simply told her that 'this number is no longer in service'. He'd either changed his number to shake her off or gone abroad to get himself as far as possible from her, and whichever it was, it was surely her fault, she told herself.

But without his overwhelming presence, her career started to fly higher than ever before – the weeks whizzing by in a blur of tournament wins and visits to see Georgie in London, where she had already found a job in a sports PR company.

She wasn't, however, managing to maintain the same sense of closeness to Max. Any messages she got from him seemed to have lost their energy by the time she replied, the time difference making everything seem impossibly hard to truly read. Her news – the little she ever had of it concerning her match results – seemed irrelevant or braggy by the time she had written it out and pressed send, and in the end the gaps between messages slipped from days to weeks, buckling under the weight of what was going unsaid. She didn't blame him for not wanting to contact her, assuming his new and exciting college lifestyle was the reason for his less-than-verbose replies. It had never occurred to her that after a full day's training in the Florida sun, he might just have been too tired to spend the evening at a keyboard.

She started to accept the loneliness in the same way that she had nearly five years ago in the months that had followed the death of her parents. Back then, her life had been in such upheaval that this more recent, but no less constant, low-level sadness felt more bearable in comparison. And this time, she had tennis – her saviour.

Rosie Forbes, the new coach at Bracken Lane, was almost the complete opposite to Cole. She was kind, gave lots of praise, and above all, she really listened. To her surprise, Abi's game only continued to improve once Cole had left the club. Perhaps, she let herself think, he hadn't been the key to her game after all. Under the more gentle but no less attentive guidance of Rosie, Abi started to develop an emotional resilience during challenging matches that she had never had before. She started to think for herself, to find solutions to her challenges and problems. And she had also started to adjust her schedule, to take proper rest days, and to pay attention to her diet at long last.

It was because she had made these tweaks that she didn't notice the tiny amount of weight that she had gained recently. Her periods had been erratic for a while, but she had been telling herself that perhaps it was just the ridiculously demanding schedule Cole had had her on – or stress, even.

So when Abi woke up the morning of the Hampshire County finals feeling a little nauseous, she assumed that it was just the usual mix of pre-match nerves and anticipation. She had no idea that this particular match was to change the course of her young life. When she lunged for a nasty low ball that was spinning away from her, her foot slipped on an uneven patch of grass, leaving her in an undignified heap on the court, as well as writhing in pain. She had sprained her ankle before, and was sure that she just needed ice and a few minutes of elevation. She desperately wanted to finish the match and tried to play on, only to feel her ankle swelling uncontrollably beneath her.

After a second set break, during which she had asked for some ice to put on the injury, she tried to stand up confidently, to show her opponent that the pain had now passed. Instead, she crumpled to the grass, unable to comfortably bear her weight on the right foot. Reluctantly, she raised her hand from where she was.

'Umpire, I don't think I can carry on,' she said, trying to sound as professional as she could while her heart was breaking for the third time that year. The tournament physio was called to the court again – this time with a pair of crutches – and confirmed that she really did need a trip to A&E.

It was Barb who took her to Southampton Hospital, leaving Mrs Forbes with the rest of the squad. But it was Grannie Annie, having followed them in her smaller car, who was sitting next to Abi when the nurse had appeared outside of the X-ray room, breezily asking, 'Before we head in, can I just check there's no chance you might be pregnant?'

The thought had never occurred to Abi. She had been so busy boxing her feelings up, packing in layer upon layer of sadness and regret, trying to hide everything in a place where nothing and nobody could find it. So when the nurse looked up for an answer to see Abi sitting there, blinking, she turned to her grandmother.

'Abigail?'

Abi's voice was gone, but her mind was whirring. Suddenly, things were slipping into place. Those missed periods, the nausea, the tiredness, the sense that her body was somehow different. And it was now more than two months since she had slept with Cole. Wasn't it? Abi had spent so long trying to forget things that dates had started to become hazy, recent events seeming so much more distant than things which had taken place a while back. They had always been so careful, hadn't they?

Well, at least Cole had been. Their sexual encounters had always been so entirely on his terms that Abi had never dared to take that side of things under her control. She felt so bound by secrecy that she had spoken to no one about what had been going on, had no one's advice to seek. If it had been anyone else, she might have plucked up the courage to speak to Barb, but that would clearly have caused more trouble than it was worth. She had been terrified to look things up on the shared computer at home, merely clinging to half-forgotten lectures from well-meaning teachers and dusty leaflets she had seen in a GP's waiting room and putting her trust in Cole. That final couple of times, though, hadn't Cole been less careful than usual? By then, the whole set-up had been feeling more urgent and less romantic than ever, but Abi had simply been too defeated by the whole thing to object. Her recollection of those last few encounters was already fraying at the edges, as if she'd been willing her memory to let go of as much as possible.

The thought of answering the nurse's question seemed like it might crack the sky in two.

'Abigail? Is there a chance?'

Still, she couldn't speak.

Her grandmother, who seemed to be seeing the pieces of a jigsaw puzzle suddenly moving closer together, slotting neatly into place, took Abi's hand in hers, resting it on her lap.

'Do you know what,' Grannie Annie said directly to the nurse. 'I think perhaps we might have to get to the bottom of this ourselves. I don't suppose you have any tests here, do you?'

The nurse, barely older than Abi herself, flushed at the prospect of crashing into the middle of such a drama, said she'd be back shortly and vanished for ten minutes.

'Abi, dear, no one is going to be cross. But they need to X-ray your foot, and they can't do that if there is any chance at all that you might be pregnant.' Annie gently stroked Abi's forearm. The glossy coral of her nails – done recently for her grandfather's birthday dinner – gleamed under the hospital strip-lighting. In the distance, she heard the squeal of trolley wheels in a corridor. 'Do you think there's a chance you could be?'

'Oh, Grannie,' whispered Abi. 'I think there might be.'

The nurse returned with a pregnancy test. Grannie Annie wheeled Abi to the disabled toilet, her leg still up, telling her she would be waiting outside, and that she would be there for her whatever the outcome.

She didn't have to wait long. The two blue lines on the test revealed themselves within seconds, and Abi, perched precariously on the loo with her injured foot out in front of her, immediately dropped it on the floor. Her grandmother, who had clearly heard the clatter of plastic on linoleum, knocked on the door.

'Abigail, do you need me to come in, darling?'

'No, thank you,' she managed to say, before tossing the test into the bin. 'It's positive,' she said, before bursting into tears. 'And now they won't be able to X-ray me, my foot will never heal and my tennis career is over before it's even really started.' Sobs racked her body now, betraying the fact that it wasn't just a foot injury she was trying to process. She had seen enough women vanish from the circuit when they had their first baby to know which was the tougher challenge to overcome – and it wasn't the foot.

'Darling girl, we can sort this out. It's not the end of the world. Nothing ever is.'

Then came the nurse's voice through the closed door. 'Don't worry, Abigail, we can work around this situation. There are other ways to find out what's wrong with this leg too. You hold tight and we'll find you a room, somewhere nice and quiet.'

The sobs wouldn't stop now. Not just about the baby, or the foot, but all of it. The secrets, the lies, the absolute exhaustion of the best part of the last year.

Eventually, Abi let Grannie Annie in.

'We've overcome more than this, haven't we?' she said. 'It's just another bump in the road for my brave girl.'

But Abi didn't feel like being brave any more.

A room was found for her, and someone from Gynaecology was with her within the hour. But when it came to giving helpful answers about dates, her memory felt blurry and she turned crimson with shame at having to peel back layer after layer of the lies she had told her family. When she was asked about boyfriends, she simply sobbed into her grandmother's shoulder, apologising for the mess.

'Don't fret,' her grandmother reassured her, stroking her back. 'You don't have to talk about all of it now. We just need to get that leg fixed up, and we can take the rest of it from there. Take a deep breath. Things always look brighter in the morning.'

Working with such hazy information and with the pressing need to deal with her foot, the doctor said that he thought she could be as much as ten weeks pregnant. There were a lot of gaps that the scan could not fill, but as Abi saw the heartbeat on the black-and-white screen, pounding away like a tiny but mighty drum, there was one thing it told her for sure: she was keeping this baby. She knew what it was to grow up without parents, and in that moment she knew with equal ferocity that this child would not grow up without her. She'd already known so much grief, she couldn't face those demons again. From now on, it would be her and this baby against the world, come what may.

An hour later, Abi left the hospital in a wheelchair, her foot in a plastic boot, with a possible but undiagnosable fracture and a baby on the way.

Chapter 25

NOW

As Abi held Robbie's hand, next to him in his hospital bed, she thought back to that afternoon nineteen years ago when Grannie Annie had sat in just the same position she was now. The protector. That was the same day she had seen that first scan. The first time she had had that overwhelming sense of 'me and him against the world' that she had always had with Robbie, her baby. It was no less strong today. But today was the first time she could see clearly the size of her mistake.

It had been years since the questions had started to ease up a bit, since the sense of the two of them as lone, fatherless warriors had started to dissipate as they witnessed fathers of his friends either disappear, or let them or their mothers down. Over time, Abi felt both of them come to realise that who your father was, or might be, needn't be the most important thing about a boy. Later still, Robbie found friendships with peers who had never had fathers, either because of fecklessness on the man's part or design on the mother's.

In time, the questions stopped, and Abi hoped that her son had come to see that his mum had always done her best, that he had wanted for very little during a childhood filled with fun and joy.

Only now that he lay in a hospital bed, a victim of the very secrets she had fought so hard to keep, she could see that he had never stopped wondering, never stopped wanting to know. She had never dodged that question at all. She had simply kicked it into the long grass, time and again, while he'd learned to stop asking for fear of hurting her. She had tried so hard, for so long, to keep a lid on it all, and now the whole thing had exploded in her face.

Abi took a deep breath, ready to start her explanation, when Max and Georgie, who had left to grab a drink, reappeared with a nurse at his side. She was a short, stocky woman, who looked like she had seen patients in every shade of distress in a decades-long career.

'Hello there, young man,' she said with a smile, lifting the clipboard from the wall beside his bed before peering over it at Robbie, who was still juddering with the aftershock of his tears. 'It's good to see you awake again. All this anaesthetic, and the pain meds we had to give you, they can leave you feeling very emotional. It's a big thing you've been through, a lot of drugs for a body to process, even a young man like yourself. My sister broke her leg last summer and the morphine had her saying all kinds of crazy things.'

Robbie gave a sheepish giggle, visibly relieved to have been absolved for his outburst of emotion.

'Is he going to be OK, nurse?' asked Abi, wiping at her own face with the back of her hand. Her other fist was clenched, even her short-clipped nails digging into the palm of her hand, willing her to keep her nerve, that her chance to speak the truth would only have to wait a minute.

There was a brief flicker in the nurse's eyes. Not enough to reveal that she had clocked who Abi was, but enough to suggest that she thought she recognised her and was trying to place her. The energy in the group paused, just for a millisecond, as each of them in the cubicle realised, and made the decision to move on.

'We have no reason to believe that this injury will not heal beautifully. It was a deep cut, and we are glad we got him back here for surgery in time, but what he needs now is to rest. We want to keep him here for a day or two, so we can make sure he has recovered from that anaesthetic, and that we've got him on the right pain-meds regime, but he should be free of us before too long.'

'Thank you so much, that's wonderful news,' said Abi, fist still clenched.

'It'll be good to get you home in time to watch your mum in the final,' said Max with a wink, as he reached out to stroke Abi's back. 'Now, look, Georgie and I are going to head downstairs and get a car ready, then we'll see you when you're ready, Abi. And thank you, nurse.'

The nurse smiled at Max, clearly charmed by him, and Abi waved at her friends, who had once again been there for her in her hour of need. Even Robbie was now smiling. The group was awash with relief after the intensity of the conversation that had preceded the nurse's arrival.

'I think that sounds like a great plan, especially as visiting hours are now over so your mum's going to have to head off too,' said the nurse, reaching to replace the clipboard and forms where she had found them. As she did so, she tapped the top sheet and said with a wink, 'And I see you're one of our special patients. Not often we have an AB negative on the ward!'

Abi felt as if she had fallen through a trapdoor.

Chapter 26

THEN

Later that evening, Abi came home from the hospital with Grannie Annie, who helped her to break the news to her grandfather. The two of them perched on the edge of the faded Laura Ashley sofa, taking it in turns to explain.

'The foot will mend and it won't affect her tennis but the thing is, we've even bigger news than that. Abi, would you like to be the one to tell your grandad the exciting news?'

Abi could have cried with relief at the gentle way her gran helped her to frame every single part of it as positive.

'Now, we've been told there's no reason she won't be able to carry on playing afterwards.'

'Quite a few of the professionals do it now, I hear. It's becoming quite a thing on the tour.'

'Isn't it wonderful, new life in this house after so much grief?'

'And I've explained we're going to help her with every single thing she needs.'

Her grandfather was lost for words. He looked dazed and exhausted, but managed to nod in agreement.

Over the next few weeks, Grannie Annie would surprise

Abi by dealing with the news better than she might ever have given her credit for. Even in the hospital, she had broken into a smile broader than Abi had seen for years. Now, as Abi sat and watched her grandmother take her husband's hand in her own, gently explaining her plans for ceaseless support of Abi, it was as if sunshine had filled the living room. After all they'd been through, the possibility of new life in the home seemed to be filling her with hope, rather than causing her to admonish Abi or overwhelm her with questions. It was only one final comment that gave away the fact that Grannie might suspect she could have done more to prevent the situation.

'And no more damn secrets from now on!'

This unexpected response, coupled with the confusion about how many weeks pregnant Abi already was, meant that any conversation about ending the pregnancy was not given much consideration at all.

Barb, who had left the hospital fully expecting no more than a severe ankle sprain, came round a couple of hours later and was told the news.

'Yes, there's no doubt it's a surprise,' Abi heard Grannie Annie saying, her voice faint as if in the distance. 'But we are thrilled for her. And we'll be here with whatever she needs.'

'Well, that's wonderful news,' said Barb, her lacquered lips breaking into a forced smile. There was a wariness there, and Abi didn't miss it. Barb never so much as whispered Cole's name, but there was something about the way she pulled Abi to her before she left, giving her an uncharacteristically tight hug and whispering, 'Let me know if you ever need anything. Or if you need me to get hold of anyone. *Anyone*,' that told Abi all she needed to know.

If her grandmother had worked out what had been going

on, she wasn't the sort to mention it, and Abi made it clear that she did not want the father of the baby involved, strongly implying that he was an overseas player, someone who would not be able to be around anyway. Clearly, it seemed so unlikely to all concerned that there might be a fleet of likely suitors to contact, that the discussion was tacitly deemed unnecessary.

Abi, who had been so lonely for so long, and aware that her existing injury had put her out of sporting action for a few months anyway, accepted that having a baby might fill the hole she still felt after a life of so much loss in such a short amount of time. Someone to love her back unconditionally. Someone to cuddle in the dark of night when the solitude usually felt the most acute. Someone to occupy the hours she had once spent lying on her front on the bed, texting Georgie about anything and everything.

For once, Abi let herself eat what she wanted, when she wanted. She truly let herself rest. And by the time her injury started to feel better, Abi was in late pregnancy and able to do some basic conditioning exercises, determined to resume training as soon as she could. The birth was a quick and simple one, and she was released from hospital later the same day. It was barely a year since her first kiss with Cole and now she was back home, a mother. She was terrified and at peace in equal measure, besotted by the peach-soft velvet of her baby's cheek and dazzled by the fact that it was up to her to keep him alive.

She looked up from the same floral sofa where Grannie Annie had explained things to her grandad and smiled.

'I've decided what to call him.'

'Have you, darling?' said Grannie Annie, with customary gentleness.

'And will you be sharing it with us?' asked her grandad with a raised eyebrow. 'Or are we just to call him "the baby" til he's a great strapping lad?'

'Oh, you are daft,' said her gran, elbowing him in the ribs as they both chuckled at his attempt at humour.

'Of course I will, you doughballs. He's Robbie, just like my dad.'

Both her grandparents' eyes immediately became filled with tears, the joy in the room undeniably suffused with the memory of grief. But Abi knew, as she saw their faces gazing down at little Robbie, that no matter how hard things got, she had done exactly the right thing. For all of them.

Within a week of Abi and baby Robbie returning home, Georgie came down from London to meet the little guy. Abi heard squeals at the door as her grandmother opened it, before seeing Georgie rush into the living room to give her the tightest hug of her life before turning to the bassinet on the armchair and squealing all over again.

'Oh my GOD, Abi, I am so proud of you. He's just too adorable,' she declared, collapsing onto her all over again, before demanding cuddles the minute that the baby was awake and fed.

Her grandfather was still at work, and Grannie Annie took the chance to head to the shops for a bit, leaving the girls to sit and chat in peace and quiet.

'Are you doing OK?' asked Georgie, in one of the brief lulls in conversation. 'I don't mean physically, I mean ...' She put her hand on her chest, mimicking a beating heart.

Abi gave a faint shrug. She ran a finger across the baby's forehead, luxuriating in the velvety smoothness of his skin.

'How could I regret this? How could he make me sad?' As if he knew he was being talked about, Robbie blew a small milky bubble between his lips. 'But, you know, I'm also not proud of myself.'

'But you shouldn't be ashamed! I mean, he should have... taken better care, right?'

Care. That was the very last thing Abi had ever felt Cole was taking.

'That guy never took much care of me. Anyway, it's done now, and I don't even know where he is.'

'What are you talking about, Abi?'

'Bloody Cole. I don't know where he is – do you? Does your mum? Either way, I won't be telling him.'

'Oh my God, I thought – oh my GOD – I thought it was *Max*.'

'No – that was just once, and Max had a condom. Plus, I'm pretty sure the dates don't match up with what the doctors and the scans reckon. And with Cole there was... more. More times. And he wasn't always, you know, taking care.'

'God, he's such an idiot. Such an absolute dick. I wish you... could have told me about it before it all got so out of hand.'

'I tried. I did try loads of times. I just didn't know how to explain it all. I think I was excited and ashamed at the same time. And he insisted it had to be our secret. I think I was just scared of how you might react. Scared of what he'd say, what the club would say, what you might say...'

'Babe, I never want you to not be able to tell me something again. You promise?'

'I promise. I really do wish I had found a way to fess up, though. I'm sorry.'

'Babe, you don't need to be sorry. You will always have me. Us. All of us.'

'Do you really mean that?'

'Of course I do, you Mama Bear! You are surrounded by amazing, strong women. This little guy won't want for anything. And no more secrets.'

'No more secrets, I promise.'

But as Abi asked Georgie to be baby Robbie's godmother and her squealing began a third time, deep down she knew that there was one secret she would be asking her friend to keep from the baby forever.

'OMG, ABI!' said her best friend, lifting the baby above her head and beaming broadly. 'You know I am the best present buyer in the world. And you know I will give the best advice ever. He'll be able to talk to me about anything!'

Again, Abi quietly thought to herself: *No, not anything.*

Chapter 27

NOW

Max's head peered round the edge of the hospital curtain, his hand patting his pockets, looking for his phone. For a second, he locked eyes with Abi as she looked up from the nurse's face.

Literally the only negative thing about me, Abi heard Max saying to the nurse at the donation centre, as if it had been yesterday.

One of our AB-negative superstars.

There was a ringing in her ears and the scene in front of her seemed to be fading in and out of focus. Max was leaning forward, reaching for his phone from the bedside cabinet. As he stretched, one of his dark curls flopped forward, almost touching Robbie's cheek. As Abi stared, she felt as if she were falling deeper and deeper through the trapdoor, the air rushing past her as her body fell limp. She couldn't remember ever having seen Robbie and Max's faces so close to each other before.

The one fact she had always been so sure of. The fact she had never said aloud in case the shame of it overwhelmed her, swallowed them both up. The fact she had spent her son's entire life guarding him, trying to preserve him from pain and judgement.

Now, for the first time, she found herself thinking – had it really ever been a fact at all?

There was no way she could talk to Robbie now, especially not in front of Max. She had so much she needed to try to find out. As well as the small matter of tomorrow's match. Her head was swimming, the voices of the others in the room seemed to be echoing from behind Perspex, nothing to do with her at all. After what felt like a lifetime, she shook herself, forcing her eyes to look properly at Max, who was repeating himself.

'Abi? ABI! The car's on its way. They told me at Reception that visiting time's over.'

'Yes, please,' said the nurse. 'It's time to let this hero heal.' Then, in a conspiratorial whisper that confirmed she had known all along who Abi was, she added, 'And it's not as if you don't have anywhere else to be.'

Abi felt flushed, panicked at trying to work out which was worse – the pure shame of having to tell Max that he had a son she had never told him about, or the horror of having her hopes dashed and finding out that Robbie was Cole's after all?

One way or another, she owed it to both of them to find out the truth. And that was going to mean a test. Which in turn presented the dilemma of how much longer she could put off talking to … either of them.

Abi gave Robbie a kiss goodbye.

'Goodbye, Mum,' he said. 'And please, don't worry about me. I'm going to be OK. And so are you. In three days, I'll be there, cheering you on in the final, I know it.'

'Oh, darling, I'll do my very best!'

'And don't worry about the other stuff, Mum. I'm sorry I let it get to me all over again.'

'You shouldn't ever have had to think about it, Rob. I'm sorry.'

'Seriously. I've waited my whole life for that chat. I can make it to the weekend.'

'My boy. You're the best. I love you so much, I'm so proud of you.'

Abi leant in, her eyes closed as she held him tight. How could this fundamental assumption that she'd had about him his whole life be shifting all of a sudden? And what did that mean for him, for them? He was just... *him*, wasn't he?

As they headed towards the hospital exit, Abi found that she could barely look Max in the eye. If she started speaking about any of this now she might never stop. Mercifully, he was heading back to his place, leaving her and Georgie to take the courtesy car home. The minute it started moving, Georgie snapped back into professional mode.

'Right. I've got a phone full of discreet calls for comment here. Nothing's in print or online, so I'm doing some damage control. It is, after all, press intrusion that has caused this. I am going to get on the case with writing and sending out a press statement: you're fine, Robbie's fine, you're looking forward to the match of your life tomorrow and he'll be cheering you on from his hospital bed. No further questions taken at this time. Oh, and we're asking for a bit of bloody respect and the family to be left alone, thank you very much. And you, my friend, are going to get some rest.'

'Right-o,' said Abi, uncertain whether to tell Georgie now or later that she really wasn't sure that she would be playing the match at all tomorrow. How could she? Her mind was swirling with questions, doubts and guilt. Her legs felt like jelly, her heart felt as if it had been driven over by a tractor, her eyes were stinging with exhaustion. How could she possibly concentrate on a Wimbledon semi-final? But Georgie was one step ahead.

'And don't give me that look, madam. Of course you're playing the match. It's been a rough twenty-four hours but tomorrow is another day.'

Georgie thanked the driver and slammed the car door behind her as the two women headed into the building. As they entered the kitchen, Barb was there already, unloading glass dishes of yet another delicious dinner from her huge catering box onto the dining table.

'Oh, my darlings, it's so good to see you!' she beamed, arms outstretched. She was wearing faux-leather leggings and a pair of white, bejewelled trainers Abi had seen in a magazine on a starlet half Barb's age. Her hair was in a chic bob in a gleaming shade of copper – any emerging greys never stood a chance under her painstaking maintenance regime. A white silk T-shirt revealed her to be as toned as ever (when did she ever actually play any tennis?). And ropes of gold were wrapped around her neck, her signature look remarkably consistent. Squished in her embrace, feeling the necklaces press against her chest just as they always had, Abi felt memories reaching out of the past, almost touching her fingertips they seemed so close.

'Hey, Mum,' said Georgie, with a less than subtle air of 'we're not expected to chat for long, are we?' about her.

'How is that boy of yours?' Barb asked Abi, who gave her an update, reassuring her that she was convinced everything would be fine. 'That is fantastic news, just super,' Barb replied. 'And please tell me you're going to go and have a rest now, before an early dinner?'

Minutes later, Abi was holding a cool, damp flannel to her face, her eyes closed beneath the fabric, her breathing still shallow with anxiety.

She just had the next twenty-four hours to get through.

Later in the evening, Georgie was at the bedroom door with a coffee, both knocking and peeking her face round with a quiet, 'It's just me – you up?'

'Well, I am now…' said Abi with a giggle. 'No, come in, it's fine – I was awake.' She clocked the glow of Georgie's iPad in her hands. 'What's that?' She felt suddenly cold, wondering if she had seen what she thought she had just before the screen had gone dark.

'Well.' Georgie plonked herself down on the bed. 'First of all – the press statement has been received well. Nothing but love coming your way – seriously, it's absolutely wild. Even Elton John sends his love!' She put an arm round Abi and gave her a squeeze.

Not too tight, thought Abi. *I might start crying again.*

'Then I thought I'd do a bit of research on Cole. He's the same as ever, and it looks as if he is here. Well, in London at least.'

'Oh no.'

'Oh yes. But look, I really don't think you have to worry.'

Georgie touched the screen, and it lit up to show a website. *Cole Connolly: GAME, SET, MATCH starring former touring pro Cole Connolly III, promising to take your tennis to a whole new level. Tips, tutorials and private tuition available online from one of America's most charismatic and respected coaches.* It linked to various social media sites and Cole's large YouTube history. Georgie flicked across a few, quickly letting Abi get the gist of his content. There were cheesy selfies from the grounds of the All England Club. One was dated yesterday.

'He looks like he's got a lot of followers and talks a big game, but I've checked Social Blade and I'm pretty sure a huge number of those are bought. Whereas you are the biggest story of the week and could take your pick of national media interviews. The ball is very much in *your* court. And the game you are playing is tennis, *not* media domination. Not yet of course.'

Abi gasped. Even at the speed that Georgie was flicking through the pages on the tablet, she could see that the years had not been especially kind to Cole. His hair – which had hardly been abundant even back then – was now barely there. All she could ponder as she saw the huge image on his home page was how he protected his scalp in the sun?

The twinkly blue eyes were still there, albeit peering out from amid significantly more wrinkles. The wrap-around shades were tucked into the neck of his T-shirt and there was a single diamond stud in his left earlobe. What had rendered him cute, approachable in a sort of boy-band way when he was in his thirties, now made him look a little daft. As did that hint of a nascent paunch.

Abi had seen enough retired sportsmen in her life to know that there was an indisputable elegance to a man approaching his sixties who a lifetime of sport had kept in great condition. And this was not it. He looked like a chancer. Maybe he always had. But now… she wasn't sure whether to be relieved that he had been out of her life for so long or mortified that he had ever been in it. Mostly, she was gobsmacked that she had let *this*… this *loser* have such a hold over her for so long.

'I honestly think that for the next twenty-four hours we can entirely discount him being a worry on any professional level.

People will see him for who he is. And if – *when* – you win tomorrow, your confidence and your profile will only grow.'

'I guess... But what if I don't?'

'That is not a topic currently open to discussion,' said Georgie in her best 'customer services' voice. 'So here we are. We don't have to do anything for the next twenty-four hours. But, of course, at some point, and if it turns out he is looking for some media oxygen, you might want to get in touch? Especially if you end up having some sort of a chat with Robbie?'

'Oh, yeah, God. Yes, I see,' Abi mumbled.

'Do you think if Robbie wants to get to know him or whatever, you might let him know in advance that he has a son?'

Abi looked blank for a minute. Then she inhaled. 'I don't think it's him, Georgie. I don't think Robbie's father is Cole.'

'What are you talking about, Abi? Are you messing me around?'

'No. I'm really not.' There was a fizzing in her ears. It was happening. She was getting into one of *the* conversations now, unavoidably. Life was shimmering around her as if this new reality, so full of truth, was arriving without her say-so.

'Abi, I don't understand. What are you saying?'

Abi's voice was barely more than a whisper. 'I think it's Max.'

'Max?' Georgie immediately covered her mouth, her eyes filling with tears, as if trying to keep the name in and the volume down. 'The same Max who just texted me to ask how you are? To say that he's going to spend the night at the hospital, sleeping at Robbie's side? I—'

Abi's heart leapt at the thought of Max taking care of Robbie, being there for him. And it leapt again as she realised he always had, and probably always would. Unless she blew things with talk of tests and results.

'You're not making sense.'

'It's a long story.'

'Sounds like it.'

'Please... Let me explain...'

'Of course. I just don't understand how you have suddenly realised – today of all days.'

'I know. It feels like I'm losing my mind. It's just... so obvious now. I can't believe—'

'Abi – Mum's getting dinner ready. You have a big match tomorrow to say the very least. Can you just explain?'

'So, it was nearly twenty years ago...'

'Well, yes, I had worked that bit out.'

Abi gave a laugh, infuriated but relieved by the avalanche of quips coming from Georgie. As ever, her coping mechanism was teasing, rather than Abi's chosen method of simply saying nothing.

'So, it was before I even moved out of home? Wow. But he adored you. We could all see it – I just wasn't sure if you ever did.'

'It wasn't like that. We weren't properly *together*.'

'OK.'

'It was just before Cole left. I'd been really down, really lonely.' Abi glanced at Georgie, keen not to apportion blame. 'It was just one time. I didn't even think it was possible. I had been missing periods the month or so before that.'

'Just before Florida, right?'

'Do you remember that day that Max took us to the blood-donation station?'

Georgie put a reassuring hand on her knee, and listened intently as Abi explained about the blood-donation bank, the comment from the nurse today about Max's rare blood type, and then the comment from the nurse today about Robbie's same rare blood.

'So they have the same blood type? This is your proof? How rare is it?'

'I looked online: one per cent of people.'

'Oh, Abi. I can't believe this. Does Max know?'

'No, the nurse mentioned about Robbie's blood type when you were both out of the room.'

'But why has he never thought Robbie was his either?'

'Because when I had him, I just strongly implied Robbie was someone else's. I kind of knew who he assumed it was, because it was who *I* was assuming it was. Cole suddenly left, and Bracken Lane was awash with gossip – most of which I am *quite* sure reached Max, even on the other side of the Atlantic. I knew that Cole hadn't always been careful, but I also thought that Max had been. I guess – well, I guess we were inexperienced teenagers and things go wrong. But when I found out in the hospital that day, I knew I couldn't get any kind of paternity test from either of them without causing so much chaos and pain. A can of worms I was determined to keep a lid on. And the shame. Shame is so bloody good at keeping you silent.

'I know I handled it badly, cruelly, even. But I was so overwhelmed, still so ashamed of myself. There was no part of me that could see it wasn't all my fault back then. I was just awash with horror and devastated that I'd blown it with Max. It hurt him terribly, I know it. And I sort of just clammed up after that. I was so frightened that saying anything about Cole would bring him back into my life.'

'I *knew* something had happened between you two!'

'I think Max thought I'd fallen for someone else whilst he was away, and I never corrected him. I messed it up. I was too scared to tell anyone the truth. So I just locked up all those feelings I had for Max and threw away the key! And pretty soon after, Robbie came along – and, well, you know the rest.'

The enormity of it seemed to be rising up towards her – a massive wave, threatening to crash over her, taking everything in its wake.

'Correct me if I am stepping out of line here, but I do not think that any good will come out of "what ifs", *or* any discussions about this with Max this week. Do you think he has any idea?'

'I don't see how he can have heard the nurse – he showed absolutely no sign of having done so,' Abi replied.

'Then we leave it. He knows what tomorrow means to you. No matter what that man is feeling, I trust him to do right by you this week. The question is, do you?'

'I do,' said Abi, as she surrendered her phone.

Now that it was the morning of the Wimbledon ladies' semi-finals, Abi was eternally grateful to her greatest of friends. She looked at Georgie, waiting on the doorstep for the car to arrive. 'Thank you, Georgie.'

'What for?'

'For getting me here. This far.'

'Abi, you were *destined* to end up here. This is what you deserve. It is what you dreamed about – longer than most. Do not lose sight of that. You have to take this chance – for yourself *and* for Robbie. You're living out his dream for you too, now, remember.' And with that, she slammed the front door shut and headed into the flat.

As ever, Abi liked her routine to stay exactly the same for each match day – the less she had to worry about as the on-court pressure mounted, the better. At least one moment on a match day, guaranteed to be the same. But last night Georgie had received an official email from the club announcing an unexpected bonus: as there were now only four women left in the draw, Abi had been invited to use the upstairs dressing room – a privilege usually reserved for seeded players only, and a significant upgrade on the regular changing facilities.

She felt a little queasy at the disruption to her routine, but what else could she do but accept the offer? Say no and stay downstairs in the shower rooms, which did *not* have a choice of private baths, showers as large as her whole galley kitchen at home, and banks of TV screens showing every match on every court across the tournament? It wasn't so long ago that she had dreamed of being allowed up there at all, let alone getting a personal invitation. And besides, after all these years, she knew that Barb would never forgive her if she was denied a full rundown of every inch of the recently refurbished facilities, from taps to toiletries.

So once Abigail's warm-up was complete and the buggy had whisked them back to the main site, the two women crept up the elegant wooden stairs to the seeded players' dressing room, feeling like teenagers who were snooping where they ought not to be. After a good nose around, checking out the sauna, the steam room and the opulence of the leather-panelled locker doors, Abigail had a quick shower and indulged herself with a few of the high-end products provided, while Georgie headed to the player restaurant to collect a small portion of penne pasta with chicken and tomato sauce. Abi would eat before she put on her match kit, just in case she spilled anything on her whiter-than-white outfit. While waiting, she fixed her hair in the same French braid she always wore, giving it a final check for any stray strands, and sifted through her racket bag to make sure she had packed everything she needed.

Her opponent, the much-feared Renate van Cutsem, had set up camp in an entirely separate area at the other end of the dressing rooms, but was managing to both quell her own nerves and make her presence felt by singing along loudly and tunelessly to Nena's '99 Red Balloons'. And Abi had thought that she was the one who was a bit of a throwback.

Georgie had headed into the dressing room with Abi, as much for a good snoop around as for moral support.

'Please, stay as late as you can?' Abi begged. 'It's so weird when it's just the two of us, trying to avoid each other.'

'You are daft. You deserve to be here, own your space, woman!'

'OK, OK, Little Miss Affirmations ...'

'Quick, let's send Rob a pic,' said Georgie, whipping out her phone and shuffling up on the leather bench to take a selfie with Abi. The women smiled at the screen and Georgie pressed 'send' with a flourish.

A reply came immediately from Robbie's phone. Thank you but FOCUS please!

Seconds later came a matching selfie of Max and Robbie in a similar pose, sent from her son's iPhone, followed by a video of assembled medical staff from the ward wishing her luck.

Abi's heart felt full to the brim at the thought of her two favourite men together, and even more so when Max sent a further text saying he was heading to the All England Club shortly.

Now, it was 1.50 p.m. – undeniably time for them to say goodbye. Georgie had left no stone unturned and made a specific trip to the club earlier today to time the route from the dressing rooms to the players' box. It took just under ten minutes to negotiate the passageways, stairs, and crowds around the side of Centre Court, and up the final steps to Gangway 211.

They walked a few steps along the expensively panelled walls towards the dressing-room exit, and looked down the corridor that each of them would shortly be heading along. It had fallen almost silent outside as pretty much everyone with a ticket was now seated. The wooden parquet floor gleamed beneath them as Georgie turned to face her friend, grabbed her shoulders and looked her straight in the eyes.

'You deserve to be here. You deserved it back then, and you deserve it now. You know what you have to do, and you know you can do it. This is your time. We'll all be there with you. For every single point. Me, Max and Barb. And Robbie and his new crew.'

Abi nodded. She noticed that what Georgie *hadn't* said was that Cole might be there too, hiding out in the crowd. Back for his moment of glory.

'Thank you,' she whispered. 'I'll try to do you proud.'

'Don't you do it for us, we're beyond proud already,' replied Georgie. 'Do it for you.'

The women hugged. Just as they had done a million times – before and after matches, at the end of parties, on railway platforms up and down the country. This hug felt like all of those previous ones and more, the women reaching across the decades and hoping that today might mean it had all been worth it. As they moved apart from each other, Abi blew her friend a final kiss and headed back through the gilded doorway into the best dressing room in the capital.

Chapter 28

THEN

Tennis never stopped being part of Abi's life once baby Robbie was born. What did change was her attendance at Bracken Lane. As far as most of her peers there were aware, it was her ankle injury that had set her back, as she tried as best she could to keep the pregnancy and birth a secret beyond her few closest friends.

Barb, assuming the baby was Cole's, had drawn a veil of secrecy across the issue and was more than happy to maintain that discretion if it meant keeping the peace and the reputation at Bracken Lane – especially after her wholehearted championing of Cole in the early days – followed by his ignominious departure.

When paying one of her regular visits to check in on Abi and the baby, she tentatively asked how Abi was feeling about returning to the club and playing tennis again, almost as if she had anticipated the response.

'Barb, the thought of going back to Bracken Lane just makes me feel queasy,' explained Abi hesitantly. She didn't want to upset Barb by saying the words 'too many bad memories', but she couldn't think of any others that explained her position any better. 'Too many conversations just seem to . . . stop short . . . when I walk into rooms. It just makes me feel like a freak.'

'Well, firstly, madam, you're not a freak. You're just someone who has had some bad experiences. And, secondly, I've got a plan. Please don't think I've been sticking my nose in, but I've spoken to Rosie Forbes and she's put me in touch with the gang at Summershall Village.'

Summershall was a smaller, less aspirational club a mile or so down the road from her grandparents' house. It was where Rosie, the coach who had replaced Cole, had started out.

'Oh, I played there as a little kid,' said Abi, her heart brightening at the memories.

'So I hear. And there's the chance that you could have a sort of shared membership over there – still be a Bracken Lane player for competitions – if you want to – but actually train at Summershall.'

'I could just cycle down there, sort of get going again at my own pace.'

'Indeed you could. Would you like to?'

'Oh, Barb, you know I would, thank you.'

From the living-room doorway, Grannie Annie raised her mug of tea at Barb and nodded her approval. As Robbie squeaked in his baby bouncer, Abi felt a wave of gratitude for having these strong, caring women looking out for her.

And it all worked out, for a while. Until Robbie was a tottering one-year-old, when parenting suddenly changed gear. Her grandparents' home, which had seemed such a haven during the first fragile months of his life, now turned out to be completely impractical for a child who was at the age where no ornament was too precious to pick up and slam down, no doorstopper too dirty to have a taste of and no garden bed too beautiful not to be ploughed through with diggers, spades and tiny chubby fingers. From the crack of dawn until the second Robbie's head hit the pillow, Abi felt herself torn between wanting to let him play, wanting to respect the never-ending patience of her grandparents and wanting to be on court, hitting balls, competing.

At Christmas, by which time Abi really was flagging, Georgie was round to see Robbie as soon as she could, sharing fistfuls of festive biscuits with him despite (or perhaps even because of) Barb's despair at the sugar content in them. A couple of days later, she suggested that Abi and Robbie joined her on a country walk a couple of villages away. The pace of life in her new flat-share in Shepherd's Bush had left her breathless, she explained. She was longing for the tranquility of the Hampshire lanes and green spaces she had grown up surrounded by, and now she wanted nothing more than to stomp through the woods with her oldest friend in the hope that Robbie would sleep for as much of the expedition as possible.

For most of the walk, Robbie was a delight. Strapped to Abi in an outfacing sling, he beat his arms up and down at the sight of the slight dappling on his hands through the trees, and was enchanted when Georgie occasionally bent to the forest floor and picked him up a nice crispy brown leaf, which he happily scrunched and rustled for nearly half an hour at a time before letting it drop.

Helped by Robbie's good mood, the exercise and fresh air, and the relief that Abi felt about being out of the house for a decent chunk of time, the women finally had the chance for a proper catch-up. Georgie, who had been so determined to save face for so long, who had been holding the party line that she had moved on to bigger and better things since long before Robbie had been born, finally admitted that, yes, London was exhausting. Blessed with a sunny nature and no small amount of Barb's can-do nature, she had sailed into a job in sports PR and now found herself organising events most weekends and frequent evenings. The line between work, sport and her personal life was constantly blurry. She was expected to be unruffled but charming at all times, and was learning at breakneck speed about how to handle the media and, on occasion, sports fans.

The shift from being a large cog in the small wheel that was Bracken Lane to a far smaller one in the nation's capital had obviously not been entirely smooth and as the women shrieked with laughter remembering the high jinks of their early teenage years, Abi could see Georgie's shoulders drop, her entire demeanour relax and her old self re-emerge. Abi, in turn, found herself admitting for the first time that parenthood seemed to be getting harder, not easier, her voice breaking when she admitted that the most painful part of it was that she could feel her memories of her own mother fading as she made new ones with Robbie.

'I hate having to tell him off, to be firm with him,' she confessed. 'I'm the youngest of everyone at every baby group I go to and I can tell they all think I'm crap.'

'Why would they think that? They're probably just jealous that you look fantastic and your baby's the best.'

Abi laughed. God, she had missed her friend.

'I just never seem to know what I'm doing now it's more than just feeding him that is required. And I feel guilty every time I daydream about being on court, or at training. Which is starting to be a lot.'

'Oh, Abi, never feel guilty. You're doing an amazing job and you're doing it without...' a pause '...without *him*.'

Abi felt her friend stroke her back, her leather-gloved hand warm where she patted her just as she patted Robbie. There was a lull between them, the question hanging in the air a moment. Abi inhaled, braced.

'Did you ever hear from him?'

Abi shook her head, silent. And as she blinked, two fat tears fell and landed on Robbie's head. She didn't know if it was the tears or just that he was due a feed, but before the conversation could continue, Robbie burst into a cranky strop, his fists clenched, mittens dangling from the sleeves of his playsuit from the string Grannie Annie had knitted him, inconsolable.

Abi tried jiggling him, shushing him, and holding his hands, which had grown cold without their mittens, but nothing worked. It was getting towards the end of a day where he'd had a lot of fun and now he was just tired and hungry – but they were still a good half-hour from the car. In the end, Abi told Georgie the best thing would be if she just fed him. So they found the least damp log that they could, and sat next to each other, knee to knee against the cold, while Abi fed Robbie.

Dusk had started to peek over the tops of the trees and an air of melancholy came over them as they realised how close they'd been and how far they had drifted. Abi, suddenly exhausted, slumped. Georgie, feeling the shift against her own body, looked at her oldest friend and said, 'You can do this, Abi. And remember, it's never a sign of weakness to ask for help. It's a sign of strength.'

She had known at the time that this was true, but she had never imagined that it would be a further eighteen years before she would get her career as a top player back on track.

Chapter 29

NOW

Yet here she was, sitting on the plushest bench in the innermost sanctum of the All England Club itself, waiting for the return of Angela Chadwick-Hall, the member of the championships committee who Abi knew would be here to get her soon. Sure enough, she entered the dressing room moments later, her patent leather pumps smacking on the parquet to announce her arrival.

'Ladies, it's time to head down for your match. I am here to accompany you to Centre Court.'

As the unseeded player, Abigail was invited to lead the way. She put her headphones on and kept her head down, following Angela. She could still just about hear the clack of Angela's shoes and turned the volume up as they descended the stairs. Through the windows, she could see the crowds outside and could sense the excitement building, but she didn't think she could bear to hear it until the last minute. The shiny wooden banister, with its iconic tennis ball shape on top of the newel, was cool and smooth under her hand, as she reached out and touched it on her way down. A moment later, they reached the trophy cabinets, filled with the world-famous silverware – the very trophies that each player there was fighting for. Next to them were the champions boards, inscribed with the names of the victors.

Angela put a hand out to indicate that they were to stop here. Had it really only been two days since Abi had last been here? It already felt like a lifetime of reliving and rewriting the past on an almost hour-by-hour basis.

It doesn't matter who or what happened in the past. You can't change it, she told herself. *It's about today. And the people who are here today. That's what matters.*

Then, as she looked up, Angela opened the doors and Abi walked onto Centre Court to face her future: a place in the Wimbledon final. Her first instinct was to try to scan the crowd for Cole, before she reminded herself that he had no part in her life and the harm he could do now was limited. She was the one here, walking towards her chair, ready to play the biggest match of her life. So, instead, she turned and looked for the players' box, for Max. And hoped that today was all about second chances.

There he was, waving calmly as if he hadn't just caught a motorcycle taxi from the hospital, but wearing an enormous smile beneath his cap and shades. She felt her heart leap, hope bubbling up once again, before she spotted Renate's formidable team on the other side of the box. There seemed to be so many of them compared to just three on her side. And at the very front was her long-term boyfriend, a Scandinavian racing driver whose peroxide hair, easy charm and ferocious driving style meant that he was as popular with petrolheads as he was with teenage TikTokkers.

Renate had, somewhat predictably, taken her time to get to

the opposite end, stopping at her chair to retie her shoelaces and to take a longer-than-necessary swig of sponsored water.

All part of the game, Abi remembered Georgie warning her. All about getting those dollars while all eyes were on her – and so much the better if it made your opponent wait.

Abi saw Georgie at the end of her parents' tennis court in that childhood home they had spent so many hours in. Wagging her finger, squinting into the sun.

'Showing me who's boss, are you?' she'd say, whenever Abi stopped to adjust her hair, or a lace. 'Well, it won't work!'

Now, Abi muttered it under her breath, jaw clenched, determined not to let Renate grab the psychological upper hand. She shadowed some groundstrokes and a few overheads, letting herself soak in the atmosphere, heavy with anticipation – and the smell of freshly mown grass. She scanned the photographers' pit. Who knew camera shutters made so much noise?

She was still on this thought when the first ball was fired across the net towards her. Renate was making her presence felt with a particularly deep and aggressive opening shot and it took Abi by surprise, causing her to clatter a forehand off the frame and into the crowd. She felt her face redden, wondering briefly what the fans and the commentators would be thinking. She could almost feel the mutters, the thrill of watching someone who simply 'shouldn't' be there…

She immediately fished into her shorts for another ball and started the rally with a forehand that barely cleared the service line. Renate stepped up to hit one of her trademark topspin backhands for a winner. Abi clenched her jaw. She had seen this so often in her coaching role: a player denying their opponent a quality warm-up in order to disrupt their confidence and their rhythm. She knew what this was: stage fright on her part, compounded by an experienced opponent stamping her authority from the outset.

Abi turned her back. She made a few shadow swings with excessive knee bends and a few fast-feet movements. She adjusted her visor and nodded to the ballboy in the right-hand corner, then seized the initiative – sending a ball straight up the middle of the court.

Play the ball, not the ranking, she reminded herself. *Not the reputation. Not the seeding. Just the ball.*

And with that, she had gained control of the warm-up, the rest of which went pretty smoothly, until she snuck up to the net to take some volleys. Renate saw another chance to impose her authority and sent every ball whizzing past her for a winner, each shot accompanied by the loud emission of air that had shaped her nickname. Renate von Gruntsem. Abi let it slide, relieved that she was anonymous enough not to have caught the public's imagination with a comparably grim nickname. Yet.

She wanted to get into Renate's head as much as she could, and took Georgie's advice to keep adjusting the position she returned shots from, trying to make her wonder what Abi was up to. *Two can play this game*, she thought, as the umpire announced time.

It turned out that Renate really had misjudged how hard it might be to psych out a competitor almost twice her age, and was continuing with her attempts to unnerve and distract. She delayed at her chair as long as possible: towelling herself down as if she were in a spa, fixing her high ponytail as if aiming to reach through the roof with it, and blowing her nose as loudly as Abi's grandad used to when the spring pollen kicked in. At last, striding imperiously towards a young-looking ballboy who was standing with his hands behind his back, quivering, Renate was ready to play.

At over six feet, she cut an undeniably intimidating figure. She had shoulders an Olympic swimmer would be proud of and an unashamedly steely gaze. Once her pale eyes made contact with the lad, standing just below the scoreboard on the left corner of the court, he looked partly terrified and partly star-struck. It took a beat, but then he raised both his hands, as he'd been trained, and threw a ball downwards towards her.

One ball was enough for Renate, Abi noted. She'd never be caught tucking a second ball up the side of the shorts beneath her figure-skimming designer dress, as Abi had been doing before Renate had even been born. Ruin the line of the technically sculpted breathable fabric? She may as well drop a set.

Renate moved slowly up to her serving position on the baseline and stared down the court, eyeballing Abi for far longer than necessary, before starting her excessive pre-serve ball-bouncing routine. Yet another tactic designed to haze her opponent's concentration, making them wait much longer than usual while they applied laser focus as long as they could before, just as they blinked, hitting them with a killer serve. It was annoying – for opponents and the crowd – but Abi had been expecting it. She and Georgie had studied it last night, making notes on how to respond, just as they had done with their old video tapes of Hingis and Davenport. And with years of coaching teenagers under her belt, Abi was more than qualified in all forms of gamesmanship and had developed an unusually high tolerance level for it. She could *more* than handle annoyance.

She knew a rocket was going to come her way, from one of the biggest servers in the game. And there it was: delivered with an almighty grunt and registering at 121 mph on the

Centre Court speed gun. Abi managed to get her racket to it and blocked it back, thankful for the countless men and junior boys against whom she had played practice points and sets. But the ball fell pitifully short. Renate pummelled it away and celebrated with an exaggerated toss of her long blonde ponytail, a clenched fist and one of those emphatic head tilts that suggested there was a bad smell under her nose.

Abi had known it was going to take a little time to settle into this match, this opponent, this occasion. She couldn't compete with Renate for power, so she would have to outsmart her and be ready to chase down every ball.

As she raised her bottle, her eyes darted into the crowd behind the umpire, landing on an elderly woman wearing an outsized straw hat covered in Union Jack ribbon and half a dozen tennis balls. Abi wondered how anyone behind her could possibly see past it, as she made her way to the opposite end. The sun was now behind her and a timid-looking ballgirl standing below the outsized Rolex clock smiled tentatively as she passed the balls. Coach-brain still engaged, Abi recognised that the girl was almost as nervous as she was and mouthed a big, 'Thank you.'

Serving was the one stroke in tennis that Abi knew she had to have *complete* control over. But she also knew that nerves linked to a big match could create a mild paralysis of her upper limbs, often referred to by the players as 'jelly arm' – so called because it made performing a ball toss feel all but impossible. And now, just as she was starting to relax a little, it came for Abi.

Chapter 30

THEN

It was when Robbie was about eighteen months old that Abi really, truly realised what having a baby as a teenager had done for her career in tennis. What followed was the hardest period of her life. In the past, when she had suffered grief or heartache, tennis had been there for her – a solace on the court, refuge in the routine, discipline and sheer joy of hitting balls. On court she was Abi the athlete, the fighter, the champion. And *not* Abi the orphan.

Now, barely twenty herself but with a grandmother aged seventy-five, Abi knew she couldn't rely on her grandparents for ever. And the mechanics of the regional tennis circuit were simply far too complicated for bringing a toddler along too. There was no one to look after Robbie while she tried to zigzag the country playing tournaments, and the costs attached to competing quickly proved prohibitive too. Slowly but surely, the reasons not to keep entering events mounted up. No matter how much she wanted to do it. And she really, really did.

So, after a few months of trying, she quietly gave up, and looked around instead for work at other nearby clubs. Frank

Johnstone, an elderly, experienced coach at Summershall Village, was the first person she had spoken to. A grandfatherly figure who had coached Rosie Forbes himself, he was now too old to test the top juniors he was coaching on court, but he nevertheless had an eagle analytical eye and an impressive track record. This was how Abi made the sideways move from competitor to becoming his top hitter, playing just as he asked for each and every training session, testing his stable of juniors to the edge of their capacity and in the process keeping her own game up. Because it was paid work, she was able to spend her earnings on proper childcare for Robbie. Sometimes the three of them would head to Summershall Village together and their soon-beloved sitter would play with Robbie in the children's area, or take him to the nearby park to feed the ducks before they all had a picnic and headed home.

Once she started earning, Abi realised that she had a chance of actually giving Robbie a decent life rather than merely making do, and little by little her ambition grew. She enjoyed seeing him play nearby as she worked at the club, and she enjoyed having a job where she was working around kids, family and community. As soon as he started at primary school, she went back to education herself, getting coaching qualifications as fast as she could, and setting herself up as a fully fledged coach by the time he was six.

Yes, there were moments – when he smashed a favourite mug, when he embarrassed her with a tantrum in the supermarket or when he simply went for a week or two of restless nights – that she felt a hot fury that she had given up on a dream she had already sacrificed so much for. She would think of Georgie, dining in London's smartest clubs, or Max networking in the sunshine on the other side of the world, and she would feel pure envy. But these moments were few and far between – because she was playing. She was still playing tennis pretty much every day, and nothing else made her feel quite like it.

Robbie was happy, and growing up playing outside, always nearby, and surrounded by friends and club members of all ages. So, slowly, she let go of the dream – the competitive side of tennis – and instead counted her blessings that she earned a living on court. She could talk about tennis all day with people just as passionate about it as her, and as her business grew she was able to encourage the next generation, to try to instil in them the passion and respect for the sport that felt so innate to her.

When Robbie was eleven, Grannie Annie passed away, only a couple of years after Grandad Bob, and once again grief was intricately stitched into the fabric of her life. When her parents had died, Abi had had her grandparents, but with them now gone, adulthood felt all-encompassing. If she were to fail, Robbie would have no one. Well, as close to no one as could be imagined. Because Barb was still there, even long after Georgie was living life to the full in London. She took full control of the funeral, sparing no expense, and made sure that Mr Blackwood was on hand to help Abi with the seemingly endless probate paperwork that followed. Abi knew she would never have coped without them, and their ongoing care and affection for her played a huge part in keeping her going during that period.

Abi and Robbie inherited the house, the same one they had now both grown up in, and that created a layer of security. But still, from this moment on, Abi took the safe choice every time, rather than reaching for the stars. Like the balloon she had once watched Robbie let go of as they had walked home after a visit to the Bank Holiday Fair, the dream was gone. It had been beautiful, but, yes, it was gone. It was a good life, even if she had felt painfully alone for so much of it. Perhaps it wasn't even loneliness, Abi reflected, rather the weight of keeping a secret from her son – and others – for so long.

She never quite articulated this sense of sorrow for what she might have been when she saw Georgie and Max, which was usually at Christmas. They'd always have their shared past, and they almost always managed to get together for a meal out around the festive period – but for years they were somewhat distant friends.

It was Robbie, as he became a teenager, increasingly curious about his past, who had wanted to see more and more of his 'Auntie Gee'. She started to take him up to London to visit the big museums, to spend long afternoons at the South Bank skate park, an occasional football match and once or twice to watch the tennis at Queen's Club, or Wimbledon if Georgie got lucky with tickets via work. But getting to know Georgie had meant getting to hear more about Max, and that in turn had meant seeing more of Max. So, over the last four or five years, the four of them had spent more and more time together, rebuilding the once unbreakable bond that they had known as teenagers.

At first, Abi had been hesitant for the four of them to hang out together, the dynamic too close to the old days, yet miles apart. Yes, Georgie had always been there for her, and Max had always been on the end of the phone. But time in person, revealing herself as a mother, not just as a mate, had made her feel intensely vulnerable. But Robbie had persisted, and as he grew older and more articulate, he also grew more persuasive – and Abi was mindful of how much parental figures like Barb had meant to her at a similar age. Why deny him that simple pleasure? So they had hung out, more and more, and despite herself, she had loved every second.

Max, too, had become increasingly involved. For years, he had seemed to enjoy being a good-looking tennis player on the tour, as much as any man would. There was a fleet of girlfriends, sometimes younger, sometimes older, but no one lasted for more than a year or so. It even became a bit of a Christmas tradition for Georgie to grill Max about what he was getting 'this year's girl' for Christmas, before determining how long the relationship would last by the quality of the gift. Underwear – she barely had until Valentine's Day. A scented candle – she'd be gone by the New Year. Jewellery – maybe she would last beyond summer.

Abi would giggle along, sometimes awestruck at how effortless he seemed to find dating, while she had never quite found her confidence. The shadow Cole had left was long, and the added extra of a young son was deemed a challenge by many of the men she met through work. Then there was the fact that, on some level, Abi was comparing the men she met to Max as much as Cole. And he was a man who really was ageing well. The awkwardness he'd had as a gangly seventeen-year-old now felt like authority on an older man. And the slight daftness, the giggle that had often stopped him from being taken seriously as an opponent, was charming, disarming even, in a man with just a couple of stray grey hairs around the temples. Best of all, the shyness that lay behind it all had now manifested itself as a peerless ability to listen – really listen – when people were talking. And that was, of course, intoxicating to most people, making him not just a great manager but clearly a great date.

Over the years, Abi had enjoyed watching both of her friends come into their own, just as they had her. What could have been unavoidable scar tissue scratched across their friendship, caused at the time of Robbie's birth, was now healed, and largely down to the insistence of the boy himself.

Until Robbie had taken that step too far. And now here she was, the eyes of the nation on her, trying to navigate the impact of her worst trauma while reaching not just for love, but the dream she had so long ago thought was impossible.

Chapter 31

NOW

Abi made a few attempts to throw the ball upwards, but each time it fell too short and too far forward, completely unusable for a serve. Her 'jelly arm' just wouldn't extend, leaving her feeling as if she was having to use someone else's limb. She let another ball drop. Then another. And another.

The crowd was deadly silent, patiently waiting for her to get it right. She longed for just a little murmur, a bit of white noise so that she didn't feel as if she had half an ear listening for any sign of Cole. Meanwhile, at the other end of the court, Renate had sensed what was going on and was doing everything she could to prolong the agony. Creeping closer and closer to the service line, her wide stance and swaying motion making her appear even bigger than usual, like a lion stalking its prey.

Abi took another breath, and tried to imagine she was on the court at Georgie's house, back in the day. Just the two of them. Barb, head to toe in Lycra, keeping a close eye on them from the patio while performing one of her aerobic routines to the best of the Spice Girls. The memory made her smile. Barb really was a dreadful singer.

Abi's facial muscles relaxed. She inhaled deeply and let her shoulders drop. She felt a cloud above shift, and the sun hit her back just as it did when she played from the house end on summer afternoons at Blackwood Towers. In an instant, she was back in those teenage years, when tennis was nothing but fun and friends. She tried to stay suspended in those memories, and let that sense of playfulness fill her body as she felt her lungs expand.

She blinked, shook her arms out a little, and finally felt them relax properly. She delivered a toss that was more or less in the right place, and with a rush of adrenaline that made her blush like a teenager, she was finally up and running. A seventeen-stroke rally followed – just what she needed to help her settle down. And, at last, she got her first point on the scoreboard with a perfectly executed drop shot. She would never be able to match Renate's effortless power, but she could expose her relative lack of mobility – and finally she did! After all, a six-feet-two player might have a large wingspan, but she was far less likely to have fast feet, and just as she used to with Georgie, Abi started to exploit that weakness.

Buoyed by the deafening applause from the partisan crowd, Abi found three more solid points to hold both her serve and her nerve. Seeing the electronic scoreboard display a one beside her name gave her a huge sense of relief, while the noise in the stadium started to sound like more like the FA Cup final she had taken Robbie to only a few weeks earlier. Yes, the crowds were very different, but Abi knew what a home crowd sounded like, and she knew that this time the advantage was hers. And there was nothing Renate could do about that. She smiled again.

The next four games went with serve, Renate holding with

relative ease while Abi struggled to do anything but defend with her returns. She kept trying to draw Renate up the court and off the baseline with low-angled slice backhands, as well as playing deep shots straight down the middle, in the knowledge that tall players hated being 'jammed up' – all part of the tactical plan she had made with Georgie and Max. At other times, she shuffled right and left, trying to distract Renate. But with her height and reach combined making well over eight feet, it sometimes felt as if Renate was serving at her out of a tree.

At 3–3, Renate abruptly went to change her racket, common practice at the top of a game, just before the balls were changed. Abi watched with interest, aware that her opponent was seeking an advantage for the seventh game when the new balls would be in play. Of course, a more tightly strung racket would help to control the lively new balls, freshly popped from their pressurised tin. But Abi didn't follow suit. There was no point in switching her routine around, and, anyway, she really hadn't hit enough shots yet. Was it ever worth it? she wondered. Or just one of those 'facts' that some hotshot trainer had made fashionable, leaving other players to do the same just in case?

As she waited for Renate to return to the baseline, Abi walked to the corner of the court and picked up her towel from the court surround. A quick glimpse up at the players' box confirmed that Georgie and Max still had their eyes trained on her, clapping and nodding in silent encouragement. For a second, she considered who else was there, but pushed the thought away in an instant.

The next two games both went with serve, and Abi felt her confidence trickling back. Renate was starting to get flustered, perplexed that her biggest weapon, the double-handed backhand, was being returned with interest, and Abi's drop shots were really finding their mark.

Then, a sort of magical alchemy started to spark between Abi and the crowd. She began to feel them moving with her, gazes following her racket as she scurried around the court, seeing for the first time this promise and talent that had once been talked about up and down the country. *This was how she had got here out of nowhere*, she could almost hear them thinking.

'I know!' she wanted to reply to each and every one of them. 'I just needed a chance!'

Sensing another unexpected opportunity for the underdog, they were now gasping at every big shot and cranking up the volume whenever Abi won a point. Were they daring to dream along with her?

When Renate's coach, Pepe Delbonis, started to make his presence increasingly felt, Abi knew that she hadn't been imagining things – the clear home-crowd advantage was getting to her opponent. Pepe was a huge influence at any match: a grizzled fifty-year-old Argentinian with dark unruly hair and weather-beaten forearms, tanned from years of coaching in the sunshine while he rolled endless cigarettes. His reputation as a hugely experienced coach who got results had only become slightly tainted by the rumours on the tour about his gambling habit – one that he was alleged to be able to afford on account of his formidable success rate. His sunglasses, as ever, were pushed back into his wiry hair, to reveal a deeply furrowed brow and to allow him to make direct eye contact with his player. As Abi prevailed, he was now standing up, fist pumping every one of Renate's winning shots, leaning over the edge of the box and repeatedly having to be pulled back by the steward. He knew as well as anyone in that box that the ledge was sacred – no one was to leave anything on it, and certainly not a body part.

Before long, his inconspicuous encouragement in the form of an occasional '*Vamos*' had been replaced by a not-so-subtle mix of verbal instruction and coded hand signals. A linesman seated below the players' box had already alerted the umpire, who eventually snapped, giving a dispassionate, 'Coaching from the stands. Warning, Miss van Cutsem.'

Abi looked down at her shoes and closed her eyes, trying to preserve what was left of her concentration and her nerves. But she couldn't block out the noise of the slow hand clap the crowd was starting, and for the first time she realised that with them behind her and Renate being so rattled, a win was really, truly within her grasp.

At 4–4, 15–15 on Renate's serve, a particularly long and gruelling rally ended with Abi outside the tramlines defending a vicious cross-court shot with a slice forehand. A lucky break for Abi gave her 15–30 on her opponent's serve. Renate had lost her footing in an especially dry patch behind the baseline and as she picked herself up and dusted herself off from her fall, she raised her hand to the umpire, asking for the trainer to be called to court at the end of that game.

More tactics, Abi thought to herself, determined not to fall for the histrionics or the gamesmanship, whether they were genuine or not. But something had changed. Walking gingerly back to serve, with a mixture of pain and frustration on her face – and a slight hint of a limp – Renate threw in an uncharacteristic double fault.

15–40. Two break points. Abi's first break points of the match.

In a way that she never had when such moments of magnitude had come her way in the past, Abi knew that what happened next had the potential to change the rest of her life. Up until now, the fatalities, the fumbles and the fight-backs that had directed the course her life had taken had all seemed to sneak up on her unawares. She'd never seen them coming, so they seemed to have *happened* before there had been any sign of them on the horizon. Now, she felt as if the world was slowing down for her, for the first time letting her *know* that this was a big moment.

She took her time. She adjusted her visor, she gritted her teeth and she altered her position, telling herself to make Renate move, no matter what she threw at her. A first serve came thundering towards Abi at 122 mph, making her wonder if those rumours about performance-enhancing drugs had ever been true. But before she had even finished the thought, she had blocked the ball back with her forehand and was hurtling to the middle of the court to regroup. She was on the back foot again as Renate stormed to the net looking to finish the point with a volley. So Abi threw up the highest lob she could muster, knowing that the sun would be in Renate's eyes. As the ball sailed down, Abi could see Renate struggling to focus on it through the brightness, and Pepe, jaw clenched, slumped back in the players' box right behind her. Just as she'd hoped, the glare proved fatal, and Renate mishit the smash over the baseline. Abi had broken her opponent's serve. Now, she would serve for the set at 5–4. But, first, a ninety-second break and another chance to hide beneath her towel.

The trainer was ready to come onto the court immediately to speak with Renate. As per protocol, she had three minutes to assess any injury and another three to treat it if required. Abi had no idea if the injury was real or invented, but she knew that six minutes would be an eternity to sit on her own with all those eyeballs on her.

Stay calm, stay focused, she told herself. She visualised shaking herself by the shoulders, speaking to herself as she would do one of her own players.

That's enough, Abi. This is about you. And only you. This is your time. Save all your energy for you. Plan the next game while you have a moment. Where are you going to serve on the first point? What do you expect Renate to do on return? What's your next shot? Visualise it. Breathe long, and slow.

But the crowd were beginning to get restless. Any break in play always led to a sort of switch-off that all players dreaded, largely because with it came a rise in rustling of food wrappers and shuffling among the seats as people took the chance to head to the toilets and bars, as well as an obvious increase in hushed chatter. It was clear that this crowd knew they were on the cusp of watching something memorable, and Abi was once again aware of the sunlight twinkling off the back of mobile phones as they were raised towards her, ready to take a shot of anything interesting she might do.

In response, Abi draped her towel over her head, the only vague form of privacy available to her. Despite that, she heard the trainer giving her assessment to the umpire – that there was a slight strain on Renate's right hamstring and that they would need a further three minutes to apply some physio tape.

In the relative shade but increasing clamminess under her towel, Abi could sense the nerves escalating. How long could three minutes actually last? Before the umpire had even called time on the treatment break, Abi decided to head back to the court and warm up her own serve. Having watched the world's best for years on TV, she recognised that sometimes mind games could only get you so far, and sometimes you just needed to keep warm, keep moving, be ready to resume at any minute.

Eventually, Renate returned to court – to huge applause. Abi gritted her teeth, accepted two balls from the ballgirl and stepped up to serve.

One point at a time. Use the slice. Swing it wide. Be ready for the short return and use the wrong-footer on the next shot.

She knew Renate had an injury concern. She also knew Renate wasn't the best mover, that she struggled with a change of direction. And she knew she had to take advantage of both.

15–0.

It had worked!

Abi suddenly discovered to her surprise that, despite years of protesting otherwise, she was the sort of player who did clench her fist towards the players' box at moments like these. *Maybe we all are*, she mused, *and you just don't find out until you're there.*

Next point. Executed to perfection. Renate was surprisingly predictable on return and Abi finished the point with an exquisitely angled forehand volley.

30–0.

Do it again. Slice serve wide. If she returns to my backhand, short slice cross-court. And if she returns to my forehand, I'm going to wrong-foot her again.

Bingo.

The backhand slice was lethal. Renate chased it, but the ball stayed low on the grass and was out of her reach.

40–0.

Three set points.

Focus on this point. Look at your target. Serve into the body. You will get a weak return towards your backhand and you're going to use the drop shot. Let's do this.

This time, the moment had passed before Abi had had a chance to savour it. The next thing she seemed to hear was the umpire.

'Game and first set, Miss Patterson, by six games to four.'

The crowd erupted. They were standing, arms waving, hats in the air, ecstatic. A sea of Union Jacks.

Abi walked to her chair, head down, in a daze. Wow, sometimes you really do get an afternoon when all your luck lines up.

Her heart was racing. She knew she had a huge job ahead, she knew it was just the first set, but she had the momentum now and she realised it was possible. It really was!

Renate started the second set with a double fault, clearly distracted by the 'Marry me, Renate' shout that rang out just as she started her ball toss, and whacked the turf in disgust. Abi silently thanked the love-struck American from the front row and momentarily dared to look up at the players' box for encouragement – and it came in the form of a fist pump from Georgie and a nod of the head from Max. Abi could picture them all discussing the match later, Max's hand on her shoulder as he congratulated her. She had to get there, she just had to get there.

Renate's boyfriend leant back, an ostentatiously relaxed pose, or perhaps just one to show off his expensive diamond-encrusted watch while the cameras were on him as he raised his hands up and behind his head.

The crowd fell deathly quiet. The hairs on the back of Abi's neck started to rise a little as she realised that they were waiting, sensing a possible upset.

But it was short-lived. Renate powered down three unreturnable serves to lead the game 40–15, before sealing it with a serve-volley combination that was reminiscent of Navratilova herself. Abi knew she had to be patient, to take her chances when they came and not be distracted by the rest. But she also knew that there wasn't much that could be done when the serves were booming down at 120 mph.

She grabbed her towel and walked quickly to her chair, purposely passing the net before her opponent and avoiding any eye contact or opportunity for the famous van Cutsem shoulder charge. There was no sit-down time as it was only the first game of the set, just time for a quick swig of her drink and to towel down her grip. Hand-held Union Jack flags fluttered all around the court, everywhere except in the royal box, where it was frowned upon to show partisan support for either player. Were there more now than an hour ago? Abi wondered.

'Quiet, please,' the umpire said. 'Quiet please.'

At 1–1, after Abi held her serve, Renate was panicking. The crowd – and Abi – had got to her. When Abi unleashed her signature backhand drop shot on the next point, she seemed completely taken by surprise, rooted to the spot. 0–40. As the crowd shifted in their seats and began that hushed chatter of anticipation that came with a big moment, Abi turned her back on Renate, faced the curtain, fiddled with her racket strings and counted to ten. She could see the second clock counting down from twenty-five, yet another thing she had had to get used to. You didn't have those in the Hampshire leagues. *Let her wait*...

Renate unleashed one of her bomb serves that whizzed past Abi and ended up in the third row of the crowd. Several hands flew up to catch it before it was eventually thrown back by a middle-aged man with a beanie hat and a *BACK THE BRITS* T-shirt. He would no doubt dine out on that for weeks to come.

Abi knew she had to find a way to get the serve back in play and work her way into a position to make Renate run. She got a touch on the return and blocked it short into the service box. Renate came forward fast, winding up for a huge backhand. Abi guessed correctly the direction of her opponent's shot and was there in time to throw up what Georgie called 'a skyscraper lob', loaded with topspin. Renate was tall, but not tall enough; although she gave chase immediately, she quickly realised it was irretrievable and let it go. Abi had broken serve to lead 2–1. If she could hold her serve just four more times, she was through to the Wimbledon final.

Abi hurried to her chair, while Renate walked slowly and deliberately. Was there a limp? There was definitely frustration, and perhaps a hint of concern? The change of ends passed quickly for Abi. Towel. Drink. Jelly beans. Notes. Locket. Ready.

The noise from the crowd was deafening. The quartet of rugby players were in the stands again. They waited for silence then rose in unison to belt out their. 'ABI DABI DOOOOOOOO!' More laughter from the crowd. Abi let the noise subside before starting her serve routine. The first two points were straightforward; she went for accuracy over power. Renate returned both serves into the net and looked disgustedly at her racket as if shifting the blame.

30–0.

The next point produced a fifteen-stroke rally, which saw both women hurtling from side to side before Abi found an opportunity to use her slice backhand down the line and approach the net. The slice kept the ball low, forcing Renate to stretch to reach it. She lunged to dig the ball up, straight onto Abi's racket, which she pummelled away for a volley winner.

40–0.

While Abi clenched her fist and gestured to the roaring crowd, Renate watched the ball land in the open court and clutched the back of her hamstring. There was a more noticeable limp as she trudged back to the baseline and Abi wondered if she had aggravated her injury, or was she just playing mind games again?

Taking her time before serving, Abi went for her towel, even though she didn't need it, turned her back, counted to ten again, shouted, 'Come on!' to herself and stepped up. She was going to serve straight at Renate, giving her no space to swing. And she did just that.

Mission accomplished. Renate hurtled after the stop volley but couldn't reach it, even with her impressive wingspan. The umpire called the score. 'Game, Miss Patterson. She leads by three games to one in the second set and by one set to love.' The crowd had gone wild. Renate stood in the middle of the court, hands on hips, head down, before walking slowly to the net to speak to the umpire. Abi waited patiently, heart racing.

'I cannot continue. My hamstring is too painful; it is restricting me to run. I am retiring from the match.'

Abi had moved up the court to hear what was being said but knew she had to wait for the umpire to make the official announcement. She hoped her face wasn't giving her away, but slowly she realised that she was about to become a Wimbledon finalist.

'Ladies and gentlemen. Due to injury, Miss van Cutsem is retiring from the match. Game, set and match, Miss Patterson.'

The crowd went feral with glee.

Abi walked slowly to the net to shake hands. 'I hope it's not too serious and that you recover quickly.'

Renate, ungracious as ever, proffered the quickest and limpest handshake that barely touched Abi. 'You know I would have won if I hadn't hurt my leg. You got lucky, little Miss Wild Card.'

Chapter 32

THEN

Abi slammed the door of her car and looked across the neat row of tennis courts to see if her students had arrived. She tipped her sunglasses down from the top of her head, tugging them from her hair, where they'd become tangled up while she was driving. She should get her hair cut, have something more grown-up, like Georgie's chic bob. But she didn't want short hair and she loved the colour of hers, flecked with copper to match her freckles. And anyway, she told herself, long hair was easier to tie back neatly than mid-length. She hadn't spent all that time teaching herself various plaits, done blind with her hands behind her back, to chop the whole lot off now. She yanked at the shades, resting them on her nose, and reached into her pocket for her phone.

Texting them would be easier than looking for her students around the courts, she figured. Her home screen displayed a text from sixteen-year-old Robbie, who was away at a football match with his mate Felix and the rest of the team.

> Got here no probs, thank you for the amazing lunch. Felix v jel. Hope today good Xo

Abi smiled, pleased that her packed lunches – a pale imitation of Barb and Grannie Annie's – always went down so well. She was equally pleased that Robbie was OK, off doing his own thing, not feeling obliged to traipse around after her but following his own sporting passion on a weekend.

'Miss Patterson!' came a voice from the other side of the car park.

'Jess!' she said, smiling at one of her young players, approaching her with a wave. 'Great to see you. How are you feeling?'

'All good, Miss P,' Jess replied. 'Gorgeous day.'

'Isn't it?' said Abi, glancing across at the hubbub of players, coaches, supporters and general organising adults. 'See you in the clubhouse in ten? Will you tell the others if you see them in the locker room?' she continued.

As she spoke, she caught sight of something she had noticed once or twice before. A young player, early teens just like Jess, talking to her coach – a man a good twenty years older than her. As they walked in the direction of the clubhouse, there was something about the closeness between their bodies that set Abi's senses tingling.

The coach's hand in the small of the young woman's back, closer than any teacher would be allowed in a classroom or any other setting. The way he was leaning down to speak in her ear, his mouth only an inch or so from her face. They were outside; there was no need to whisper. But the way he was imposing his physicality on hers was unmistakable. Abi followed them with her eyes, watching the young woman twist her body, trying to create space between them as they walked.

She had been that girl, unsure what to do with the attention she was receiving. Unsure if the attention was even for her or for her game. Doubting its sincerity, fearing its power, longing for its approval. Oh, how that sort of attention had bent and shaped her identity. And for how long.

The first time she had seen the dynamic elsewhere, she had almost gasped, having to take herself to the bathroom and splash her face with cold water, reminding herself that she was an adult now, that she was only noticing it because she was safe, no longer a beacon for that sort of older male gaze. The second time, the truth started to set in: it had never been her fault. She hadn't done anything to make a man unable to control himself. The third time, she realised it wasn't even that uncommon. After that, she saw that she was in a position if not to be able to save her past self, then at least to keep an eye out for any future versions.

'Excuse me!' she called out to the young woman. After she called out once more, the girl eventually looked round.

'Hey,' she replied with a shy smile. Was that relief on her face?

'Hi – and sorry for interrupting,' she said to the coach who was now glowering at her. 'I thought for a minute you were one of my old students. Emma Keane?'

'No, that's not me,' said the young woman.

'Oh, my mistake – you look so similar, and I was wondering how she was getting along only the other day.'

And with that, Abi kept up her chit-chat with the young player, all the way to the locker room, where she handed over her business card.

'Just in case,' she said, keeping her tone breezy. 'I've been mentoring young women on the tennis scene for a while now. You know, girl stuff, if you ever need someone to talk to in confidence. No pressure, it's just I know that sometimes there are things it's not so easy to talk to a male coach about. So, if you ever need to, well, I'm around. Looking forward to seeing you play later!'

She left it at that. But she had done the same or similar on a handful of occasions since. Because once Abi had realised the abuse of power she had suffered, she didn't want any other players to go through the same. And this was her way of helping to ensure that other young players' spirits were not crushed along the way.

Chapter 33

NOW

Abi's hands were shaking as she tried to stuff her belongings into her bag, before waving to the crowd – all of whom were still roaring with delight for her. The sound of thousands of voices, hands and feet blurred into a sort of white noise, like the buzz of static she sometimes heard as she was waking from a dream.

But this wasn't a dream. She wasn't going to wake up. She was here. She was a finalist.

She repeated this to herself, before she stood up with her racket bag over her shoulder, giving one last wave to the sea of smiling faces looking her way. She tried to make sure that she caught the eye of as many enthusiastic youngsters as she could. But while she was doing it, she was also scanning, checking, listening out for Cole.

It was – thankfully – almost impossible to make out any of the individuals, let alone find one she hadn't seen for decades. She would have to hope that he wasn't there, that he had realised the error of his ways and wasn't going to make waves.

Because Abi's common sense told her that causing trouble for her was surely likely to cause trouble for himself too.

She headed back to the dressing room, wanting to text Robbie, to send a little flurry of WhatsApps, letting her friends know that she was through ... before she realised that they had all been there, or at the very least, watching. They all knew. She felt unsure how to adapt to such unblemished good news and chose to hide in the dressing room as long as she needed. Barb would never forgive her if she rushed, anyway.

Renate was already leaving the dressing room as Abi headed in. Her hair was still wet, her chin lifted, gaze averted. She wasn't interested in acknowledging Abi – nor, Abi suspected, in acknowledging the fact that she had been losing the match to a newcomer. Oh, well. Abi had come across enough haughty teenagers in her time as a coach not to be intimidated by Renate's theatrics.

Abi flopped herself down on the plush seating in the dressing room, having asked one of the staff to prepare her an ice bath. Her phone buzzed, with the one name she wanted to see on it. Robbie.

'MUM! You did it! OMG, you're in the final!' There was the sound of a whooping nurse in the background. 'It was amazing. We all watched it on the ward; you had that Renate *on the ropes*!'

Abi laughed, mumbling thanks and trying to shout down the phone to the nurses, 'You look after my boy! And thank you for all the good wishes!'

'But listen – you have to turn the TV on now. They've got a load of Summershall kids on there – Jess, Laura, and some faces we haven't seen for years!'

Robbie was right. Abi ended the call and turned to the plasma TV on the wall, showing the same stream that she had seen her son on only two days ago. Had it really only been two days? It felt like a lifetime. Today, Sarah Jones had managed to find a group of Abi's previous students in the crowds. Of course she had. How extraordinary, she thought, forgetting where she was, entranced by seeing their faces on screen. The hours she had spent watching them over the years, and now they were watching her. They were kids only Robbie's age, some even younger, now standing together on Murray Mound, grinning as they listened to each other recount memories of being under her tutelage.

'She's a really good coach,' said a gawky boy she remembered as having been a spindly twelve-year-old only a couple of years ago. 'But she really loves winning.'

The group descended into giggles. 'It's true!' said one of the girls. Abi instantly remembered Emma, a young player who had been bursting with talent but crippled by a lack of confidence. 'But she loved us winning too. Seriously, she was, like, the most encouraging person ever.'

Abi put her head in her hands and felt the warmth of her own tears as they trickled down her cheeks.

'So do you guys reckon she has got it in her to go all the way?' asked the reporter.

'One hundred per cent.'

'Yep, she can do it.'

'We all really want that for her.'

Sarah Jones turned to camera to wrap up her piece.

'There we have it – a vote of confidence from some of the few people we've managed to find who actually know Abigail Patterson as a player and a coach, all of whom are one hundred per cent behind her.'

Just as Abi thought she might dissolve entirely into tears, she was told her ice bath was ready. By the time she had taken it, followed by a warm shower under the multiple jets of the club's deluxe suite, the roving reporter was elsewhere in the grounds.

Abi had her head tipped upside down when she first heard his name again. She was running a wide-toothed comb from the back of her scalp to the ends of her hair, waiting for her leave-in conditioner to work its magic, when she caught the end of the reporter's sentence. '…Cole Connolly, who is here with us now.'

She flipped her hair back, leaving a spray of water from her hair across one of the mirrors. The sight of Cole's face on the huge screen made the shock of the ice bath feel like a pleasant memory.

'So you coached Abi as a teenager?' Sarah Jones was asking, but Abi barely heard the reply.

There he was. In a pair of navy chinos and a slightly too-small sports jacket. He was, mortifyingly, wearing a Wimbledon baseball cap, presumably to keep his balding scalp out of the sun. But, from beneath it, he was still grinning. The confident curl to his lip as he smiled. That lupine smirk. The twinkle in his eye that was always just one millimetre from sarcastic, mocking.

The comb fell from Abi's hand. She shook herself, determined not to get lost in the interview. Cole seemed to be burbling on about what he had taught her back in the day, the reporter nodding along, lapping it up. But Cole had apparently forgotten the biggest lesson he had ever taught her: that she owed her talent to no one, and she made her own luck.

Abi grabbed her phone, her first instinct to text Georgie and let her know he was here, and he was talking. But just as she moved to type, a message arrived.

Seen it. Seen him. On it. On my way round to you too. Do NOT lose your nerve. G xx

As she was about to shove the phone in her pocket, a message came through from Max.

Am outside. Ready to take you to press. Georgie sorting media statement now. Xxx

Abi all but ran to the door, and straight into Max's arms.

'Abigail Patterson, you superstar!' he whooped, but Abi had almost forgotten the match, and was still shaking from seeing Cole on that huge screen.

'He's here,' she said. 'Cole is here.' And as she said it, she realised that she had never really had a proper conversation with Max about Cole. About what had really gone on. About what it had done to her. For years, he had been the great unspoken ravine, the unsurpassable gap that had kept them from getting as close as she had longed to be. Now, here she was, burbling in a corridor about him on the way to the media centre.

Max grabbed her arm. He pulled her to the side, so her back was against the wall and he was looking at her straight on, his face hidden from view of anyone passing by – but all that she could look at.

'Listen to me, Abi, you have just become a Wimbledon finalist. This is a dream you have held for a lifetime. And it is within your grasp. No one else got you here. Not Robbie and his form-filling. Although he did deserve a bit of credit for kick-starting it all. Not Barb and her diet plan. Not Cole and his training. *Especially* not him. *You* did this. It is *your* day. Embrace it.'

Abi felt the warmth of his hands on her upper arms. She could feel his breath on her face as he spoke, barely more than a whisper. But she didn't want to move. She knew he was right. She nodded, glad she had just had a shower. They hadn't been so physically close in years.

'I mean it, Abi. That guy is nothing. He was a bully, he always was.'

And as he said it, his head nodding emphatically, the same dark curl she had seen a thousand times flopped over one eyebrow. Exactly the same as Robbie's hair so often did.

For all of her son's life, Abi had never considered that anyone but Cole could have been Robbie's father. But now, with Max as close to her as he had been since that night so long ago, she realised how blind she had been. She knew that she was going to have to talk about a paternity test with him in the coming days, but as she watched that curl fall, she also knew that she barely needed a DNA test. But now she was in a situation more precarious than ever before: to be free from Cole forever, she had to confront her demons and tell both Max and Robbie what she now suspected was the truth – and face the possibility of detonating those relationships.

'Do you promise me, Abi?'

For a moment, she had stopped hearing what Max was saying, lost in her own panic. But as she watched his hand move that stray curl up and off his face, she felt two things above all else. That at last she was ready to admit to herself that she longed to kiss him, and that she had to stop panicking about Cole for long enough to get through this press conference and to focus on the final.

'I promise you,' she replied. 'He's nothing.'

'You got it.' He kissed her on the cheek. She could feel it

burning as he turned and led her down the corridor towards the media centre. 'Now, I've just listened in on Renate's media round, and don't worry, it isn't anything you can't handle. She was pretty blunt about the fact that she is sure she would have won if she hadn't been injured. So that's going to come back to you. But you can handle this.'

Abi nodded, suddenly very hungry. 'Gee, thanks, Renate.'

'You know what she's like, she hates losing so she was trying to own the fact that she didn't actually lose. No one wants to fuck up making it to the Wimbledon final, so she's trying to spin it that she didn't actually fuck up.'

'Fair enough,' said Abi, wondering if she had the courage to be as blunt about her own fuck-ups, while Max led her into the room.

The press conference went almost exactly as he had predicted. He stood at the side of the room out of shot, as did the All England Club moderator. The first few questions were celebratory, asking if she'd ever imagined such a turn of events, what she might do to prepare, how she felt about each of her two potential opponents in the final. Then, as expected, came a sly little query about what Renate had said. She saw Max's shoulders stiffen in her peripheral vision, but Abi actually felt pretty relaxed. She only had to tell the truth, so she did.

'I can't comment on Renate's language – I wasn't aware that she had a problem until she brought the trainer on at the end of the first set. I hope she makes a quick recovery, but I'm focusing on my game. I'm playing really well, I have a lot of variety in my game and I guess that might have been a challenge as there aren't a lot of my matches on record for players to study. It's a big advantage that the players here don't know me.'

She paused for a moment, feeling in control of things for the first time since her match had ended.

'I guess I am your genuine wild card.'

There was a ripple of laughter through the room, and as Abi glanced over and saw Max beaming with pride at her, she felt a surge of confidence. She deserved to be here, and he was right, she had got herself here. Each small decision, from going back to Summershall when Robbie was a baby to raising a son who cared enough to have fought for that wild-card place for her, had been a step towards today. At last.

'Time for one last question . . .' said the moderator.

Abi's eyes scanned the room to see who had raised their hand. She noticed the reporter she recognised from the last week, and felt a small lurch in the pit of her stomach. Did she trust her? The moderator nodded at her and she started to speak.

'I was interviewing some of the kids you yourself have coached over the years, and also had the chance to speak to your own former coach Cole Connolly. I know your path to the final has not been a conventional one, so I was wondering if there were any mentors – Cole himself, or anyone else along the way – who you'd like to acknowledge? Your journey has been such an inspiration to so many – like you say, you're a true wild card – so our viewers would love to hear more about the people who helped to hone your game over the years.'

When Abi realised where the reporter was going with her questions, she thought she might hear that rushing in her ears again. The sound of true panic. Instead, this time it felt as if the entire room had fallen more silent than ever. She patted her hair, still damp from the shower, and put her hand up to her locket, once more around her neck. Then, at last, she took a deep breath and decided that a place in the final was worth nothing if it came at the cost of even more lies. Not for her, and not for the girls who might come after her.

'Thank you for your question,' she said, sneaking a quick glimpse over to Max, who was looking directly at her, nodding softly, encouraging her. 'It was great to see you speaking to some of my old students earlier. I have learned so much from coaching over the years, not least from their imagination and confidence. And yes, there are a couple of people I would love to thank.'

Another breath. She could do this. For them, for the girls who might come after her.

'First of all, I should pay tribute to the love and support that I received from my family over the years. My parents died when I was twelve and my grandparents took over the reins of bringing up a tennis-obsessed kid and they did an amazing job.

'I have also been incredibly lucky with my team, which is largely made up of people I knew back as a junior on the circuit. An important figure during that time was Barb Blackwood, who was the mother figure I didn't know I needed, and she has played a huge part in getting hundreds of kids to play tennis over the years.

'As for coaching. Yes, I did once work with Cole Connolly. And yes, I would like to take this opportunity to thank him. To thank him for teaching me exactly how not to coach. I am reluctant to dwell on the negative experiences of my past today; my absolute focus now has to be on Saturday. But it would be a lie to say anything beyond the fact that working with him was not a happy period of my life, and nor is it one that I would recommend to any other young women hoping to reach the top of the game.'

The silence in the room was broken by a couple of gasps, then the sound of rustling as people reached for phones and further notes, looking to check out who this man was. But Abi was now undeterred, determined to say her piece. She had spent enough time wondering if she should have spoken out sooner, fretting that there were other girls she could have – should have – protected, so she couldn't stop now.

As she drew breath, she saw that every eye in the room was now on her, including Max's. But, for once, she didn't look across to check for his approval before speaking. Because at last she truly believed that she had survived her experience with Cole, and she was going to make sure that neither Cole nor any other such coach could do this to anyone else. No one was more surprised than her, but, yes, today she finally felt strong enough to look that part of her past square in the eye and not just face it, but try to change it.

'If there is a coach who deserves praise from me, it is Mrs Rosie Forbes, who I worked with when my son was very young. She was hugely encouraging to me at a time when I had been written off by many. But she saw potential when I had lost hope, and she always saw me as a whole person, not just a tennis player, and I learned so much from her.'

Abi felt the power of that last half-sentence ripple through the room, reporters reaching to post social media updates and grab her attention – desperate for more details. Over half the room now had their hand in the air, seeking out the moderator to take further questions. The other half were muttering to each other. Had they really understood what she had been implying correctly? What did this mean for the sport? And tomorrow's front pages? But Abi, for so long so paranoid about being discussed, now found them easy to ignore. Having taken control of things for the first time in what was far too long, she simply turned and smiled at Max and Georgie, who had slipped into the room, before leaving her seat and heading out of the room.

For the first few strides, neither of them said anything, until at last Max asked if Abi was OK.

'Do you know, I think I finally am,' she replied with a grin. 'I don't care what Cole thinks any more. I don't care what he says. I'm done. In fact, no, I'm not done. I'm just getting started.'

And with that Max and Georgie whooped, high-fived each other, then gave Abi an enormous hug. It was far more than a match they were now proud of her for.

Chapter 34

Twenty minutes later, Abi and Max had wound their way back up into the maze of concrete that surrounded Centre Court before, at last, emerging in the secluded players' area high up behind the royal box. As Max had predicted, they were the only ones there.

Max patted the seat next to him and handed her a bottle of water, whispering, 'We can chat later, but let's watch this live.'

Abi was more than happy to shuffle up and sit next to him, their thighs touching. Georgie was somewhere down there in the inner sanctum of the corporate areas, taking back-to-back meetings about what the next forty-eight hours might hold for Abi. There was so much hubbub out there, and it was only going to get louder between now and Saturday. So Abi had snuck off with Max, safe in the knowledge that Georgie had eyes on everything and Robbie was doing well in hospital. Cole couldn't get to her now, she realised. In speaking out, she had ensured that she would probably never hear from him again. If only she had had the strength to do so sooner – well, if only she'd had the platform.

They had missed the first set, which had been won quite emphatically by Kristy Hampton, a popular American with a ferocious forehand and a patterned bandana. The second was going with serve and Olivia 'Livi' Delgado had just whipped up a couple of aces to lead 2–1.

Max put his arm up and then round her shoulders. 'You've done an incredible thing, Patterson,' he said, smiling but looking straight ahead. 'Absolutely incredible. And you're not done yet.'

Abi wasn't sure if he was talking about her match or her press conference, but, either way, she wanted to melt into him. She felt a wave of exhaustion wash over her, and had to fight an overwhelming urge to put her head on Max's shoulder and close her eyes. Just like she used to on the train home from county matches or tournaments. Sunday night, a warm carriage, darkness closing in as the train trundled through Birmingham New Street, and there would be Max. And, just like there had been all those years ago, there was that crackle between them, the electricity that Georgie had always been right to tease her about. What did each touch mean? How far might each touch go?

This time, newly aware that everything she did might be caught by a roving lens, Abi managed not to give in to the instinct. Instead, she stared forwards, gave a quiet smile and said, 'Thank you.' They could talk more later. After this match.

Unlike the general sense of indifference that the home crowd had had for Renate van Cutsem, there was an unabashed adoration for Livi in the stands. She was one of the most charismatic players on the tour, with pop-star good looks and a smile that felt like the sun coming out. And she was one of the smaller players, a left-hander nicknamed 'the Mosquito'. When Abi asked Max why they called her that, he replied, 'She gets to everything. She's fast, and she buzzes round the court. The other players try to swat her away but they can't. So ... *Mosquito*.'

'This sounds like something you've made up to wind me up – are you *actually* telling the truth?' she asked.

'This time, I'm for real,' he said. 'You're a Wimbledon finalist – I'm not going to let you go out there and make a fool of yourself. And thank you, by the way, for crediting me with one of the tabloids' daftest nicknames. Very kind.'

Abi reasoned that the nickname wasn't all that bad; Livi was very clearly not the sort of player who stood on the baseline terrifying people. In fact, to watch her play was almost like watching her dance.

On top of this natural abundance of personality, Livi was also kitted out in unfailingly chic sportswear, and her trademark dark ponytail shone like polished wood. Her nails were alternately red, white and blue on one hand, and the green, blue and yellow of her native Brazil on the other. The minute the match started to go her way, she treated the court to flamboyant whoops of joy, and at one point Abi was convinced she was about to cartwheel. In addition to her intensely watchable on-court display, there was also a bank of international celebrities in the back row of her players' box. Then there was her rapper boyfriend, whose rippling biceps were scrawled with multiple tattoos, and whose muscly neck was supporting an array of huge gold medallions. This afternoon, he was wearing enormous shades and a T-shirt with *LIV AND LET DIE* emblazoned on the front in neon font. His earrings glinted in the sun, as did his short blond hair.

All in all, Abi started to feel less sure that she would be carrying much of a home advantage with her when she took to the court on Saturday.

'She's good,' said Max reassuringly when Abi muttered something about not having a hope in hell, 'but she's not flawless. And you know *way* more about her game than she does about yours. So we're going to have to use that. Anything is possible'

As the match ended and the crowd took to their feet, thrilled at having witnessed two such dramatic matches in a row, Abi and Max stood up to leave their seats as fast as possible. Max had already arranged to have one of the tournament's courtesy cars waiting at the players' gate for them and handed Abi his baseball cap as they left the stadium. She put her shades on and pulled the cap down over her face as the three of them criss-crossed through the amassed crowds to collect her bags from the player-services desk before jumping in the car. Now she just had to get through the evening, stepping delicately around the question of Cole and Robbie. Which of them to talk to first?

Chapter 35

Abi had already spoken to the hospital to make sure that the staff were briefed not to talk to reporters about Robbie, and that Robbie knew not to take any visitors he didn't know. Georgie had also been in touch with the hospital to alert them to potential media 'guests', as well as making sure that all key media personnel knew that all access to Abigail Patterson was to go through her. As Georgie sat at the kitchen island back at the flat, their de facto boardroom table in their de facto headquarters, what was going unsaid was the fact that Robbie might have seen the press conference himself, and might even be reaching his own conclusions about his paternity in the very near future.

The second Max got up to take a call, Georgie watched him head into the small backyard and started speaking as soon as he was out of earshot.

'I really don't think we need to worry about Cole at this point. I am quite sure he will have been taken aback by how forthright you were when speaking to the press – bloody well done by the way – and he's hardly going to want to have his actual part in your story splashed across the front pages now. I reckon he didn't think that was a risk before, and now he's realised it really might be.

'I've also made it very clear that it's me looking after you, and I am willing to bet that he *doesn't* want the Blackwood family out there raking up the reasons he stopped coaching at Bracken Lane.'

'I get it. And thank you.' Abi was twiddling nervously with the hairband she had now taken out from the end of her plait. But when she spoke, she was no longer the fretful person she had been a couple of days ago. Something in her was unfurling, setting her free. 'But if the press find out, they find out. I never said anything before because we knew he was no longer in junior coaching. But for years I have wondered if he was still out there, doing more harm.'

'Abi – you don't have to take this crusade on, certainly not this week—'

'I know. But I might not get this platform again. And the situation has changed with Robbie.'

'Have you spoken to Max yet?'

'No, not yet. There's so much at stake. This of all weeks. It's too much.'

'I hate to keep repeating myself, but I really don't think you need to worry. Especially after seeing him with you the last few days. Nothing has changed.'

'Everything has changed.'

'You know what I mean. How he feels about you. It's like the last twenty years never happened.'

'But they did and it's just not a can of worms I think I can open before Saturday. The fallout could spread too far.'

'As long as you do. I can't stand much more of him mooning over you.'

Abi flushed. The women stared at each other. Yet again, something that had gone unspoken for all too long had now been said.

'And nor can my mum!' said Georgie with a giggle. 'Honestly, she's been going on about it for bloody ever.'

Abi gave her a friend a shove. 'Do I not have *enough* on this week?' she muttered, to an eye roll from Georgie.

Within minutes, they were back to strategising about the next day or so, Max back in with them moments later. But the anticipation about what on earth to say to him continued to grow inside Abi, a bubble that might burst at any point.

Focus, Abi, focus . . .

There was a lot about Livi Delgado that was potentially challenging, not least the fact that she was a leftie. And Georgie in particular was determined that Abi would not be thrown by this when play began on Saturday. They couldn't do much about the ridiculous dances that her TikTok fans would almost certainly be performing in their seats, inevitably taking up time and sapping concentration on court. And they couldn't do much about the intimidating bank of celebrities who usually turned up to watch her play, creating a flurry of camera shutters to whir when they took to their feet to celebrate her winning shots. But they could practise with someone who had a similar playing style, and they intended to make that a priority for the next day.

'Seriously – tomorrow we are in the business of getting to know whatever we can about the Mosquito,' said Georgie, with Max listening in.

'What isn't there to know about someone who seems to spend their whole life online?'

Abi was referring to her forthcoming opponent Livi Delgado's fifty million TikTok followers. The Brazilian superstar was perhaps the biggest of the next generation of sporting mega-brands. Having had a social media presence for the best part of a decade already, Delgado had an instinctive gift for showmanship both on court and online, which had created a legion of devoted fans who weren't just rooting for her to win, but also enjoyed copying her celebratory dance moves in their own TikTok accounts, buying whichever kit she was endorsing that year (always a glitzy white and gold that gleamed against her tan, regardless of the sponsor) and following every development in her very public romance with rap icon Big Mo.

They were the king and queen of the digital generation, which in turn made her a favourite of the big brands. She was an endorser's dream ticket – but, worst of all, instead of letting it divert her from the job in hand, Livi seemed to be able to make this unique relationship with her fandom fuel her, the sheer energy of their interaction creating relentless distraction for her opponents. It wasn't just the noise, but the glint of her earrings, the weight of Mo's presence as a spectator and, of course, her irrepressible vitality on court. Time after time, it left opponents seeming old, out of touch, a little plodding. And those were opponents who had thus far been more or less her own age, rather than fifteen years older.

But Abi knew all this, and Georgie knew her friend well enough to understand that she didn't need anyone in her close-knit team to keep banging on about it. What they needed to do was to discuss strategy for overcoming it, rather than to rehash the problems it might cause.

'At least you're not going to be in for any surprises,' offered Georgie.

'I guess not, even if she does make me feel like the maiden aunt of Centre Court.'

Georgie let out a snort of laughter at this image. 'What she's got in online presence and frankly bonkers super-fans, you have in experience.'

'But it's not Centre-Court experience, is it.'

'Does it matter? Really? You can only play the ball, not the personality. Or the ranking. How many times have I heard you say that over the years?'

'True.'

'Of course it's true! I got that little gem from you! Hampshire v Berkshire 1998!'

'Fair play. I was wise before my time.'

'Too damn right, and now's the time to use it. You really just have to get used to playing a leftie for a while tomorrow and the rest is going to be a case of holding your nerve.'

Georgie also explained to Abi that as well as getting a leftie lined up for her to practise with later in the day, the best way to spend Friday morning would be to do a complete 'run-through' of what would happen on Saturday, in order to get the whole plan as foolproof as possible and to help settle Abi's inevitable nerves. From what time they should book a car to leave the house, to how big breakfast should be, to how long she would need in the warm-up area and on the practice court.

Once they had agreed on a schedule for the morning, booked in an appropriate hitting partner from the list at the practice-court desk and sent a quick message to Robbie to let him know their plans, they all headed to their bedrooms, hoping that adrenaline would not prevent too much sleep.

*

To her credit, Georgie's plans for Friday ran almost like clockwork. There wasn't a peep from Cole, the press were kept away from Robbie, and Max was able to work his magic with sponsors. In a strange way, it started to feel like any other pre-match day, the three of them keeping their heads down and getting on with things.

Apart from, of course, the tsunami of hype and goodwill that was coming Abi's way from the outside world.

Celebrities from both the sporting and entertainment world, and a handful of politicians, including the prime minister, were getting in touch via social media. 'Desperate to be attached to your success,' said Georgie dismissively about anyone who had contacted her publicly. She discreetly slid over a list of names who had been in touch personally.

There was also a file of asks from people she barely knew for tickets to the final, alongside bouquets of flowers from the sports minister, a Hollywood A-lister and the chairman of the All England Club, as well as bottles of champagne delivered to Player Services from various news outlets and random fans.

And it didn't end there. There were seemingly endless gifts of toiletries, clothing, jewellery and even an iPad and headphones from brands keen to be associated with her winning streak, alongside real offers of racket and clothing deals that were springing up apparently by the hour. Best of all was the small package with a tiny lavender pillow from an elderly neighbour left on the doorstep of their rented flat 'to help you have a good sleep tonight'.

The media were still frothing with anticipation, with interview requests from daily and Sunday papers mounting up, and her local paper and radio station, as well as all the national broadcasters, each looking for an exclusive. She even had her pick of the chat shows, should she want to do some more glamorous slots.

Despite all this, something continuing to nag at Abi was the way that she hadn't had a second alone with Max. Yes, it had been cosy up there watching the match. But they'd been surrounded by people, even if it had felt like it had been just the two of them. And it had been this way for so long, since before the tournament had even started. He was trying to work on US time as well as being constantly available to her, and they both seemed to be surrounded by people – endlessly. Abi would catch his eye from time to time: in the car, in a hastily held meeting in the club room at the All England Club, and even across the room while Georgie was talking her through the magazine interviews she was hoping to line up. But a proper conversation, it just didn't seem possible. Just as Georgie headed out for some meetings and Abi thought there might be a moment, Max sprang up from his position at the kitchen island.

'Right. I need to head back to mine for yet another change of clothes and another bloody laptop charger as mine's given up the ghost. You going to be OK?'

'Sure. I'm exhausted actually. My head is spinning.' If only he knew that it wasn't just exhaustion causing it.

'Right, leave your phone here and take a couple of hours' nap.'

He slid his laptop into the side pocket of his overnight bag and stood up, looking as if he might be about to kiss her. He leant in, that curl bouncing forward as he reached towards her, and his phone began to ring again.

'Yep, it's me … Yes, she is …'

He blew a kiss at Abi, mouthing, 'It's about you!' before heading out. Another moment gone.

Abi closed the bedroom door behind her and began her

stretching routine to a spot of Handel. She did some of her oldest Pilates moves, the ones she had relied on time and again when Robbie had been a fractious toddler and she'd needed to remind her body that she hadn't forgotten about it altogether. She let her breath take over as she slid from move to move, counting how long she held each position for, trying to clear her mind of everything but how each muscle felt, how strong her heart was, carrying the fresh blood to every inch of her body, how ready she was for whatever tomorrow brought.

You have the strength for this. Know you do.

And for the first time, Abi had a sense that rather than trying to persuade herself, she genuinely believed it.

A two-hour nap, a final huge breath and she was ready to leave the calm of her bedroom for the dining table in the open-plan kitchen. Despite her reservations about making chit-chat when her mind was buzzing like it was, dinner with the gang proved to be exactly what she needed. Max and Georgie were back, and Barb – who had proved unable to surrender her position in the inner sanctum – had stayed for the meal, and Abi was genuinely glad of the chance to thank her in person. The spread of delicious grains, roasted veg, organic chicken fillets and a side bowl of pomegranate seeds ('for bejewelling') was exactly what her body needed, and none of them could deny that Barb's new-found talents as a nutritionist meant absolutely no scrimping on flavour. She had been so far ahead of the curve when they were kids, endlessly marinading halloumi and doing new things with tahini, that Abi and Georgie had laughed at her new concoctions more often than not. It was Barb who had had the last laugh, though – looking fantastic on it and charging a fortune to jet-set clients.

Just as Barb was bringing a bowl of extra-dark chocolate and berries to the table, Robbie FaceTimed from hospital, causing all four of them to crouch around Abi's iPad, grinning and waving like relatives on Christmas Day.

'How are you doing? You bored yet?' asked Max. 'Console come in handy.'

'Are you eating properly?' asked Barb. 'It'll help so much with faster healing!'

'No strange visitors?' asked Georgie. All three of them were talking over each other, and Robbie eventually managed to calm them down.

'Jeez, guys – no need for the third degree!'

'Rob, are you really OK?' asked Abi in a steady, serious voice. Her right hand was lifted to her neck, fiddling with her locket.

'I am, Mum, and the good news is they're going to let me out tomorrow.'

'For real? Can you come to the match?'

'Well, that's why I was calling – I don't know when they'll let me go. Have to get the once-over in the morning. I want to be there for you, but I just don't know if I'll make it in time.'

Barb's eyes lit up. Perhaps, after all this time, she really *was* going to get her seat in the players' box at a Wimbledon final.

'Darling, don't think about me at all. If you want to come, come. If you want to rest, rest.'

Out of the corner of her eye, she could see Max and Georgie muttering to each other, strategising.

'I'll do my best, but I don't want to disrupt…' said Robbie.

Max leant his head into shot, smiling at the younger man. 'Rob, don't worry about it – we'll make sure Security know you might, you might not. Let's keep everyone safe and well, eh? Your mum likes to pretend she's all about the big wins, but not at any cost.'

'Thanks, Max, thank you – for everything.'

Max high-fived the iPad screen, then blew a goofy kiss, which Robbie chuckled at before returning his attention to Abi, who was still trying to hide the way her heart was galloping after that interaction between Robbie and Max.

'Goodnight, darling. Rest up. I love you.'

'And you, Mum – I'll be thinking about you all day tomorrow!'

Then, just as the call ended and the evening looked as if it might lapse into another round of thank yous and well dones, Georgie started to reminisce about how Barb's business had started – which in turn led to the four adults exchanging memories about key characters at Bracken Lane over the years.

There was Miles Minihane, the retired Coldstream Guard who had had a soft spot for Barb, a passion for discussing his time with the military in Belize, and who'd waged a years-long campaign to turn Bracken Lane into a haven for Real tennis players. His mantra had been: 'Real tennis is the sport of kings, but we all deserve to play it!'

Then there had been Barb's great rival, Dotty Lambert, who was far better at tennis than Barb had ever been, but had been cursed with catastrophic organisational skills. The girls had never recovered from the Christmas do at which they had spotted her wearing a devastating backless silk dress which owed more than a little to vintage Pucci – with odd metallic-leather shoes. 'One silver, one gold? HOW did she not notice?' Georgie had managed to gasp before collapsing into further giggles at the memory of Dotty gamely trying to dance with one leg slightly shorter than the other.

And so it continued, with Barb sharing confidences about the extramarital high jinks some of the parents had got up to, and then Georgie finally confessing the truth about the summer barbecue where she had spiked the 'Pimm's Punch' with extra vodka.

As they wiped their eyes, their sides aching from laughter, Abi knew with overwhelming certainty that she had never felt safer than in this company. Yes, the path of friendship had been far from easy, but it truly had endured. Each of them danced deftly around the topic of Cole, each as determined as the other to keep him from entering Abi's headspace in any way. Because he didn't matter right now – instead, all of them, instinctively, were celebrating how far they had come, and how much tomorrow would mean to each of them.

It was Georgie who decided to break up the party, announcing that she was heading for a shower and an early night.

'As for you, young lady, I don't want you to be far behind me, please!' she said with a flourish as she left the room. The similarity to Barb was unmistakable, thought Abi with a quiet smile.

The room fell quiet for a minute, before Max's phone buzzed and he headed out of the room, talking business as ever. Abi helped Barb load her catering equipment into the back of her car, before turning off the lights and heading to her bedroom. She could hear that the shower was no longer running as she pottered around her room, then she made her way to the bathroom with a towel wrapped around her.

Only a few hours till she'd be back in the luxury of the seeded players' dressing room, with its deep ice baths and state-of-the-art facilities, she thought as she went to open the bathroom door, only for it to pull away from her as she reached for the handle.

'Oh God, sorry!' said Max, who was emerging just as she was going in.

For a second, the two of them were standing under the unforgiving light of the bathroom fixture, Abi in nothing but a towel. She was reminded of the night after they had been to donate blood as teenagers. How could time have moved so fast and yet so slowly? She felt like exactly the same girl who had stood before Max that night, barely daring to reach for the love she feared she might be imagining. Yet the existence of Robbie, the scars her body now bore, and the knowledge that tomorrow she would be playing on Centre Court in front of a global audience rather than enduring another grim training session with Cole – they all told a different story.

Max opened the door to let Abi in, putting a hand out as if to invite her to the sink. She suddenly felt self-conscious under the brightness of the light, even though she knew it made no sense.

'I'm heading home in a second. You all set for the morning?' he asked, turning to face her. His skin was glowing from the heat of the small bathroom. She wanted to lift that curl from his eyes as he looked down at her, but she didn't dare. She didn't dare do or say anything, for fear that if she started talking she'd never stop. It would all come tumbling out: the timings, the suspicion and, above all, the feelings. He was one of so few people in this world that she could truly trust, so Abi knew she could not jeopardise things now, for the sake of emotion.

'All good.' She smiled, convinced he might be able to see her heart hammering away inside her chest.

'Listen to me, Patterson,' said Max, as he put out his thumb and forefinger to raise her chin to face him. 'Don't go out there tomorrow and play because you think you owe us lot anything. Do you promise me that?'

'Obviously it's a team effort, though, isn't it? I wouldn't have got this far without you. I owe you guys everything.'

'But you *don't*. I want you to let go of that. I have seen you this last couple of days – you still believe that you should win to please *us*. There is a part of you still trying to right the past, but we don't need that. You've got to let that go. You owe us nothing. You owe yourself everything. You sacrificed enough back then. Tomorrow is all yours.'

Abi could feel the tears welling, but knew she couldn't let go now. One more day. Just one more day of holding this heavy heart full of secrets. Instead, she nodded, looking down at the mosaic bathroom floor. And when Max opened his arms for a hug, she fell into them, hiding her face against the warmth of his chest.

Tomorrow. They'd talk tomorrow.

Chapter 36

'BUT, ABOVE ALL, TODAY IS ABIGAIL PATTERSON'S DAY, AND IT DOESN'T LOOK AS IF THE CROWDS ARE GOING TO LET HER FORGET THAT.'

Abi woke with a start, memories and dreams tumbling around her. Cole … Dotty Lambert … Barb … and the warmth of Max's chest. Was that really her name being blared across the flat? Was she really waking as a Wimbledon finalist?

Yes, she was. And it was Max's fraught, 'Shit! Sorry!' as he hurriedly turned down the TV in the kitchen that yanked her back to reality. 'I think I had been sitting on the volume control; I only wanted to turn on the news!'

And today, Abi was the news.

She had slept better than at any time during the fortnight, a sense of release had flooded over her as she'd hit the pillow, acknowledging at last that there was no more she could do to prepare. The last three decades had been her preparation. Now, she just had to live it.

The three of them had a quiet, relaxed breakfast, the routine now a well-oiled machine after two weeks of repetition. Max made them omelettes in between fielding calls, and Georgie discovered with a whoop that Barb had left home-made granola in the fridge too. Robbie, as promised, wasn't bombarding them with texts, but had checked in with Max.

'Waiting for the doctor to do his rounds. Poor lad's going spare not knowing if he will get out in time, but I've told him to chill. What will be will be.'

Georgie made a face of yogic calm behind Max's back before rolling her eyes at Abi, who was relieved to let out a burst of laughter.

For the first time in days, Abi leant back in her seat as the forest green Wimbledon car ferried her out of Belvedere Villas, and towards the All England Club. What more could she do? May as well enjoy the ride, as it was unlikely to happen again, she thought as she waved at the next-door neighbour who was pretending to fill her bird feeder … As for the rest of it, those emotions were on ice for now. One thing at a time, she told herself. One thing at a time.

A couple of hours later, she was waiting outside the frosted-glass door that opened onto Centre Court. Next to Livi Delgado. Next to the Wimbledon trophies, the champions boards and those famous words from Rudyard Kipling. This time, it felt like an eternity. She had removed her headphones way too soon and was pretty sure that, as a result, she could actually hear her stomach churning. Her mouth was dry. Her legs were like lead. And she stuck her hands in her jacket pockets to stop them from shaking.

Livi, meanwhile, was bouncing around on the marble-floored foyer as if she was the most enthusiastic guest at a silent disco

– arms above her head, hips swaying, jewellery jangling. Her shocking-pink headphones were still blasting music at her. Had it been 'Livin' la Vida Loca' Abi had heard as she'd put them on? Kind of cheesy, she thought. Abi couldn't help but notice the huge diamond ring on her right hand and wondered if it was a gift from her Big Mo and whether she would take it off to play the match.

She knew she should be focusing on herself, but her thoughts were apparently doing their own thing. For a change, she decided not to berate herself for this – after all, it really was impossible to avoid this curly-haired bundle of energy who seemed to have not a care in the world. It was almost thrilling to see someone this age so self-assured, so excited by doing her thing. She seemed to find sheer pleasure in every part of the game, and she had her whole life ahead of her to enjoy it. Instead of feeling jealous, Abi found it hugely empowering to see women living and loving life to the max.

Once the ball kids, line judges and umpire were all in place, the announcer called them onto court.

'Ladies and gentlemen. Please welcome the finalists for the Wimbledon ladies' singles title. From Brazil, Olivia Delgado.'

Livi literally skipped through the door, grinning broadly and waving enthusiastically to the crowd. The noise was deafening. Abi waited, wondering whether she would get a louder roar from a largely home support. Or whether she would get muted applause as the underdog, the unknown, the wild card.

As the clapping subsided, the voice boomed out again. 'And from Great Britain, Abigail Patterson.' *How very formal*, thought Abi. *Using our Sunday names again.*

She had barely finished the thought as she stepped through the doors and onto the court, nearly finding herself bowled over by the roar from the crowd. The applause was off the charts, Union Jacks were everywhere, and people were on their feet shouting her name. She waved tentatively and walked up to where Livi was waiting for her. They both turned and curtseyed in tandem to the royal box before heading to their chairs. Abi took the time to look around her, letting it all sink in. How many times had she watched these finals on TV and wondered what it felt like for the players?

She had requested the chair to the umpire's right as it was closest to the players' box, meaning she could more easily make eye contact with Georgie and Max. As she sat down, she checked out the members of the armed forces, standing proud in their military uniforms as they guarded the court. Her gaze skimmed the photographers' pit opposite her; they were already audibly clicking away. She marvelled at the size of their lenses and wondered if any of them were those who had cornered Robbie.

As she unpacked her rackets and removed her locket, the umpire called them to the net for the coin toss, which would be performed by a student from a local college. As he was presented to the crowd, Abi gave him a huge grin. He was the spitting image of Felix, one of Robbie's oldest mates, and appeared to be every bit as nervous as Abi.

'Heads or tails?' he asked Livi. Of course he asked *her*. She drew everyone's attention.

Livi smiled sweetly at him, chose heads and gave him a high five. He flushed from the neck up and dropped the coin. She bent down to pick it up and handed it back to him with a flash of her whiter-than-white teeth. Abi wondered if she had a toothpaste sponsor among her burgeoning portfolio of endorsements.

The red-faced youth managed to flick the coin in the air, catch it and slap it down on the back of his hand. 'Heads, it is,' he said, looking more than a little pleased with himself.

'I'll serve,' said Livi.

'And I'll take this end,' retorted Abi, repeating what had worked for her in the semi-finals. Choosing to have her back to the royal box so as not to be distracted during the warm-up by a front row that included the Princess of Wales and the Queen Consort, tennis legend Billie Jean King and the super-slick David Beckham. It crossed her mind that Robbie would be hyper that one of his footballing heroes was watching his mum play a tennis match. His street cred would go through the roof when he returned to his cricket club.

'Five minutes, ladies…'

The umpire set his timer and Livi fired the first ball down the middle of the court.

The warm-up passed without incident. Everything felt surprisingly relaxed, that sense of release she had felt on the way returning to her as she eased into the mood on Centre Court. Abi was pleased to have got a good feel for her opponent's pace and spin – as well as an uninvited introduction to the four-man boy-band in her corner, who were sporting matching white T-shirts with one gold letter on each to spell out *LIVI*, and were standing up and sitting down in unison like a well-choreographed dance troupe, singing or shouting the LIV-mania chants that had made her into a global sensation. The crowd loved them.

Where's Cliff Richard when you need him?? thought Abi, before reminding herself that being relaxed was one thing, but spending too much time distracted by her surroundings was another. Then again, if it was keeping her nerves at bay…

'Time, ladies. Prepare to play.'

She smiled at the thought of Georgie's mantra. *This is it. Play the ball, not the opponent.*

Not the occasion. Not the circus around her, Abi added, just for luck.

Abi lifted her water bottle, took a few gulps, tightened her plait and picked up her towel.

The crowd were on their feet clapping and yelling as the players jogged to their respective baselines. As the din subsided, the boy band broke into a version of 'Mickey', changing the lyrics to 'Hey Livi!'

Abi remembered hearing the Toni Basil original blaring out at one Bracken Lane Christmas do, Barb up there on the dance floor, her boobs jiggling in her low-cut silk dress.

Livi looked up in their direction before she started her service motion, waggling a finger at them with a naughty grin. She knew what she was doing. She was here to put on a show. And they were part of it.

Abi bounced around on her toes, swivelling her hips and loosening her shoulders. She had seen many newbie finalists crumble through nerves on these big occasions and was determined it wouldn't happen to her.

Pressure is a privilege, she reminded herself, echoing the words of former champion Billie Jean King, who was seated just a few feet behind her. She glanced up towards the players' box once more – her own side was noticeably empty compared to Livi's, despite the added presence of Barb. Her enormous sunglasses almost needed a seat to themselves. Was she trying to be noticed or not? She also seemed to have grown about six inches thanks to an outrageous but glamorous bun piled high on top of her head. Abi smiled, wondering how long and how much she had spent in the hairdressers to cultivate that Audrey Hepburn look. And what time had she got up?

Beyond the bun, she could see several of her protégés from the tennis club and Frank Johnstone, the coach for whom she'd worked when she'd quit playing. Everything and everyone else was a blur, but she was sure Rosie Forbes was out there somewhere too – Georgie had promised to get tickets to her. And, of course, Robbie was watching from his hospital bed, perhaps even with a passing nurse or two if they had time. But despite herself, there was one person Abi was hoping to impress more than anyone else while she was on court. And, at last, it wasn't Cole.

Cole. What a fool she'd been to let him cross her mind, even for a second. Maybe he was out there, maybe he wasn't. He was a fragment from her past and he would have no part in her future. As Max had told her last night, '*No more looking back. The future is all yours.*'

Chapter 37

The Brazilian bombshell threw the ball high in the air and struck her first serve crisply down the centre line. The final had begun. White chalk billowed up, causing the first 'Ooohs' of the match, as Abi stretched but struggled to make contact as the ball swerved away from her.

15–0.

As she moved to the other side to receive the next serve, Abi came close to the cohort of Chelsea Pensioners' resplendent in their red jackets and seated proudly in the first row. They reminded her of Grandad Bob, who would have been about their age had he lived to see this day. How proud he would have been to watch her during these championships. 'Give it your best shot,' he'd always said before a match. He'd never cared whether she won or lost, only that she had tried her hardest.

Concentrate.

Abi slapped her thigh and leant forward, twirling her racket in her hand. Livi's giant gold hoop earrings glinted in the sunlight as she reached up to smack another curling serve towards the sideline. Abi scrambled to block it back and hurled herself across the court to cover the open space. A seventeen-stroke cat-and-mouse rally ensued and though it went in Livi's favour, it was exactly what Abi needed to help her settle into the match.

The women were a contrast of playing styles and personalities, which produced an intriguing match for a noisy, appreciative crowd. Abi slicing and dicing, chipping and charging, with a single-handed backhand. She knew it was uncommon in the modern women's game, aware that the more mature commentators called it 'good old-fashioned tennis'. But it worked. And it was working.

Livi was all topspin and controlled aggression, content to roll the ball from side to side, chase every ball down and wait for an opportunity to step up the court and rattle any short balls into the corners. While Abi's winners were celebrated with a largely unnoticeable clench of her left fist, Livi's were accompanied by whoops of delight, pirouettes and exaggerated nods to the crowd. And shared on social media, of course. Livi had an entire team doing point by point live commentary on Instagram and TikTok.

The first six games went with serve, but at 3–3, Abi missed a simple volley on break point. The crowd gasped and groaned. The Chelsea Pensioners looked devastated, hands clasped across their foreheads. It was a golden opportunity to take the lead, but instead Abi had handed up Livi a 'Get Out of Jail Free' card, which she accepted gratefully and went on to lead 4–3.

The ball kids collected in the tennis balls and opened fresh cans for the ball change that was mandatory at the end of the seventh game. Abi hated new balls. They were too lively for her precision game and they were perfect for the high-bouncing groundstrokes of her opponent. She struggled to dismiss her disappointment and annoyance at wasting a golden opportunity to take the lead and immediately made a number of uncharacteristic errors. Livi took advantage of the new balls, cranking up the pace, breaking serve quickly in the next game. She celebrated with her signature 'break dance', which involved throwing her racket high into the air, spinning a full three-sixty on her left foot, clapping twice and catching the racket by the handle.

The crowd went bananas. The boy band broke into their own version of 'You're the One That I Want' for Livi, and Abi realised they had deliberately picked songs that the vast majority of an older crowd would recognise. Was this for maximum effect? To distract her? Livi really was a box-office draw and Abi briefly wished that Max had tracked down that rugby quartet from the semi-final and offered them seats today. That at least would have evened things up a little in terms of the sideshow.

While she waited for the boy band to stop, Abi turned her back on the court and her opponent, fiddling with her strings and giving herself a good talking-to. Coach Abi took over.

It's just the first set. Early days. Your tactics are sound and you're matching her from the baseline. It was just one stupid mistake.

Just one stupid mistake. Words she had said to herself time and again in her past. But the last few days had finally taught her, you could let your mistakes define you or you could learn from them and grow.

Livi was in full strut mode now. She was buzzing off the energy around the court, all flicks and spins. It was so difficult to get the ball away from her. She seemed to be everywhere – of course, her nickname was the Mosquito, Abi thought, remembering what Max had said about other players being unable to swat her away. Abi noticed that Livi had even tucked the right side of her skirt into her undershorts to showcase the tiny mosquito tattoo on her right thigh. Despite Abi's best efforts to slow her down by mixing the pace and the height of the ball, and the partisan shrieks of encouragement from the crowd, Livi powered on and took the first set 6–3.

As Abi made her way to the courtside chair, she turned to look at her team, who stood up immediately, cheering. She sat. She towelled down. She drank. She nibbled her banana. She chewed some jelly beans. She closed her eyes. For a moment, she wondered if it would come. That drawled 'Abi-gurrrl'. But it never did. She breathed a huge sigh of relief, with a silent 'thank you' to whatever forces were working in her favour, and walked slowly to the press-box end of the court to open the second set.

Yes, Livi had her fans. And they had their tactics. But what Abi hadn't counted on was the enormous goodwill and sheer volume of the crowd supporting her. They were on their feet, clapping, shouting, willing her on at every turn. On and on it went, the legions of fans apparently competing with the same intent and ferocity as the players, until the umpire, the very debonair Italian, Giorgio Carratini, had to call, 'Quiet, please,' more than once. Abi didn't care, though: the noise ringing in her ears had drowned out all thoughts of mystery voices, as well as any hope of distinguishing any individual in the crowd. It bolstered her resolve.

She nodded assertively to the ballgirl positioned under the Rolex clock and checked the four balls sent to her before selecting the two newest. The less they had been hit, the more pace they would add to her serve. 'Take advantage of all the little things that can make a big difference' was a favourite mantra of Max's, and Abi realised, once again, that he was absolutely right. Her eyes flicked towards the players' box and she was momentarily reassured by seeing him on his feet, sending one of his trademark wolf whistles in her direction. She smiled and felt a lump rising in her throat. He had always been in her corner, sticking up for her, whistling for her, making her feel good about herself.

Could she do this? Damn right she could. She hadn't been *that* far away in that first set, after all.

Playing with a renewed purpose and taking advantage of a lapse of concentration by her opponent, Abi stormed to a 3–0 lead. Her serve was working a treat and her slice backhand was causing all sorts of problems for the queen of Tennis TikTok. At the change of ends, Livi brought out a bandana, white with gold stars dotted around it. She made a big drama out of putting it on, standing up as she did so and encouraging the crowd to show their appreciation. Abi felt like a weary coach, waiting for a teenager. She covered her head with her towel and blocked out the sideshow.

Livi sprinted to the baseline before the umpire called 'time'. There, she treated the crowd to another of her trademark moves while she had their full attention. The ballboy in the left-hand corner had thrown her two balls. It was her turn to serve after all. She proceeded to bump one ball up into the air to play keepy-uppy with her racket, her feet and her head. Cue thunderous applause, which totally overshadowed Abi's return to the court and would surely make the highlights reel. Abi marvelled at her opponent's confidence and ability to work the crowd. Oh, to have had that level of self-assurance at twenty. Instead, she had been wrangling with potty training.

Livi may have set out to distract Abi and swing some sectors of the crowd in her favour, but her antics proved only to have distracted herself. Two double faults in the next game and she found herself trailing 4–0. She screwed up her face in disgust and cracked her white-and-gold racket – or as she preferred to call it, 'the wand' – into the grass. The crowd tutted and shifted in their seats, sensing an opportunity for the underdog.

Abi sensed the opportunity too. She had a two-break cushion. Simple? This was Wimbledon. The final. Abi tried to remain calm as Livi unravelled, her timing and her confidence had deserted her, as had the boy band, who seemed to have taken an ill-timed Pimm's break.

Big Mo looked petulant. He sat with his muscular arms crossed over his white leather waistcoat, which Abi was pretty sure squeaked when he moved. Beneath it was a black vest and on top of that was his gold medallion with thick gold chains. Abi noticed Livi look up in his direction – he barked something at her in Portuguese and she pointed a manicured finger at him. Even her nail polish was white.

Abi scanned back to Max, seated just six seats away from Big Mo. She felt a glow at knowing that twenty years of shared history worked better. She knew he was gunning for her, even as he sat there, the epitome of transcontinental cool. That instant of shared eye contact was all it took – she wrapped up the second set 6–1 and walked slowly to her chair, soaking in the moment.

'Game and second set, Miss Patterson, by six games to one.'

Wow. Did that really happen? Could she win this? If Livi didn't get her act together, it was quite possible.

Control what you can control. Look after you. And your side of the court.

Abi checked her notes, devoured some jelly beans and looked at her locket, thinking of Robbie, imagining him and Max as they had plotted to get her that wild-card spot. She changed her racket. New balls. Tighter strings would help her control them. She felt her heart racing again.

Nerves are good. Shake them out. Keep moving. Smile.

Nobody and nothing could have prepared her for what she was feeling now and it was threatening to overwhelm her. She could feel it. She had spent the best part of twenty years in the tennis wilderness and had no experience on such a huge stage. A trickle of sweat crept down her back, her hands were starting to shake again. She stood up and requested a bathroom break.

Lifting her towel and armed with a fresh shirt from her kitbag, Abi headed off the court, eyes firmly on her feet. Livi decided to follow suit, eyes firmly on her team. Her coach was pumping his fist at her. Big Mo was making a heart shape with his thumbs and forefingers. The boy band were back, standing up and pointing their opened palms at her and belting out 'She's the One'.

Abi sprinted up the stairs, followed by a tournament official, and into one of the private cubicles in the locker room. Stripping off her sweaty top, she splashed water over her face and neck before looking at her image in the mirror. The sun had brought her freckles out and her mascara had smudged slightly where she had rubbed an eye. She was still slightly out of breath after legging it up the stairs, and as she stared back at her reflection, she saw a woman she never would have dared dream she could become. Just that one glimpse of that woman left her empowered, determined and ready to do battle again.

Fresh shirt. Fresh start. She might not have much experience on Centre Court, but she had experience at life. Who was to say that she didn't have the nerve for it when she had had the nerve to bring up a baby despite the sniggers of her one-time peers. Was she really expected to *care* that Livi could do a cool dance when she knew that she could change a nappy while taking a call from a coach and still make it to training on time twenty minutes later? Was she supposed to feel *nervous* about an international audience when she'd had the most painful of rejections, not just from the man she'd thought had loved her, but from her entire social circle, and, for a time, from the game she loved? While still having the guts to make it back here? *As if…*

Abi pushed any stray hairs back into the twists of her plait as she walked back down the stairs and out onto the court. She took deep breaths – in through the nose, out through the mouth, just as Barb's yoga teacher had taught her all those years ago when she and Georgie were subjected to yet another of her mother's efforts to 'gain an edge over the opposition'.

She was done with nerves. She was done with telling herself this was her 'one big shot'. She was done with the idea that this was the end – why couldn't she have years left in her yet?

The future is all yours.

The entire crowd, including the Chelsea Pensioners, were on their feet. 'Come on, Abi, love,' one of them called as she walked past. She glanced towards him and smiled broadly as Livi made her entrance with a brand-new dress and bright-red lipstick. *Lipstick!*

Then, as she turned to look away from Livi, Abi came to face the players' box and in it, the face she had longed to see there. Robbie – being helped to his seat by Barb and Max. She knew she didn't have time to dwell, to look up at them, but even that brief glance was enough. He was safe. He had made it. They both had. Centre Court. Finals day. Together.

Abi picked up her towel and racket, and made her way to the baseline as the applause rang out around her. She stared across the net, waiting for Livi to serve with the new balls. She was, of course, taking her time – picking at her strings, then bending down to touch her toes before swishing 'the wand' in several shadow motions. Abi looked up at Georgie, who was shaking her head and mouthing, 'Oh, get on with it.' Abi giggled to herself and wondered if any cameras had picked it up.

Eventually, Livi opened up with a 120 mph ace, which she celebrated by licking her forefinger and chalking up an imaginary '1' in the air. The first game was a bit of a blur for Abi. Livi served three aces and a serve-volley combo, which prompted gasps of amazement from the crowd, then did one of her trademark pirouettes. She raised her fist in the air as she waltzed to the changeover. She was back.

The second game wasn't much better for Abi. The afternoon sun had broken through the clouds and affected her ball toss. Just one first serve on target allowed Livi to step up and take potshots off the returns. As Abi scrambled from corner to corner, she marvelled at the suddenly renewed power of her young opponent and wondered briefly what on earth she'd taken during that bathroom break.

The crowd were treated to another 'break dance' when Abi's defensive backhand sailed over the tramline.

2–0.

Round and round went Livi on her right foot before catching her racket by the handle and dropping into a curtsey.

Abi turned her back. Counted to ten slowly. Smoothed her skirt. She suddenly felt tired. It had been a long four weeks, and it had involved more than just tennis, to say the very least.

'Stay with her, Abi!' Georgie shouted, urging her friend to hang in there, that the purple patch wouldn't last.

'Find a way, Abi!' This time, it was Max's voice, telling her exactly what she needed to hear.

Then, the words that had sustained her so many times in the past. 'Love you, Mum. You can do this!'

Abi reached for her towel and wiped her face before the cameras could zoom in on her. No more tomorrows.

Chapter 38

Abi somehow managed to hold serve in the fourth game thanks to a net cord and two outrageous drop shots, which led to a surge in support from the crowd.

When Livi slid at 3–1 and ended up doing the splits, Abi found herself hoping that might derail her, but it did the opposite. Livi held the splits position for several seconds, putting her hands on her hips as she did so and pouting towards the photographers' pit. Another Hollywood moment – just the sort of thing Max had warned her about. But that life looked as exhausting as hers had felt in its own way.

Who would want to be on show like that, all the time? Abi had had a taste of that this past week and it hadn't given her the buzz it clearly seemed to be giving Livi.

Try as she might, Abi couldn't break back. She threw herself into every point, but she always seemed to be on the run, never able to get on the front foot. It was like playing a ball machine that kept firing everything into the corners. She clung valiantly on to her own serve but found herself trailing 5–2. Livi was within a game of clinching the Wimbledon title.

But Livi wobbled. The enormity of the occasion and the crowd's last-ditch efforts to propel Abi to victory seemed to rock her confidence and her concentration. Her nerve shattered and her forehand went to pieces.

She's choking thought Abi and continued to play almost every ball to the left side of the court. Time and again it paid dividends. The crowd whooped and hollered as Abi pumped her fist repeatedly and reeled off three successive games for the loss of just one point to level at 5–5.

The crowd were on their feet. The Chelsea Pensioners looked like they might pass out. Livi bounced the ball repeatedly before lining up to serve. She had gone from being a game away from the title to being in real danger of losing. Abi, on the other hand, had gone from being a game away from defeat to being in with a real chance of winning. But in that moment, it no longer seemed to matter. She had won the bigger battle because, despite it all, she had got here, to this moment. For the rest of her life, nothing could take that away.

At the other end of the court Livi was prowling the baseline, taking her time, muttering to herself and slapping her thigh before lining up to serve.

Abi narrowed her eyes determinedly and continued to pressure the forehand corner when she could but Livi had somehow found her focus and her rhythm. Four consecutive first serves meant Abi was under pressure from the outset of each point and despite throwing every ounce of energy at the returns, she couldn't penetrate the court enough to do any damage. Livi stepped up and pummelled the short balls away with both power and accuracy, then celebrated with a twirl and her trademark '*Vamos*'. 6–5. Now Abi must serve to stay in the match.

At the changeover, Abi sat and gazed around her. The crowd

was willing her on, the stadium almost rocking. The chants, the flags, the T-shirts and the occasional calls of 'Come on, Tim!' She took a bite of banana, a couple of sugary sweet jelly beans, a swig of water and a long deep breath. *Here we go...*

Before she could toss the ball up to serve, a mobile phone went off in the crowd. The umpire called for quiet. Livi was smiling. She knew how distracting that was when you were the server and she sensed an opportunity. Abi took a deep breath and bounced the ball seven times before glaring across the net and firing down her biggest serve of the match. 117mph. 'FAULT' shouted the umpire. Her second serve was a nervy powderpuff which floated wide. An audible groan echoed round the crowd. 0–15.

Livi jumped up and down on the spot then skipped across the baseline to get ready for the next point. Abi gave herself a serious talking to, closed her eyes, shook out her shoulders and decided to serve and volley. She won the next two points with wicked slice serves and drop-dead stop volleys. 30–15

The crowd were at fever pitch. Abi felt sick. She missed her first serve and saw Livi creeping closer and closer to the service line, swishing 'the wand' and ready to swat away a weak second serve. Abi resolved not to give her that chance and whacked the serve as hard as she could down the middle. 'FAULT' cried the umpire as the ball missed the box and the crowd groaned once again. 30–30.

'Make her play' she told herself and rolled in a medium pace serve into Livi's body and rushed to the net. Up went the defensive lob from the Brazilian and Abi, sun in her eyes, scurried back to the baseline to retrieve it. When she looked up, she saw Livi had moved up the court and was preparing for a backhand drive volley. Abi gave chase and countered with the highest lob she could muster – the type that comes down with snow on it. A wonderfully entertaining 23 stroke 'cat n mouse' rally ended with the cruellest of net cords. A low chipped backhand from Abi, designed to draw her opponent up the court, hit the top of the net, rolled a couple of inches along it and dropped back on her own side. 30–40.

Match point.

Abi could hardly breathe. Her heart was pounding so hard that she felt sure it was audible, even though she could barely hear herself think. The noise had gone through the roof. She looked up at her team. She felt her eyes welling up once again and turned her back. The umpire waited for the applause to stop. Abi checked the three balls that had been thrown to her. Selected two and began her routine. She served wide to Livi's forehand but hadn't noticed that her opponent had adjusted her position in anticipation of that exact serve and was lining up to throw the kitchen sink at the return. And she did. Down the line went the forehand. Abi threw herself after the ball but couldn't reach it.

Up went the arms of the Brazilian bombshell along with a shriek of '*Vamos*!' and her customary twirl. Abi picked herself up, smoothed her skirt and walked to the net to shake hands.

'You're dynamite,' she said to Livi, and she really meant it. 'It was a joy to play against you.'

Livi's smile was mesmerising. Her whole face lit up. 'And you, Miss Abigail, will be a lifelong inspiration to me.'

Tears were welling in Abi's eyes, but the roar of the crowd seemed to carry her emotions, higher and higher, keeping the smile on her face as she turned to the players' box once more. The moment she had dreamed of so often, yet it felt like more unreal than any of those occasions. They were all there, waving, cheering, jubilant. As she looked at each of their faces, it was as if she could see their younger selves alongside them. The teenagers she had grown up with, as well as the adults who had helped her get to this stage of her life. The baby she had cradled, as well as the man he had become. And the mother figure who had always been there for her, no matter what.

The match might be over. But her future had just begun.

Chapter 39

The second the match finished, the crowd erupted into applause that left decibel levels reeling, topping anything Abi had ever heard before. The combined efforts of Livi's youthful prancing and Abi's status as the unlikely comeback kid had offered something for everyone. As Abi walked up to the Princess of Wales to collect her prize, she spotted Barb wiping tears from her eyes. It finally occurred to her that perhaps Livi's literally show-stopping antics weren't the only reason that people wanted to watch the tennis. She was no longer an impostor, an also-ran, or a has-been – she was part of the spectacle itself.

As she looked around the crowd, Abi realised that despite the result of the match, she felt as if she'd won. She beamed from ear to ear and waved to fans, as the cheers grew louder and louder. After she had packed up her bag and was ready to leave the court, she waved again, spinning round to address all four sides of the court, before stopping to sign some programmes for those seated in the front rows. Fans screamed for her towel, her sweatband and her visor. She obliged, aiming each item towards kids that she knew would be taking massive inspiration from being just feet away from a Grand Slam finalist and the hallowed turf of Centre Court. Despite offloading whatever she could into the crowd, her bag was still heavy. But her heart felt immeasurably lighter.

Livi was already showering when Abi got back to the dressing rooms – her gold jewellery was scattered across one of the beautifully upholstered leather banquettes, her phone buzzing away with notifications.

Abi pulled the band from the bottom of her braid and shook her hair out, running her hands through it. There wasn't much time to dwell. She knew she had a press conference still to go, before she could relax properly. When she glanced at her phone, messages were stacking up almost as fast as Livi's.

She plunged herself into the ice bath, feeling the contraction of blood vessels in legs that had worked so hard for this, and for so long. Moments later, in the shower, Abi felt the warmth of the water running through her long hair and down her back. The shampoo swirled around her feet towards the plughole. She reflected on how much else she had washed away this afternoon. Was this how she had long imagined coming off court would feel after a Wimbledon final? Was it what she had dreamed of as she had played Wannabe Wimbledon with Georgie, the two of them barely teenagers? Or as she had hopped on her bike to Summershall Village, leaving infant Robbie in his great-grandmother's arms? Or even last night, as she had leant into Max's warm chest?

Hardly. And, to her surprise, she wondered if perhaps this felt better than she had let herself imagine. Because for each serve, each lob, each volley, she hadn't just been playing tennis, she had felt as if she were batting away the demons of her past, the memories and fears that had flown at her time and again over the years. She had held her own, she had told the truth, she had, at last, become herself.

There was, of course, the small matter of the conversations she still had to have with Max and Robbie. God, she was dying to see Robbie, to hold him tight, to know that he was safe, recovering. But would he think she had been keeping this information from him all this time, denying him a paternal relationship he had always dreamed of? To explain the silence, she was first going to have to explain Cole, and that was going to be painful.

Abi couldn't bail out now, though. Anyway, instead of the churning in her guts leaving her paralysed by fear, she now felt galvanised. She'd seen that woman stare back at her in the closing stages of that match, she knew she couldn't let her down. She just had to keep going, to address what had been postponed for so long and to embrace it. For years she'd asked herself – what was the point in aiming for the WTA Tour again? Why dream of winning Wimbledon when you probably wouldn't even make it into the draw? And now she had her answer: she should always have tried, because sometimes it's not just about the winning. It's about what else you gained.

As if to prove it, Max was waiting for her as she stepped out of the dressing room, and pulled her into the most enormous hug as soon as he saw her. He lifted her feet clean off the ground, whispering through her loose, damp hair and into her ear, 'You're a superstar. You're a role model. What you've achieved is nothing short of miraculous. You're everything I always told you you were.'

Abi burrowed her face in his neck and never wanted to let go.

The mood in the media room was very different from the one she had left two days ago. She was treated like a victor, with the entire room standing to applaud as she entered. There wasn't a question that was not preceded with profuse congratulations for all she had achieved, and this time she had the added bonus of speaking without fear of her past being unpeeled before her eyes.

Abi wasn't sure she would have minded either way, though. After decades of feeling guarded about almost everything she said – trying to protect her son from his father, her perceived mistakes and the shame that had for so long accompanied them – she now spoke the truth with the conviction of a woman unburdened.

She happily answered questions about where she might have done better in the match, how she would train and prepare differently in the future, noting with interest that the prevailing mood in the room seemed to be that she did now have a future, that she had done well enough in this match to prove that it wasn't a mere one-off. And she answered honestly about Robbie's condition and how the best thing for him, for all of them, would now be rest and privacy.

As she looked across the room to Max, her jaw was aching from grinning. And the way he smiled back at her – well, that only intensified things. She felt herself flush. Could the rest of the room see this?

As soon as she was done with her obligations to the All England club, Abi was back in a car to the flat, only this time with Max, who warned her that the volume of press and fans outside was far larger than at any time all week. And he was right, except now they felt less predatory, more celebratory. She even wound down the window as the car approached the driveway, waving, signing autographs and admitting that she was looking forward to some rest and the safe return of her son.

None of this meant that she wasn't longing to get inside and away from the glint of sunlight on lenses, though. And when she did, she flopped onto the sofa and closed her eyes for a minute, wondering if, when she opened them, it would turn out that the last week had never happened. Instead, it was Max yelling, 'He's here!' that yanked her back into the present.

On the driveway, Georgie was opening the doors to an enormous taxi, before helping Robbie out on his crutches, while the driver retrieved a wheelchair from the back. Abi darted out of the door, arms open. She barely dared hug him in case she hurt him, but she wanted to hold him as if he were a baby.

'You made it,' she said, holding him as tight as she dared.

'No, Mum, you made it,' he replied. 'And I'm so freakin' proud of you.'

Abi felt a sense of peace for the first time all week, to see her son back, and smiling. She had come so close to losing him – in so many ways – that the day's sporting excitements almost paled into relative insignificance. He was here, on the sofa, safe, gibbering on about how he was desperate for a decent shower, a shave and to wash his hair properly.

'That hospital was so hot! I missed Barb's food, and my hair stinks!' Georgie took a sniff and declared it the truth.

Abi set about helping him to cover his wound and its dressing with the bizarre rubber thigh-high sock he had been sent home with for the purposes of bathing, before dispatching Max to help Robbie if needed. As they hobbled off down the corridor, the women could hear them laughing, the burr of their voices rumbling over the sound of the running water. Abi wanted it to last forever.

Max seemed not to have a care in the world, chuckling at Robbie's indignity, momentarily free from the avalanche of phone calls he had been taking since the minute they had returned. Now that Abi had a Grand Slam final under her belt, she had a thousand ranking points, which meant she would get into most major events on the tour. Her run of sudden success was clearly making her very attractive to tournament directors for some of the biggest and most lucrative events and they were now offering huge fees to sign her up. Then there were the clothing and racket sponsors, the TV shows, the fashion magazines and even the influencers desperate to meet her. In her own way, she was proving as popular as Livi, and was blown away by the interest, promising to get back to people once she was home and Robbie's recovery was underway.

An hour later, Robbie finally emerged, as smooth-faced as the cheeky ten-year-old she used to pick up from cricket practice, with his curls still damp from the shower. He was wearing a huge pair of Max's tracksuit bottoms, the only things they had found that were loose enough not to disturb the large dressing on his leg.

Abi beamed, but part of her was still trying to fathom when – or if – there would be a good time to speak to Max. One minute she was giddy with her new-found freedom, the next, she felt perilously close to throwing it all away again.

Barb, who had arrived with more food for the gang, was finding it impossible to hide the fact that her ears were flapping as they discussed plans around her. After dinner, Abi watched as she unpacked what seemed like vast quantities of breakfast into the kitchen cupboards, only to discover the next morning that half of it was in fact for the amassed fans and photographers outside. So thoughtful, she commented, before being reminded by Georgie that several national papers were now familiar with the Barb's Bites branding and could attest to its quality. Abi couldn't help but admire the hustle.

Without the hubbub of the rest of the team, an awkwardness descended like a blanket the next day. Max was mostly working and when he was off his phone, Abi had no idea how long she would be able to hold his attention before he'd be back in business mode. The sense that she was slipping from simply 'not sharing a hunch' to actively lying was becoming all-consuming, but she couldn't find a way in to the conversation. Their chat suddenly seemed slippery; she couldn't get any purchase on the mood, or what he might be feeling, how he might respond. Last night was fading into the rear view, the closeness they had shared at risk of becoming a strong professional alliance – and one that she could be putting at risk if she didn't get talking, and soon. As Abi headed out of her bedroom, dressed ready for that evening's champions ball, Robbie and Georgie having already gone on ahead, Max was waiting for her.

'Thank you,' she said. And as her hands touched his, she realised that she couldn't live her life with a single second longer of deceit. Like a tide coming in, the confidence she had felt yesterday was returning. She had twenty minutes. Then the rest of her life.

'Listen, Max…'

'Yes.' They were walking into the living area now. Abi was too scared to sit and crease her dress, so she stood at the fridge, pressing a glass to the lever in the door to get herself some water.

'There is something we need to discuss – not work stuff – and I don't know if there is ever going to be a right time for it, but I can't hold it in any longer. I don't want to keep any more secrets from you—'

'Abi, it's OK, I know what you're going to say.'

'No, Max, I don't think you do. This isn't about me and you. Well, it is. But not like that...'

'Abi.' Max was standing by the fridge now, too. He took the glass from her hand and put it on the side. Taking her hands in his, he said, 'I know.'

'What?'

'I spent the whole night with Robbie in hospital. And, if you remember, we medical marvels rather like to tell everyone we can how special we are...'

Abi gasped, covering her mouth with her hands. She felt weightless, unburdened, the tears now so close to pouring out of her.

'I couldn't believe it when the nurse said it. I didn't know what to think. Max, you have to believe me, it was the first time I knew. The first time I'd even considered...'

'I believe you. Of course I believe you, Abi.'

'I mean, we don't know for sure. But—'

'He's mine, Abi. I'm sure of it.' He was smiling now. 'I never let go of that night, even if I always believed you had. And now I know why...'

'You remember it?'

'Of course I do! How could I ever have forgotten it! I think I lost my heart to you forever that evening...'

Abi was stunned. Silent. He'd lost his heart forever?

'Why didn't you say anything?'

'You know why. It was the day before the semi-final. And as Robbie said, he'd waited eighteen years, he could wait a few more days. And if a teenage boy could wait, so could I. Although it has been killing me...'

'Me too. I can't believe I got as far this week as I did with the weight of that information hanging over me.'

'I can. You did that because you're a pro. You're an incredible player – and an incredible mother. You were both out there this week.'

Max reached up and stroked her face, pushing back a wisp of hair that had fallen across her eye.

'Listen,' he said, his face so close she could feel his breath. 'We need to talk to Rob. What are we going to tell him?'

'Let's start with what we do know, shall we?'

'What? That I love you?'

'Max!'

'But it's true.'

And with that he kissed her. At last. And when he stopped, his hands around her face, he continued.

'We'll tell him about the blood type, shall we, and take it from there?'

'Take what from there?' Abi asked in reply.

'Well, a proper test. But also this.' He kissed the tip of her nose. 'And this.' He kissed her hands, clasped between his. 'And obviously this,' he said, as he kissed her on the lips again. She kissed him back, thinking how long she had waited, how long she had wanted this, and how her dreams had finally come true.

'Game, set and match, Abigail Patterson,' she whispered to him. 'The future is all ours.'

Acknowledgements

When you set out to do something totally new, the most logical first step is to find people who have been there and successfully done it before. I was pointed down the fiction-book route by my *Strictly* dance partner Anton du Beke, who has written a series of novels set in the world of ballroom.

With over thirty years of experience of the domestic and professional tennis circuits, there was always going to be plenty of behind-the-scenes content for me to work with, as well as opportunities to explore some of the challenges that still exist for women and girls at all levels of my sport.

With the expert backup of my literary agent Kerr MacRae, the invaluable expertise of my fabulous author friend Alex Heminsley and the trust, guidance and encouragement of my editor Charlotte Mursell and her fabulous team at Orion, we have created *The Wild Card*.

It's a tale of one woman's triumph over adversity and a reminder that it's never too late to follow your dreams…

Credits

Judy Murray and Orion Fiction would like to thank everyone at Orion who worked on the publication of *The Wild Card* in the UK.

Editorial
Charlotte Mursell
Snigdha Koirala

Copyeditor
Suzanne Clark

Proofreader
Jade Craddock

Finance
Jasdip Nandra
Nick Gibson
Sue Baker

Contracts
Dan Herron
Ellie Bowker

Design
Charlotte Abrams-Simpson

Editorial Management
Charlie Panayiotou
Jane Hughes
Bartley Shaw
Tamara Morriss

Marketing
Ellie Nightingale

Production
Ruth Sharvell

Audio
Paul Stark
Louise Richardson

Publicity
Elizabeth Allen

Operations
Jo Jacobs

Sales
Catherine Worsley
Esther Waters
Victoria Laws
Rachael Hum
Anna Egelstaff
Frances Doyle
Georgina Cutler